DUSK AVENGER

FLIRTING WITH MONSTERS

EVA CHASE

Dusk Avenger

Book 3 in the Flirting with Monsters series

First Digital Edition, 2020

Cover design: Yocla Book Cover Design

Ebook ISBN: 978-1-989096-78-9

Paperback ISBN: 978-1-989096-79-6

1

Sorsha

I wouldn't have thought my journey toward ending the world would involve a glamoured RV plastered with copious amounts of glitter, but hey, we couldn't always choose our fates.

At least the glitter was all on the inside—at least, as far as I knew. At this point, I'd only seen the outside in its various glamoured states. With a push of the button on the dashboard, the luxurious ride could appear to be anything from a school bus to a military submarine.

We hadn't tried out the latter of those just yet, more's the pity.

Right now, the RV was in its tour bus guise—an excellent multipurpose façade that could fit in just about anywhere. Like, for example, the parking lot outside a state park's nature center. The building with all its displays about local flora and fauna was closed for the night, but we weren't here to brush up on our environmental acumen anyway. About half a mile off one of the forest trails lay a rift that connected this mortal world to the shadow realm.

The seven beings who stood around me—or in the case of my little dragon, Pickle, *on* me, in his favorite perch on my shoulder—all belonged to that other realm. Only three of them were returning to it this evening, though.

Gisele adjusted her stance next to her partner, Bow, who had his arm around her torso to help her keep her balance. A few days ago, the unicorn shifter had been nearly mortally wounded in a battle with the Company of Light, a secret organization we'd discovered that was dedicated to ridding all worlds of the shadowkind by whatever means necessary. Gisele, Bow, and their friend Cori were heading back to their natural home so she could hurry along her recovery.

She gave the RV one last mournful glance. "You take good care of the Everymobile, all right?" The three of them were kindly lending us their vehicle, glitter and all, to continue our quest to take down the Company. As a thank you slash apology, we'd fixed up the broken windows and other bits that'd been battered in that recent skirmish.

Ruse shot the unicorn shifter one of his typical smirks, making his gorgeous face even more roguish, and patted the RV's side. "We'll treat her like a member of the family—the best of everything."

I jumped in before Omen, the leader of our little group, could bring up the fact that I'd supposedly gotten two of our previous vehicles destroyed—as if it were somehow my fault the Company's mercenaries had decided to target our means of transportation.

"You've been healing so fast," I said. "I bet you'll be back to collect her in no time."

"Back to rejoin you in crushing those assholes," Gisele muttered, her voice managing to keep its sparkle even when she was grumbling. "There are consequences to messing with a unicorn."

Omen tipped his head with its tawny, slicked-back hair to her—just slightly, but a major show of respect from the hellhound shifter, who was the most powerful shadowkind I'd ever met. An air of menacing authority radiated off him, as consistent as his breath. "We'll continue paying out those consequences until you return. We've got plenty of bones to pick with the Company."

"I'm looking forward to clobbering many more of them," Bow announced. He'd done a good deal of clobbering already with the massive haunches and hooves of his full shadowkind form. After seeing him as a centaur, I couldn't quite accept the standard human appearance he took on to blend in with mortals. Like all the shadowkind who traveled here, he did keep one of his monstrous features no matter how human he tried to pass as: in his case, a glorious mohawk mane of chestnut hair.

Thorn, the third of my current companions, straightened his considerable height even taller with a flex of his bulging biceps. The moonlight glinted off the one shadowkind feature *he* couldn't hide: his crystalline knuckles, also highly useful for bashing our enemies. His deep, gravelly voice came out as somber as always. "The villains have much to answer for."

They did. Just remembering Gisele's crumpled form after the ambush, smoke billowing off her like blood would have poured from a mortal, sent a prickle of angry heat through my chest. The sensation flared hotter at the thought of what the murderous Company pricks might be doing to the fourth member of my monstrous quartet now.

Snap had been the sweetest, gentlest being I'd ever met, humans included—even if, yes, he was also capable of inflicting inexpressible pain by devouring mortal souls. He'd been so ashamed of using that power to save me that he'd taken off on his own and been captured by the Company. Their scientists ran torturous experiments on the shadowkind they imprisoned. Imagining the devourer on one of their steel lab tables brought the searing heat to the base of my throat.

In the last week, I'd discovered a supernatural power inside myself, one no mortal should contain. So maybe I wasn't all mortal, even if neither I nor the shadowkind with me had been aware that was possible. I didn't know *what* I was, but I did know I'd happily send anyone who laid a hand on Snap up in flames. I didn't think it'd even be difficult to summon the fire inside me now. The Company had messed with the wrong gal.

As if sensing my mood, Pickle squirmed from one shoulder to the other and pressed his scaly neck against my cheek. As we waved our good-byes to the equines and their friend, I reached up to scratch the dragon's belly. He let out a pleased snort.

Maybe I should have been sending him back home along with the others. He wasn't equipped to fight in what had become a full-out war. But there was a reason I'd kept him after rescuing him from one of the collectors of the supernatural whose menageries of beasties I'd enjoyed freeing. His jailor had gotten Pickle's wings clipped so he could barely fly. I suspected that on the other side of the divide, he'd quickly become prey to other sorts of predators.

Could I even call the shadow realm his "home" now that he'd spent the past two years living here with me?

Gisele glanced back at us one final time and blew us a kiss I'd swear twinkled in the deepening dusk. Then she and her companions vanished into the shadows between the trees. The late-summer breeze twined around us, cool enough now to raise goosebumps on my arms. We turned back toward our ride.

Omen folded his arms over his chest and gave the RV a rare approving look. "We've got a long road ahead of us, Darlene."

I bit my lip and exchanged a glance with Ruse, barely holding in a snicker. Omen liked to name his vehicles, from his now-demolished station wagon—R.I.P., Betsy—to the motorcycle he called Charlotte that was currently mounted on the Everymobile's back end. Of course, this time there was one small issue that I couldn't help raising.

"You know, I don't think you should really be naming things that don't belong to you."

Omen let out a huff. "She does for the time being. All right, folks. Let's get on this thing and point her toward Chicago."

A shadowkind who knew his way around computers had been able to determine from the Company's files that

Snap had been sent to the Windy City. Before we tackled the head of the murderous organization, who as far as he'd been able to determine operated out of San Francisco, we were getting our devourer back.

Of course, that was easier said than done.

As Ruse took the driver's seat with a twirl of the silver spangle dangling from the rear-view mirror, I sank onto the white leather sofa that curved around a sleek dining table. Omen propped himself against the kitchen's marble counter. The hellhound shifter seemed to be most comfortable on his feet.

"How hard do you think it'll be for us to find the facility where they're holding Snap once we get to the city?" I asked. In my hometown, I'd relied on the connections I'd spent over a decade developing, and Omen had been able to call in a favor from a local shadowkind gang that had owed him. I didn't know anyone in Chicago.

There was probably a branch of the Shadowkind Defense Fund there, but I couldn't expect the people back home to provide introductions. I'd burned through a lot of bridges—metaphorically speaking, but we wouldn't get into what I'd *literally* burned—in the last few days.

"It's easy enough to sniff out the beings with the most influence if you know what to look for," Omen said with his usual aloof confidence. "If they haven't picked up on any hint of the malevolent organization rounding up their own, then they barely deserve to be called shadowkind."

Thorn had come to stand beside the sofa. He squeezed my shoulder with one of his large hands. "We'll rescue the devourer, m'lady—and make the miscreants regret ever ensnaring him. No matter what it takes."

Yes, we would. We'd managed to take on a local head of the Company operations and raze his home to the ground—and that after freeing all my city's imprisoned shadowkind and uploading a virus that would decimate their computer systems as well. But my stomach stayed knotted.

It was possible that Snap's capture was a teensy bit my fault. We'd gotten... close over the weeks since he and his companions had shown up in my apartment unannounced. In every meaning of that word. He'd become as devoted to me as he was to sampling every edible item he could get his hands on. I didn't know exactly why he'd left, but I wouldn't be surprised if it had at least a little to do with the fact that when I'd first seen him in full devourer form, I'd been horrified. And I probably hadn't hidden my reaction all that well.

My momentary horror hadn't changed how much I trusted and cared about Snap. I'd tried to show him that, but in the chaos afterward, he'd slipped away before I'd gotten much chance. If he'd had any idea how much I missed his divinely golden beauty, the possessive tenderness with which he'd doted on me, his awe at every new discovery he made in the mortal realm...

My throat constricted. *I* hadn't realized just how much I'd miss him either. I wasn't in the habit of getting all that emotionally attached to my lovers since years ago, when a long-time boyfriend had ghosted me out of the blue, leaving nothing but a note and our apartment half-empty. Snap's earnest affection had been like a balm on the wounds that had never quite healed in my heart.

But we'd be on the road all night before we made it to Chicago and could even start our search for him. There were other people I cared about that I might be able to help right now. As I sank deeper into the cozy leather cushions, Pickle cuddling against my thigh, I dug my phone out of my purse.

"I'd better touch base with Vivi—let her know what's happened."

Omen made a derisive sound at the mention of my mortal best friend and turned away to consult his own phone.

"I'll keep watch over the road behind us," Thorn said, and stepped into the shadows to give me a little privacy.

Vivi answered on the first ring. I guessed she didn't have a whole lot to keep her energetic mind occupied on the houseboat we'd turned into a sort of safe house for her after some Company goons had attacked her.

"Sorsha!" she said. "I've been going crazy here wondering what's going on. What's happened? Did you crush the bad guys?"

The corner of my mouth twitched upward, but the knots in my stomach tightened at the same time. Vivi was an enthusiastic supporter of our cause, but we'd had a bit of a falling out over her treating the conflict like an adventure rather than a potentially lethal clash.

"We got all the shadowkind out," I said. "And we destroyed as much of the Company property as we could. But... it turns out their organization stretches way beyond the city. They've got other bases of operations all across the country."

"Shit." I could practically see my bestie's grimace over the phone. "They're like some kind of cockroach hydra, more creepy hairy legs springing up every time you think you've cut one off."

Vivi had a way with metaphors. I couldn't say that one wasn't accurate.

"Yeah." I made an answering grimace at the cupboards across from me—which probably still contained the equines' treasured stash of grass, hay, clover, and... the other kind of "grass." "So, that means it *might* be safe for you to go back to life as usual, but I don't know for sure. Maybe they'll focus on ramping up their security everywhere else, or maybe the other 'legs' will send more people your way looking to strike back any way they can."

As usual, Vivi didn't sound particularly fazed. "I'm keeping in touch with the Fund people. If no one comes sniffing around—or worse—in the next couple days, I'll risk showing my face again. I've got enough food here to last that long, but I can't hide away forever." She paused. "Ellen got out of the hospital, by the way. They say she's recovering quickly."

A rush of relief swept through me. "That's really good to hear." The co-leader of our branch of the Fund had nearly been another casualty of my involvement in this war. The Company had beat her up to send a warning my way—and turned the rest of the Fund members against me in the process.

"What are our next steps?" Vivi said, breaking into

my uncomfortable reverie. "How are we taking down these assholes?"

The "we" made me wince. What had happened to Ellen—and nearly happened to Vivi—was exactly why I had to give her an answer I knew she wouldn't like.

"I'm already on the road with my shadowkind friends to see about that. You just focus on staying safe. If there's anything you can do to pitch in from there, I'll let you know."

"What, you took off on me? Sorsha..." Vivi couldn't disguise the disappointment in her voice.

"I couldn't ask you to uproot your whole life when this feud has already sent you into hiding twice," I said quickly. "You've got a job; you've got family—and we don't know what else these psychos are going to throw at us."

"Hey, if *you* can stand up to them, there's no reason why my mortal self can't too."

Other than that I wasn't sure exactly how mortal—or not—I was. But I hadn't told Vivi about my newly unearthed powers. Either she'd get all excited like they were a cool new app I'd downloaded into my personal operating system, or... or something would shift in her tone the way it did when she talked about the shadowkind. Because she'd see me as something not-quite-human too.

I kept my tone breezy. "No reason except for the ones I just gave you. Trust me, the best thing you can do for the cause right now is keep out of trouble and be ready for when a good opportunity for you to step in *does* come up."

"All right, all right. But I expect regular updates. No holding out on me, Sorsh."

"Of course," I said with a pinch of guilt.

When we'd said our good-byes, I tucked my knees against my chest and gazed gloomily out the window at the darkening sky. I didn't like this weight of worry pressing down on me. I was the Robin Hood of monster emancipation—I laughed in the face of danger.

It was just a heck of a lot easier to do that when the danger was only coming at you and not everyone else you cared about too.

I pushed my posture straighter and gathered my resolve. Auntie Luna, the fae woman who'd raised me—and who'd died evading the Company's hunters—had given me a lot of things, not least of which was a thorough indoctrination in the joy of all things '80s. There was nothing for honoring her contributions to my life and pumping up my spirits like mangling an excellent song lyric or two.

"Never gonna give it up, never gonna fret and frown," I sang into the quiet of the RV, ignoring the face Omen pulled in my direction. "Now we're gonna run you down and see hurt through!"

I pictured Snap standing beside me while another building burned down in front of us. One more Company facility destroyed; one more set of baddies slaughtered. The villains had it coming to them.

Without even trying, a surge of heat seared through me. My fingers curled around the edge of the seat. I closed my eyes, the swell of sensation inside me so intense that I lost my breath.

Burn it. Burn it all down like they deserve.

In that moment, I felt as if I could have leveled the entire city of Chicago with one blast of the rage inside me. My pulse hiccupped. The flames were rising higher, slipping between my ribs and out through my skin, faster and more furious than I could control—

A sharp sting shot across my fingers. I jerked my arms toward me, biting back a yelp. My gaze dropped to my hands, and a chill settled over me that doused that inner fire.

Holy mother of magma. My fingertips shone red, still stinging with the brush of the air. As if I'd set *myself* on fire.

2

Sorsha

Walking up to the clubhouse of Chicago's premier shadowkind criminal syndicate, I had trouble telling whether the gang had been going for unsettling or brutal with their décor. Either way, it was safe to say they'd shot well past the mark on both.

With the narrow two-story building tucked in between a tattoo parlor and a motorcycle dealership, they definitely had their clichés in order. But the front of the place was painted entirely black—including the first-floor window, because apparently curtains weren't enough for these dudes—other than stark white skull symbols on either side of the door and threads of pale gray that crept across the darkness like a massive spider web. They hadn't bothered with a sign or any other pretense of this being a regular place of business.

I stepped inside half-expecting a collection of

Halloween store paraphernalia, but what I got wasn't much better. The walls of the small front room were painted the same black as the outside. No spider webbing here, but the single lightbulb overhead cast a red glow over the room's limited furniture, which included a metal desk that had rust creeping along the corners, a matching bench sporting spikes on its supposed arm rests, and a display rack of ornate swords and daggers that looked much more authentic than anything our superhero hacker associate back home had owned.

A sour, slightly metallic scent lingered in the air, as if the room had recently hosted a blood bath. Not exactly a place of friendly welcomes.

Omen didn't look concerned, though. He stalked into the middle of the room and stood there, his eyes narrowing. He'd told us the shadowkind who operated this syndicate would be expecting us, and I could tell he wouldn't be happy if they kept us waiting long.

Before it got to the point of his hellhound fangs coming out, three figures wavered out of the shadows to meet us.

The one in the middle was obviously the leader, nearly as tall and broad-shouldered as Thorn, though packed with leaner muscles. The speckling of pale stubble on his scalp gleamed in the crimson light, and a patch of scales glinted on the backs of his hands just below the cuffs of his suit jacket. Reptilian in nature, presumably.

He was flanked by two other men. The slender, sallow one on the left I immediately pegged as a vampire

—which wasn't hard when his lips had curled back to bare his fangs in implicit threat. That explained the painted-over window and the weird lighting. The guy on the right was trickier to pin down—literally. His eyes darted this way and that, his wiry body never quite settling from its twitching and fidgeting even while he stood in place next to his boss.

When his gaze did come to rest in one spot for a couple of seconds here and there, it was on me. The vampire was ogling me too. Possibly Boss Man was as well, but it was impossible to tell thanks to the thick sunglasses that hid all hint of his eyes. I was pretty sure Omen would have given this bunch a heads up about the mortal he was working with, but I was used to the extra scrutiny my presence provoked. You didn't see shadowkind and humans getting chummy all that often—if you could call my relationship with Omen anything as warm as "chummy."

Omen was sizing up the syndicate guys in turn. "You'd be Talon?" he said with a nod to the boss and a razor-edged tone that suggested the dude had better be or there'd be hell to pay.

"As you requested," Boss Man replied in a liquid voice so dark it seemed to blot out the dim glow of the bulb overhead. "What brings us to the attention of a hellhound and his cohorts? We don't have much time for entertaining unexpected visitors."

Despite myself, a shiver shot down my spine. Unlike the other gang leader we'd dealt with, this one didn't speak with any noticeable deference to Omen. For him to have agreed to his impromptu meeting in the first place, Talon must have recognized the hellhound shifter as a larger power, but he wasn't offering much in the way of respect besides that.

As happened sometimes, being intimidated annoyed me, and when pissed off, I didn't always make the choices most likely to keep my innards intact. I'm sure you have your flaws too.

I waved to the closed door behind the syndicate dudes. "What, have you got a full schedule of polishing torture devices and laying down a few more coats of black paint? You know, putting so much effort into showing how badass you are only makes it look like you're trying to distract anyone from actually measuring your dicks. Maybe if you cared a little more about what's happening out *there* and not how cool you look wearing sunglasses in a room that's barely lit, we wouldn't have needed to interrupt your busy day in the first place."

The boss's head turned in a smooth, serpentine motion. He was *definitely* looking at me now, whether I could see his eyeballs or not.

"The sunglasses," he said, equally smoothly, "are to ensure I don't extinguish your life with a glance—unless I absolutely want to. But I can remove them if you'd prefer to play that game of Russian Roulette. With an attitude like that, I don't think your odds are great."

Son of a shih tzu. As Thorn stepped closer to me with a threatening flex of his muscles, the details added up in my head, and I almost bit right through my tongue. Luna had told me plenty of stories about her shadowkind brethren over the years. I hadn't forgotten the tales she'd spun of basilisks, giant lizards that could kill you with a look, although I'd never met one in the flesh before.

Probably best to avoid getting into a pissing contest with one. I gave him a little smile. "My apologies. I wouldn't want to let any games distract from our very important mission."

Omen cleared his throat, shooting me a glare *he* might have wished could kill me. "Maybe you can manage to keep your mouth shut for the next five minutes?" He turned back to Talon. "If you have as much sway over both shadowkind and mortals in this neck of the woods as I hear, I assume you'll have caught on if there were humans gathering our kind in a far more organized way than the typical hunters."

The twitchy guy finally gave in to his restlessness and drifted over to the display of weapons. He plucked up a dagger and spun its blade on the tip of his finger. "There's the type with the nets and the whips. Obsessive bastards."

Thorn frowned, his muscles appearing to bulge even more. "Those would be the ones we're after."

"I don't suppose you've done anything to rid the city of them," Omen remarked.

Talon shrugged. "They catch little pests that are no concern of mine. The occasional higher being they might sweep up should have been watching its step better. I protect those who seek our protection—what happens between mortals and the rest is their business."

That was the standard line of mortal-side shadowkind. Why should they think of the greater good

—or the good of anyone at all who wasn't licking their boots?

To be fair, there were an awful lot of humans who approached life that way too.

The tightening of Omen's jaw was the only sign of his disgust with that kind of self-interest. "Understandable. We need to tangle with them, though. They've come into possession of one of our associates, and we intend to get him back."

"Well, I certainly won't stop you from tearing a few heads off if that's what gets you off," the basilisk said.

No offers to pitch in, not that I'd really expected one. Ruse gave my ponytail a teasing tug and leaned over my shoulder. "I don't suppose you gents with all your connections could direct us to this group's center of operations? That would speed along the tearing of heads quite a bit."

"I suppose that wouldn't be too much trouble." Talon turned to his frenetic companion, who was now flipping the dagger from hand to hand. "Jinx, a moment?"

The wiry guy tossed the weapon back at the display—in a perfect arc that sent it dropping right back onto the metal pegs that had cradled it. "What're you after, boss?"

"See if you can fetch Grit—he's the one we had keeping an eye on the museum. Maybe he can cough up a few more details for these 'gents'."

As Jinx darted into the shadows to follow that order, my ability to keep my mouth shut ran out. "Museum?" I asked. "We're looking for living shadowkind, not stuffed ones."

The vampire let out a chuckle almost as dark as his

boss's voice, but he didn't bother to enlighten me. I got the distinct impression that Talon had rolled his eyes behind those shades.

"Humans work in bizarre ways, as you should know, mortal," he said. "The museum gives them a front—a large building to work from and presumably a reason for money to change hands. I doubt many of the beasts that go in come out alive, though."

And I'd bet I'd freed more of the lower beings of his kind than he'd ever lifted a finger for. But with another warning glare from Omen, I managed to keep that thought to myself.

A jitter through the air that made the blades rattle in their holders, and Jinx reappeared. "Grit is stationed down by the lake today. I can take you to him if you make it snappy."

Through the shadows, he meant. I opened my mouth to protest, but Omen held up his hand. "You don't need to be involved in every piece of this operation. Wait for us back on Darlene."

Oh, he was doubling down on the name, was he? I might have had a few choice words about that, but before I could voice any of them, Talon approached me. He peered down at me through his sunglasses, cocking his head. My shoulders stiffened, but you'd better believe I held my ground.

"Can I help you with something?" I asked, raising my chin.

I might not have been able to see his eyes, but I thought I could feel his attention pass over me like a cool draft grazing my skin. His mouth tightened into the kind of smile that ate children's laughter for breakfast.

"There's a burning inside you," he said. "But it might not stay in for long. If you're not careful, you're going to sear away with it when you decide to let it loose."

3

Sorsha

The Company of Light's main Chicago facility resembled nothing so much as a shoe box—albeit one the size of a city block. That resemblance might have been intentional, because their front wasn't just any museum. It was a Museum of Footwear.

As we cruised by, I squinted at the pale gray walls from the window over the RV's sofa. "Why would anyone think you need a building that big just to show off a bunch of shoes?"

Ruse chuckled from the driver's seat. "You fail to recognize the multitude of items mortals have worn on their feet over the centuries, Miss Blaze."

I rolled my eyes in his general direction. "I'm sure there are plenty of interesting slippers and sandals and galoshes or whatever, but who wants to spend a day looking at them all?"

"Enough people to keep the Company's front in

business," Omen said from where he was standing near the door, watching the street through the windshield. "The dwarf said quite a few ordinary-looking humans go in and out on an average day."

"Well, there's no accounting for taste, I guess. I don't see much in the way of security on the outside, at least not right now." There wasn't much room for guards to take up posts along the narrow strip of lawn between the building and the sidewalk. I'd spotted a figure just inside the glass front doors, though. "If they mostly stick to lesser shadowkind here, maybe they haven't felt the need to really lock the place down."

Thorn appeared across from me so suddenly that Pickle startled where he was curled up on my lap. The warrior must have leapt straight from the shadows along the road into the RV and then into physical form so fast even his fellow shadowkind hadn't been prepared.

"The building appears to have an inner sanctum," he reported without preamble. "The galleries form a square around an area that only a single locked door leads into. The door and the walls around that area contained enough noxious metals that I couldn't slip past while the entrance was shut. No telling how many mortals might be stationed within, but I counted six guards patrolling the outer rooms."

A thin smile curled Omen's lips. "They're definitely not expecting us, then. The Company must not have realized how far we got into their computer system before we burned that last place down. It'll be simple enough to blaze through this spot to wherever they're holding Snap."

His words were enough to set off a flash of heat in my chest. My hands tightened around Pickle.

A couple of days ago, I'd have welcomed the searing power that stirred with my anger. After scalding my fingers and hearing the basilisk's warning, my body recoiled at the sensation.

I'd only just discovered this power—or acknowledged it, anyway—a week ago. I'd barely scraped the surface of learning how to work it. Which was to say, I didn't have much of a clue what all I might be capable of, for good or ill.

Besides, did I really want to go charging at every enemy we faced from now until the end of this quest, burning them alive as my opening move? The shrieks of the people I'd sent up in flames in the last facility echoed through my memory, leaving me faintly queasy. Omen and Thorn wouldn't have batted an eye at that tactic—Ruse and Snap might not have either—but murder was a tad more taboo among humans than it was among the shadowkind.

Just how much of a monster was *I* going to become while we saw this mission through?

An unnerving prickling crept over my skin with that question, as if some of my inner fire was already rising to the surface. I wet my lips. "Before we do any blazing, could we find someplace for me to get in a little fire-throwing practice? I'd like to make sure I still have a good grip on my powers after the downtime."

No need to mention that I already suspected I was losing my grip.

Omen frowned as if he resented the delay, but then

he sighed. "It isn't as if we'd go barging in there five minutes from now anyway. You can toss your flames around while we discuss our plan of action. The dwarf did mention a place where we should be able to park Darlene without being observed or disturbed."

He pulled up the map on his phone and barked a few directions at Ruse, who gamely drove us through a sprawling residential neighborhood and out to a strip mall where all the store windows were boarded up. They formed a perfect C around the parking lot Ruse drove into. Plenty of room and no witnesses—just the way we liked it.

I stepped out into the cool night air and rolled my shoulders, willing my nerves to settle. That little accident the other day was no big deal. So my powers were a little capricious still. What else would you expect when I was some weird type of mortal who occasionally bled smoke as well as blood?

There was no guidebook on being... whatever the hell I was. I just had to get used to my unexpected abilities. And as for Talon and his sunglasses, he'd probably been pulling crap out of his ass, hoping he'd freak me out as payback for mocking his interior design sense.

There'd been a time only days ago when I hadn't been able to summon a flame except under terror of death. Now, I fixed my gaze on a paper bag drifting along the asphalt, and the surge of power swelled inside me so swiftly my heart started thudding *because* of that magic instead of the other way around.

"Burn," I murmured with a flick of my fingers.

Heat shot through my arm, and the paper bag

exploded into flame. In seconds, it was nothing but a little heap of charred black flakes.

Ruse clapped his hands for me where he was conferring with Omen and Thorn beside the Everymobile. "Bravo!"

I grinned at him in return, but my face felt stiff. The prickling sensation that had welled up inside me before was spreading all through my chest and down to my gut.

As long as it stayed there, I was just fine. No self-roasting today; no problem.

I swiveled around in search of more targets. A tattered flyer for a small-time theater production—with one sharp look, it was ashes. A paper plate with grease stains in the shape of a slice of pizza—cinders. An empty pop can that rattled as it rolled in a gust of wind—why the hell not?

I stared at it, my gaze narrowing to a glare. Heat blazed from my chest through my throat to the back of my eyes, and—

A rush of fire burst up not just on the can itself but several inches around it too. The heat of those flames flared so intensely that it lashed across my body from five feet away.

Or was that the heat *inside* my body flaring at the same time? The sensation whipped up in a whirl that sizzled up my spine and across my shoulder blades, and pain stabbed through my back.

A cry caught in my throat. I winced, drawing my arms toward my chest, and both the pain and the fire around the pop can shimmered down.

Or rather, around the smear of melted metal that

marked the ground where the pop can used to be. Holy liquified lizards, I'd reduced the aluminum to a puddle in just moments. A little more practice and I wouldn't even need to miss my titanium scorch-knife with its magically heated blade anymore.

A slightly hysterical giggle tickled up from my chest. Watch out, Company of Light.

As I adjusted my stance, the fabric of my shirt shifted against my back, and a fresh sting jabbed across my right shoulder blade. I tensed instinctively. With careful fingers, I prodded the flesh just below the collar of my shirt.

Even that tentative touch provoked more stinging. Small ripples met my fingers, as if the skin there was blistered.

I wasn't just melting down metals—I was barbequing myself.

That had never happened when I'd used my powers in the first several days. Why was the fire lashing back at me now? A scorching churn remained inside my gut even though I wasn't trying to summon it now, fierce enough that my stomach lurched with the thought that it might not be just my skin getting scalded.

Maybe this was just how this impossible power of mine worked—the more I wielded it, the more it leached from me in turn. Why not, when mortals were never supposed to work magic in the first place? At least the burns on my fingers had healed with shadowkind-esque swiftness. I hadn't done any permanent damage to myself.

Of course, that didn't mean I *couldn't*.

When I looked up at the strip mall, the heat inside me bubbled up eagerly. The sense came over me that I could have burned that whole stretch of buildings down with just a little push of my will...

I closed my eyes. Fuck this. I was all for kicking butt and pummeling the assholes who treated shadowkind as lab rats and worse, but a gal needed to have some kind of limits. I didn't understand what was going on inside me, and the more my powers grew, the more dangerous that ignorance became. Playing with fire was only fun if you were truly in charge of the matches.

We had other options beyond bringing a full maelstrom down on the shoe museum, right? There had to be room for a little subtlety in between "stand back and do nothing" and "burn everything and everyone to ashes."

As I walked over to the shadowkind men, I braced myself. I could predict how at least one of the three would react to the suggestion I was going to make.

Thorn had been saying something, but he fell silent as I reached them, looking to me as if he realized I had something to say.

Omen considered me with his icy blue eyes. "Finished your flambé practice?"

"For now." The jolt that rushed through me at those words, both giddy and rattled by the impression of all the things it could be in my capacity to incinerate at this moment, only bolstered my resolve. "I think it might be best if we come up with a plan that doesn't count on me using my powers."

The hellhound shifter grimaced before I could get

any further. "Don't tell me you're doubting your abilities all over again. You burned down a whole mansion a few days ago. I saw you lighting up trash over there just now. The fire's in you—you know how to use it. What's the problem?"

The heat inside me flared with a prickle of frustration. I resisted the urge to hug myself as if the press of my arms would force the inner flames to simmer down. "The problem is it feels... different from before. Bigger. Fiercer. I know how to bring it out, yeah, but I'm not sure how well I can keep it in check once it's out there."

Omen shrugged. "So you might char a few other establishments around the museum. The mortals never seem to care how many shadowkind they mow down in their crusades."

"You might care if I charred *you*," I retorted.

"I think I'm safe from your incredible talents. I know you think very highly of yourself, but you *really* don't need to protect me from you."

Would he be so sure about that if he could feel the building inferno of my power the way I could?

"I think I do," I said stubbornly. "Especially since you can't be bothered to listen to me. I don't think it's safe for any of us—including *me*—if I keep throwing my powers around when none of us has any clue how I even have supernatural skills in the first place."

Omen squared his shoulders. "Look, Disaster," he said, his voice flat but cutting. "I know the fact that there's something not entirely human in you unnerves you. The fact that the rest of you is human unnerves *me*. I've gotten over it, so you're going to find a way to come to terms with it too. Preferably soon. Stay focused and committed, as little practice as I'm sure you've had with that kind of discipline, and you'll control yourself just fine."

"Maybe if you were focused on something other than giving me a hard time, you'd be able to think of a plan that's better than 'fry all the villains to a crisp.' Brute force isn't the only skill we've got. Look at... Look at how far Ruse has gotten us with his incubus charm. Why don't we have him beguile all the guards into being on our side, and then we'll be able to waltz right through the place and get the cells open without running for our lives at the same time?"

Ruse blinked at me, apparently startled that I'd singled him out. He ran a hand through his rumpled chocolate-brown waves, past one of the small, curved horns that poked through them. "As much as I appreciate your faith in me, Miss Blaze, I can't easily charm more than a couple of mortals at the same time—not to the lengths we'd need to override their devotion to their cause."

"You wouldn't have to win them all over at once," I said. "They're not expecting us to be here. We have time. We watch the museum, follow the guards when they go off duty so we know where they live, and you can bring them around to our side one at a time. If we can get a few of the syndicate's followers to help us track them down, we could probably have them all dancing to your tune by tomorrow evening."

The incubus tapped his lips, but a soft smile was starting to tug at them. "You know, that might work. And

I *would* love to see a whole company of Company goons following my every command."

Omen still looked skeptical. "We have no idea of their shift structure or how many staff might be working in the inner chambers of that place. Miss one, and we'll still have a mess the second we get in there."

We might have been able to sort that out if we'd had weeks to survey the museum's comings and goings, but I wasn't going to leave Snap at the Company's lack-of-mercy for that long. I spread my hands. "So what? You and Thorn can take care of one or two stragglers if they get in our way, can't you? Or we let the guards deal with their own." I liked that way better than being responsible for several deaths-by-charbroiling—and who knew what other havoc on top of that.

Thorn cleared his throat and rested his hand on the small of my back, a solid, comforting pressure that offset the faint stinging still radiating through my shoulder blade. "You know I'm most at ease with physical combat, Omen, but I believe Sorsha's plan has its merits. The incubus has proven just how much influence he can wield. We'll have more time to uncover information on our enemies' weaknesses and policies if we enter through non-violent means. Any records we can obtain could make the difference between succeeding against the larger organization."

For the warrior to support a strategy that involved him standing back while someone else took the lead role was as huge as, well, the warrior himself. I would have kissed him if I hadn't suspected that would only undermine his larger point with his boss. I settled for giving his brawny forearm an affectionate squeeze instead.

Omen's mouth went as flat as his voice had been. I hated it when he ramped up the cold-and-hard-as-ice façade he turned to more often than not. Hated it so much that I'd never been able to resist poking at him until I found the right angle to provoke some of his own inner heat to the surface.

To be clear, dealing with a hellhound shifter in a rage was no laughing matter. But I'd take being terrified over condescended to any day.

We could get along; we'd proven that while making our final plans to take out the facilities back home. But Omen had been particularly stick-up-ass-ish when it came to my unexpected voodoo skills from the start.

"Are you sure this isn't all about giving you more excuses to hide away your powers?" he demanded. "Because it sounds an awful lot like that."

I gazed right back at him. "I've gotten so far from hiding them that a whole bunch of shadowkind and at least a couple of human beings who are still alive witnessed my flame-throwing last time. And I've spent my whole life toeing the line between risky and outright suicidal, so you'll just have to trust that I know when I'm on the verge of crossing it."

"Maybe you simply need a little more practice at exercising that discipline you struggle with." He loomed on me abruptly, a flash of orange light darting through his eyes, and somehow my body reacted with both a panicked hiccup of my pulse... and a tingle of a different sort of heat low in my belly.

We should probably get this out of the way up front—I have a unique taste in men. Deal with it.

I hadn't given in to any of those flares of attraction the hellhound shifter occasionally set off, though, and I wasn't about to start simpering now.

"Let's go," he said, jerking his hand toward the open lot behind us. "We'll see what you've got."

I jabbed him in the—very well-built, I had to admit—chest with my forefinger. "No. I've had enough for today. I need some simmering down time, not more stoking of the flames."

"So you say. There's one very simple way to get over the fear that you'll somehow reduce me to cinders. Give it a shot—your best one."

My power shifted inside me with an uncomfortable crackling. I swallowed hard and played one card I knew for sure would rankle him. "Leave it, Luce. Haven't you ever heard that no means no?"

A while back, Ruse had mentioned that long ago, Omen had pretended to be Lucifer—the devil himself, who apparently didn't actually exist—to frighten old-timey mortals. Usually pulling out that nickname was a sure-fire way to break him out of his own taut self-discipline. Tonight, a few tufts of his hair rose from its slicked-back surface, but his gaze kept its cool blue. A slightly dry note crept into his voice.

"I say when you're done. Come on and get this over with, Disaster. There's nothing you can—"

"I said *no*," I interrupted, with a burst of heat I hadn't meant to unleash. Flames sprang to the surface, but not on Omen. My clenched hands lit up like glowing embers

—and with agonizing throbbing as if embers were burning against my palms.

"Shit." I pressed them to my body as if I could extinguish a fire that hadn't even leapt all the way to the surface of my skin and choked on a gasp of pain at the contact. The agony faded with the glow, leaving my hands faintly pink and my heart pounding all over again.

Omen considered my hands with an unreadable expression. His gaze rose to meet mine. For just an instant, he hesitated.

"All right," he said brusquely. "You're frayed enough for one night, then. We'll deal with your fears and whatever else tomorrow. It can't hurt to have Ruse pave our way into the facility whether you bring your blaze or not. Go get some rest."

Both Thorn and Ruse were eyeing me with obvious concern. "M'lady?" Thorn started, but I waved him off.

"I'm fine. But I *could* use that sleep. Go track down some guards while I get my mortal beauty-rest, all right?"

I kept my tone breezy, but as I climbed into the RV, my lungs had clenched. *I'd* thought the new direction my powers were taking was freaky, sure, but this was all new to me. Omen had hundreds of years of supernatural exploits under his belt... and what he'd seen in me had freaked *him* out enough that he'd backed off without one more word of argument.

Just how fucked was I?

4

Ruse

"Two down, three more to go," I said, taking in the squat brick home our next target had vanished into after leaving guard duty at the museum. "This is the one we think will be working the inner rooms, isn't it?"

Sorsha nodded where she was lounging on the RV's sofa next to me. "That's where he was this morning, anyway."

"You'll want to prime him to not just let us pass but also so that he'll bring any colleagues he's working with out where you can work your charms on them too," Omen reminded me, leaning to eye the building over my head. "I can't believe it'll just be him in the inner sanctum. And since our Disaster here wants to spare the poor little mortals..."

Sorsha shot him a half-hearted glare over her shoulder but didn't bother to comment. The movement sent a whiff of her fiery sweet scent into the air. Fucking delicious. What I wouldn't have given to be spending the next hour in the bedroom down the hall, drinking that scent right off her skin from every part of her body, rather than chatting up another of the Company's dupes.

We did have our devourer to break out of imprisonment, though. And besides, even if I had let myself indulge in Sorsha's allure alongside Snap not long ago, I suspected making a solo venture of it wasn't the wisest idea. Not if I wanted to stamp out the longing tug in my heart that no incubus had any business feeling—something I should have been doubly sure of after the last time a mortal had turned my head around.

Still, I allowed myself the luxury of a fond smile and pretended it didn't send a ridiculous giddiness through me when she returned the gesture. It was because of her suggestion that I'd ended up spearheading our current plan of action.

I hadn't really seen myself as the leader type. It'd certainly been less pressure hanging back in the shadows during our previous operations and only popping in for the rare occasions when my talents were needed. There was a bit of a thrill in knowing that when we stormed the museum facility tomorrow, it'd be my persuasive skills rather than Thorn's brute strength and Omen's houndish savageness that paved the way.

And maybe there was also a thrill in knowing Sorsha had believed in those skills enough to point to me rather than them in her moment of uncertainty.

"I remember the whole strategy we discussed," I told Omen, and gave him a teasing salute. "Off I go to meet my fate."

I leapt through the shadows, peered through the slightly hazy view of the world they gave me until I was sure no one was nearby to see, and emerged into physical being on the house's doorstep. Since we already knew this fellow's feelings about shadowkind, I'd brought my favorite cap into being with me. As Sorsha caught up with me, ready to take on her mortal part in this role-play, I adjusted the hat's angle over my horns and knocked on the door.

The sinewy young man who opened the door frowned as he looked the two of us over, clearly not expecting any stunningly handsome gentlemen callers, at least not in the middle of the afternoon. His gaze lingered on me. I couldn't read his emotions at the moment, but his expression suggested he didn't find me entirely unappealing, if I'd happened to swing that way—and if I hadn't had other more urgent concerns.

I couldn't read his emotions or work any of my other skills on him just yet because he was still wearing a protective badge made of silver and iron over the general area of his heart. Not the same design as the one Sorsha tended to keep pinned to her undershirt, but for the same purpose. How kind of him to have left it uncovered so we could carry out this part of our plan with minimal struggle.

"You've got something on your shirt," Sorsha said as if spotting an embarrassing stain, and jerked the badge off with one deft yank.

The guy had barely let out a yelp before I let the full force of my seductive power trickle up my throat and into my voice. "I'm sorry to interrupt you, sir, but there's a matter of grave importance I need to bring to your attention. Lives could be at stake."

From the conversation with a colleague I'd overheard while watching him from the shadows, I'd already known he saw himself as some sort of champion of the people. The appeal to his heroic aspirations gave my magic an extra hook into his mind. He still looked discomforted, but he appeared to have forgotten Sorsha's manhandling already. An avid gleam had come into his eyes. "What are you talking about? How do you even know me?"

"There are many of us who study the Company of Light and reach out to its most promising members," I said, letting my smile turn conspiratorial. "Are you ready to step up to the next level in the war against evil?"

Dashing darkness, was he ever. The peek I took inside his head only confirmed the eagerness that lit up his blotchy face. "Absolutely," he said. "Come in—whatever you need, I'll do what I can to help."

Sorsha's part here done, she gave my arm an affectionate squeeze and hustled back to the RV. I ambled after our target into a living room with a leopard-print sofa, a zebra skin rug, and a very large cat—no, by the realms, that was a living, breathing tiger cub bounding across the floor to pounce on a ragged chew toy.

"Oh, don't mind Elsa," my host said with a careless wave. "She never bites that hard."

Our aspiring hero was also an owner of illegal wildlife and possibly a new Tiger King in the making. Wonderful. If Omen didn't end up tearing his throat out when this was through, I'd bet Elsa would once her fangs had grown. I only regretted that I wouldn't be around to see it.

I settled onto the sofa and put on my "serious business" expression, mainly inspired by Thorn and his vast range of sternness. Another thread of magic wove through my voice. "It's particularly important that you don't mention our meeting to anyone. Not everyone in the Company of Light is worthy of our trust. Which is precisely why we need your assistance with a vital matter..."

It took more than half an hour of tempting and cajoling before I was sure the hopeful hero was 100% committed, but by then I could have told him the security of the planet depended on him jumping off the roof of the museum, and he'd have happily run off to do it. Luckily for him, the use I needed to put him to was much less hazardous to his health, at least in the immediate moment. What the rest of his Company would do to him if they realized he'd been compromised—well, I expected he'd receive his just desserts for his horrible life decisions.

As I sauntered out of the house, the sun had just touched the rooftops of the buildings opposite. I kept walking until I was out of view and then dashed through the shadows back to the RV where Omen had brought it around the other side of the block.

As soon as I appeared with an okay signal to Omen, he revved the engine as if the vehicle were his motorcycle and not the sort of thing in which retirees took off to Florida. It rumbled on down the road, and Sorsha poked her head out of her bedroom.

"Did it go all right?" she asked.

I gave her a thumbs up. "Got him eating out of my hand in no time. He had an important bit of info to pass on to us, too. They're expecting an inspection from a couple of higher-ups tonight. They run most of their experiments overnight when there wouldn't be any patrons around if a creature escaped. Smaller staff during the day. In light of that news, I primed him to make our introductions tomorrow while the place is open."

I glanced in Omen's direction with a flicker of anxiety that the boss might not appreciate my taking that initiative, but his grunt of acknowledgment was approving enough. He might be the man of plans, but I had enough wits to contribute in that area too, didn't I? More than just a pretty face and a sweet voice, thank you very much.

As Sorsha had clearly trusted. There was no surprise tempering the relief that crossed her face. "Less than twenty-four hours until we get Snap out," she said. Then her exhilaration dimmed. "Assuming he's still there. Assuming they haven't been even more horrible to him than the other shadowkind."

There was definitely something wrong with my incubus inclinations that her fretting wrenched at me as much as it did. Well, our companions didn't need me until we made it to our next target. I went over to her.

She leaned back against the closed door with a dip of her head. "I know, there's no point in worrying about it when we won't find out until tomorrow anyway."

I brushed a few locks of her red hair back from her cheek and let my hand linger against her warm skin. "Of course you're worried about him. We know what these fiends are like." And as much as our mortal had woken up passions I never would have expected in the devourer, he'd woken up a tenderness in her that I wasn't sure she'd ever expected either. Something softer than the playful affection she'd offered me as she'd started to open up to my attentions, but why shouldn't it be?

She sucked in a breath and appeared to gather herself, resolve steadying her posture. Never did she look so gorgeous as when she was preparing for battle, and damn if I hadn't had plenty of opportunities to witness that in the past few weeks.

"They have no idea what hell they brought down on themselves when they took him." Her gaze darted to Omen in the driver's seat. "Maybe literally if it comes to that. And they'll deserve every bit of it." She shifted her attention back to me. "*You* know I didn't suggest a change in tactics just to avoid having to fight, right?"

Rarely had I wished quite so much that I could take a glimpse of the contents of her head without breaking her trust. Something about her powers had unnerved her since we'd come to Chicago, but I wasn't sure why now or what exactly was going through her mind.

It didn't matter, though. I could still answer truthfully, "Of course. I'd be less surprised by you giving up your '80s tunes than by you running from a brawl where you're needed, Miss Blaze. Woe betide anyone who messes with our mortal." I stroked my fingers down her jaw, resisting the urge to lean in to claim more than just a caress. "We'll get Snap back. These pricks don't stand a chance. And just imagine how overjoyed he's going to be to see you again."

"The feeling will be mutual," she said. From the momentary dreaminess that came into her eyes, she was picturing that reunion right now. If Snap could have seen her like this, he'd never have doubted her devotion enough to run off in the first place.

If she could accept all the monstrous parts of him—the jaws, the whole eviscerating of mortal souls bit—was it possible she might accept all that I was as well, without the lingering fear of how I might pry inside her mind or sway her to my whim? The one thing I knew above all else was I wouldn't want this woman coming to me on any terms other than her own. It wouldn't have been worth it to win her by magic, not when I'd had a taste of utterly unclouded yearning.

I shook that desire off like I had so many times in recent days. It was nothing but noise and clutter. But perhaps it wouldn't be such a bad thing if I presented a distraction in this moment that we'd both enjoy quite a lot?

The ring of her phone served as a cockblocker. I managed not to glower at it as she pulled it out of her pocket to check the number. Her jaw tightened.

"Vivi," she said, and to my surprise, hit the button to dismiss it.

"Did you two have another argument?" I asked.

"No, nothing like that. I just—with everything that's going on—" She made a face as if she couldn't find the words to express her reasoning. Then her phone pinged again, this time with a text alert.

As Sorsha read the message, she let out a disbelieving laugh. "Oh my God. I can't believe I forgot." Shaking her head, she looked up at me with a twist of her mouth. "She's wishing me a happy birthday."

My eyebrows jumped up. Then a smirk crossed my lips. I could give her something even better to take her mind off everything that troubled her. "It's your birthday today? Oh, Miss Blaze, you'd better believe I'm not letting that pass uncelebrated."

5

Sorsha

"This really isn't necessary," I said as Ruse guided me down the street with his hand shielding my eyes.

"Oh, no, I think it is," the incubus said by my ear in his chocolatey voice. "Since you met us, we've lost you your apartment, your friends, and practically your life on multiple occasions. The least we can do is give you a proper birthday celebration to make up for it."

He said "we," but as far as I'd been able to tell, he'd been doing all the actual planning. While Omen had stayed at the wheel of the Everymobile, Ruse had confiscated the hellhound shifter's phone to do some research on the city, with Thorn looming over him offering not much more than uneasy humming sounds. Once the incubus had worked his charm on the last two guards we'd been able to track down, he'd given Omen directions that the hellhound shifter had accepted with a long-suffering sigh.

I wasn't sure how much of a birthday celebration I wanted in the first place. Normally I'd have gone out with Vivi and maybe a couple of the other younger Fund members to chow down and let loose, but the thought of the friends I'd left behind made my gut twist now. It was hard to say no to the incubus when he was charging full speed ahead with all his charming enthusiasm, though.

Now we were at our first destination, although I couldn't tell where the heck that was since Ruse had insisted on escorting me over to it blind.

"You could at least let me see where I'm going," I groused.

The incubus chuckled. "But making it a surprise is more fun."

"Maybe to some humans. I prefer a full view of my surroundings."

"Don't worry, Miss Blaze. I'm sure the lunk here is doing enough scanning for danger to protect us all."

The "lunk" let out a wordless grumble. "You look ridiculous," Thorn said. "I really don't see why—"

"Oh, the mortals around will understand how we're playing. We're fine. And... ta da!"

Ruse whipped his hand away from my eyes. For a few seconds, I could only blink at the mass of lights gleaming against the deepening evening across the face of a... tiny palace?

No, not an actual palace, but a restaurant in the shape of one. *Regal Thai* said the sign that was almost lost in the glow over the arched doorway.

A hint of curry drifted to my nose, and my mouth immediately started watering. Maybe a little celebrating wouldn't be such a bad thing if we were going to do it in there.

Ruse ushered me inside while he sang the restaurant's praises. "It's just opened—with a top chef who spent ten years running a four-star establishment in Bangkok—and as you can see, they've pulled out all the stops with the décor too."

The smells grew even more enticing when we stepped inside. I managed to keep my drool in my mouth, but it was a near thing. Columns painted in what I assumed were traditional Thai designs of gold, red, blue, and green stood in rows down the eating area, marking off sections filled with booths painted the same hues.

The hostess ushered us to an alcove where we settled onto seats padded with scarlet silk cushions. Sweet silver sand dollars, the fabric was so soft it felt like a crime to sink into it.

Our server gave Ruse's cap a bit of a side-eye, but he'd exchanged his typical baseball one for a subdued black number that gave the impression of religious significance. I couldn't have told you what religion or whether that religion even existed outside of the incubus's imagination, but it was convincing enough that the woman didn't comment.

Thorn rubbed his hands together in the fingerless leather gloves that hid his knuckles as he contemplated the menu. Ruse snatched it from under his gaze. "I believe Sorsha should do the ordering. She's the one who'll get the most satisfaction out of this meal, after all."

Just a glance over the offerings had me drooling all

over again. "I can order us a perfect feast," I promised, and started making a mental list of all my favorites.

When the dishes arrived, they were delicious, but the best parts of my birthday dinner had nothing to do with the food. There was watching a warrior angel—excuse me, *wingéd*—attempt to manipulate chopsticks between his massive fingers, and the look of awe Omen quickly tried to disguise when he lowered himself to tasting the pineapple fried rice. And what could be better than letting an incubus offer a morsel of fried banana while his hazelnut-brown eyes lingered on my face, as sweet as the dessert tasted?

By the time the last dishes had been cleared, my stomach felt as if it'd expanded to about ten times its previous size, but the ache was more satisfying than painful. I leaned against the silky cushions and patted my belly. "Okay, you did well, Ruse. Just as long as Omen's not going to roast me now that you've stuffed me."

"Don't tempt me," the hellhound shifter said, but the slant of his lips was *almost* a smile. We'd come a long way from the early days when he nearly had gotten my ass roasted taking on his tests.

Ruse grinned and pulled out a handful of cash that I was probably best off not asking the source of. "Better to support good food than the putz who contributed this," he said to me with a wink as he set the money on the tray with the bill. "And we're not done. You're going to peel yourself off that seat so I can stuff even more fun into this evening."

I groaned. "I'm not sure I can walk at this point."

Thorn glanced up with a hopeful expression, looking

pleased to have found some way he could contribute to the party. He moved as if to scoop me up in his bulging arms. "I could convey you back to the vehicle, m'lady, if that would—"

I miraculously found the motivation to shove myself onto my feet after all. "No, no, that's totally okay, thank you all the same." As much as I enjoyed the feel of those muscles against me, I'd like to keep a little of my dignity.

I wouldn't have thought the night could get much better, no matter what the incubus had planned next, but my heart leapt when the RV pulled up at our next stop: a karaoke bar decked out with neon lights. Not that singing was my most favorite activity—it was the thought of watching my companions take a shot that had me grinning.

"We've got to take equal turns," I announced as I bounded to the Everymobile's door. "No one sits out, or you'll have a very sad birthday gal."

"We wouldn't want that, now would we?" Ruse said with amusement.

My demand worked on two thirds of my shadowkind crew. Omen plonked down in a corner of the private room Ruse had booked and refused to do anything with his mouth other than scowl. But it was pretty easy to ignore his lack of participation when I got to belt out "I Love Rock 'n' Roll" to Ruse's enthusiastic whooping and Thorn's applause, followed by the incubus strutting around with the microphone as he instructed us all, "Don't you forget about me."

The highlight, though, had to be Thorn gruffly but gamely giving "Sexual Healing" his best shot while he held the mic as if he expected to need to club someone with it at any moment. Believe me, you've never seen any performance to top that.

I nearly exploded holding in my laughter, but the flush that darkened the warrior's tan face made me want to offer him a little sexual healing to his ego after he'd finished. I wasn't quite so wanton as to get down and dirty in a karaoke booth, so I settled for planting a kiss on him long enough to bring a rumble into his chest before I went to pick my next song.

When our hour there was up, it turned out Ruse wasn't done with us yet. "One more stop," he said, with an affectionate tap of my chin. "But you can stay there as long as your feet will hold you up."

I understood what he meant when Omen parked the RV across the street from a dance club. A dance club with a sign in the window gleefully announcing that tonight was '80s night. The smile that sprang to my lips brought a bittersweet pang with it.

It was impossible to indulge in my love of all things '80s without thinking of the woman who'd passed on that love to me. Before I'd really had friends, when we'd moved from city to city so often I didn't have the chance to get close to anyone, my birthdays had been spent eating ice cream cake that Auntie Luna glamoured glittering sparkles onto and having private dance parties in the living room of whatever house or apartment she'd managed to arrange for us in that town.

She should have been here to celebrate more of those birthdays—to see the woman *I'd* become. The Company had stolen her in a way I could never get back.

Ruse obviously hadn't realized the connection I'd draw. His own smile faltered when he took in my expression, which must have shown a little of my sense of loss.

"It's great," I told him before he could think I was at all disappointed with his choice of activity. "It's perfect. Just brings back some memories."

I'd dance for Luna and amp myself up to strike tomorrow's blow against the organization who'd caused her death.

Thorn studied the building's front with obvious hesitation. "I don't know if it would be wisest for me to—"

"Nope, no backing out now—I want to see *all* of you on the dance floor." I grabbed his hand and tugged him toward the door. "If you're not sure what to do, just shuffle from side to side a little. No one's going to dare to even think anything judgemental when they take a look at you, I promise."

Omen stretched where he was still sitting in the driver's seat. "I'll come, but only to keep an eye on the rest of you fools."

"The fool is often the one who sees things most clearly," Ruse informed him with a smirk that practically twinkled, and led the way across the street.

It wasn't that late in the evening yet, but the place was already packed. I squeezed into the center of the dance floor and let the familiar music wind around me. Ruse kept pace, his hands grazing my waist, my hips, and my arms as he moved with my rhythm.

Thorn, well... Thorn did a very good job with his side-to-side shuffle. He even bobbed his head a little with the bass line. I gave him a thumbs up when I caught his eye, which I figured he deserved for the effort.

Putting in absolutely no effort at all was our defiant hellhound leader. After a few songs, I shimmied on over to where he'd staked out a spot by the wall between the pink-lit bar and the coat check.

"All right," I declared. "Onto the floor with you. You've been around umpteen centuries—you've got to have at least a few moves."

Omen didn't budge. "It might surprise you to hear this, but the fact that it's your birthday doesn't put you any more in charge than you were before."

"Maybe it does. How would you know? Shadowkind don't have birthdays, do they? Maybe it's a rule you just never heard about." I prodded his arm and then, with a rush of boldness fueled by the synth-pop beat, grabbed the front of his shirt, willing myself not to notice the sculpted muscles of his chest my fingers brushed or just how far I'd stepped into his aura of dominance.

The song playing over the speakers gave me the perfect lyrics to spin to my purpose. "Get up on your feet," I sang with a teasing edge, giving him a tug. "Yeah, step up, don't cheat. Boy, what, will you flee?"

Omen's eyes flashed, whether at being called a "boy," accused of turning tail, or simply because of the way I was manhandling him, I wasn't sure. He gave me a little shove backward—but he followed, to the fringes of the crowd.

Content with that victory, I did a spin and sidestep, daring him with a glance to keep up with me. His eyes stayed narrowed, but his body started to sway with the rhythm. When I swung closer to him again, he caught my elbow and added a little heft to my whirl. His touch left a tingling heat coursing over my skin.

This was playing with an entirely different sort of fire, but taunting flames had been one of my favorite pastimes. I sashayed around the hellhound shifter, trailing my fingers across his back, wanting to wake up more of the passion in him. Where he ended up aiming that passion, well, we'd just have to wait and find out, wouldn't we?

"Like what you see?" I asked with a waggle of my eyebrows, turning so he could check out the whole package. My gaze slid over the crowded floor—and caught on a glint of golden hair with a stutter of my pulse.

The jolt of emotion only gripped me for a second. It wasn't Snap—how could it have been?—but a young woman with gleaming curls twice as long as those the devourer had sported. But the momentary association had already sent me tumbling back through my memories to the night a few weeks ago when Ruse had set up an impromptu '80s dance party in my apartment living room.

Snap had joined us then, with a sinuous, unself-conscious style that had fit his godly beauty perfectly but would have looked awkward on anyone else I could think of. No one around me now could match it, that was for sure.

All these people dancing away with no clue or care what torment was being inflicted on all sorts of beings from beyond this realm...

A ripple of a much sharper emotion raced through

me, propelled by my inner blaze. It surged up so suddenly I lost my breath, my skin seemed to crackle—and a couple dancing next to me leapt apart with a gasp and a scream as flames leapt across both their shirts.

My heart lurched, and my arms seared from wrists to elbows. Other dancers spotted the fire with more cries of alarm. As the girl sobbed in pain, Omen grabbed me with a solid arm around my waist.

"Let's get you cooled off," he muttered, his breath tickling over my cheek, and hauled me toward the exit.

"But—" I started to protest. It was my fault. I should do something. What, I didn't have the faintest idea—and one of the bouncers was running over with a fire extinguisher, already taking care of the catastrophe I'd almost sparked. As the hiss of escaping foam melded with the music, Omen dragged me out of the club.

The hellhound shifter didn't let go of me until he'd yanked me into the alley beside the building. He let me go so abruptly I stumbled into the wall. As I whipped around to face him, he rounded on me.

"What kind of crazy stunt were you trying to pull in there?"

I gaped at him. "I didn't do that on purpose. Do you think I'm a total idiot? I just—it just came out, out of the blue. I don't even know why." I'd barely even been aware of feeling anything like the kind of anger or panic that had riled up my powers before. "This is why I've been balking about using my powers. They keep doing crap like that."

Omen leaned in, his proximity and his dry sulphuric scent sending my pulse into overdrive all over again. As his gaze pinned me in place, an orange light flickered in his eyes. "If this is some stupid move to convince me not to push you to get your act sorted out..."

"Of course it's not," I snapped. "I didn't want to set random people on fire, for fuck's sake."

"Well, maybe if we hadn't been spending the whole night wasting time on inane mortal pursuits, you wouldn't have had to worry about that."

Was he kidding me? "None of this was my idea. If you have a problem with tonight, take it up with Ruse."

Omen let out a growl that left my skin quivering in ways somehow both eager and unnerving at the same time. "He was busting his ass to please *you*. You seem to think you can have us all wrapped around your finger and doing whatever you want, but what I say still goes here, and you're not shirking your part."

The quivering had brought back the sting in my arms. I wrenched them up to thrust my forearms between our faces. "I'm not shirking anything. I'm trying not to be the fucking *disaster* you keep calling me."

Even in the dim light, the reddened, blistered skin made my stomach lurch. I hadn't realized I'd burned myself quite that badly this time.

The sight seemed to stop Omen in his tracks too. He paused, taking in the burns. With surprising gentleness, he slipped his fingers around mine to lower and turn one arm and then the other, studying both sides.

"Why would you do this to yourself?" he demanded, but the accusatory note had left his voice. He sounded almost... concerned. About me? Let demons sing "Hallelujah."

"I don't know," I said. "It just keeps happening now. Maybe... Maybe I wasn't meant to wake up those powers after all."

"No. You don't get a gift like that unless you're meant to use it." He raised his head to peer into my eyes again. I wasn't sure what he was searching for. He might not have been quite as stunning as my original trio, but there was no denying he was a looker too—and doubly so when his icy mask fell away.

"Would have been nice if it came with an instruction manual, then," I heard myself saying, and miracle upon miracles, something that might have been a smile tugged at the hellhound shifter's lips.

He was still holding my hand. His thumb stroked across my knuckles in a firm caress. "We'll figure it out," he said. "Lucky you—you've got the expertise of three incredibly skilled shadowkind to help guide those shadowy powers. Four, when we get back our devourer tomorrow."

"Assuming I don't incinerate us all while we're trying to accomplish that."

"I don't think you need to worry about that."

I restrained a grimace. "Because you don't believe it could get that bad?"

"No, because I'm saying you don't have to try to use them. In fact, consider that a direct order. We're taking your 'charming' approach tomorrow, and if anyone ends up needing to be destroyed, you can leave that to Thorn and me."

"Oh." I hadn't expected him to give in that far, even after this incident. "Well, er, thank you."

His mouth twitched. That was definitely a smile now. "So polite when you get your way."

I did grimace at him then, but it didn't diminish the weird fondness that was rising up in me. "I mean it. I..."

I didn't know how to express my appreciation of this non-dickish side of him other than to push off the wall and brush my lips against his.

I couldn't tell you what kind of response I was anticipating. Omen's hand shot to my hair, and I started to brace myself for him to yank me away—but instead he jerked me closer, taking the kiss from a peck to a branding in an instant.

A fire I didn't mind at all flared all through my body at the hot crush of his mouth. I would have reached for him in turn if he hadn't ripped himself away a second later.

The orange glow faded from his eyes, but his tawny hair had become thoroughly mussed without my even touching it. His jaw clenched at a harsh angle. There was Mr. Ice again.

He swiveled on his heel as if we hadn't been twined like lovers just a moment ago. "We're gathering up the others and getting out of here. That's been enough commotion for one night. We've got a shoe museum to scuff up come tomorrow."

6

Sorsha

As we strolled up to the museum entrance all casual-like, Ruse offered me his elbow as if he were a Victorian gentleman. The effect might have worked better without that goofy baseball hat perched over his horns.

"M'lady?" he said in a near-perfect imitation of Thorn's somber voice.

I poked him with my own elbow instead. Thankfully, with some aloe and the healing powers that seemed to come with my ability to barbeque myself, the burns on my arms from last night were already pretty much gone. "Let's save the joking for *after* we've gotten Snap and all the little beasties out of here."

"Ah, you wound my heart," he teased, but his warm eyes took in the foyer with total alertness. For all his playful nature, he was taking this operation seriously.

There were actually a shocking number of patrons

browsing the glass cases holding various styles of shoes. A tourist couple snapped photos while their two kids tugged on their shirts, looking like they'd rather be anywhere else. A young guy in sneakers so puffed up he could have pulled off an excellent Donald Duck imitation exclaimed about the history of sporting footwear to a girl with glazed eyes. Good luck hitting a home run on this date, dude.

We passed boots worn by soldiers—not anyone who'd seen much action, from their pristine condition—and slippers supposedly possessed by emperors, with an obscene amount of gold thread. The celebrity hall of fame boasted diamond-encrusted stilettos worn by some pop star on a recent tour. Did she still have working ankles after stomping around a stage with those things strapped to her feet? Or vision, for that matter? Their sparkle was blinding. Luna would have approved, anyway.

We came up on the inner sanctum, its doorway discreetly tucked down a little hall between *Put Those Soles To Work* and *A Watery Good Time*—boat shoes and diving fins for the win!

Ruse didn't give any noticeable signal, but he must have primed the guards he'd charmed well. A muscular woman in a tan uniform approached us with a respectful tip of her head.

"Everything's in order, sir," she said. "Let me know when you're ready to begin your final inspection."

Ruse put on an expression of total professionalism, but a hint of his roguish smirk showed through. I bit back a smile.

"I'd like to meet the other guards on duty out here first," he said. "Everyone except Mack, I already spoke with him. If you could escort them over to the vestibule one at a time, so we can keep this discreet...?"

"Absolutely, sir, absolutely."

"The vestibule?" I repeated with another twitch of my lips as she hustled off.

Ruse let his grin slip out. "One of my favorite words. Can't go wrong with a good vestibule. Now let's get over there so I can have the rest of this contingent singing our praises."

There were only two other guards patrolling the collection during the day—the Company must have thought it was unlikely anyone would risk an invasion while there were so many witnesses around. Of course, that fact worked in our favor now. And once we had what we needed, we could clear the innocent bystanders out of the place with a pull of the fire alarm before any real fires got started.

As long as we kept the situation totally under our control.

Ruse made great friends with the other two guards in a matter of minutes—easier when he only needed the influence to last for an hour or so now. As much as I hated these people who'd dedicated their lives to eradicating the shadowkind, watching the incubus work his charm was still a little unnerving. I couldn't completely suppress the faint but chilly quiver as I remembered the other shadowkind who'd toyed with me as a child using his own brand of persuasive voodoo.

But Luna had chased the jackass off, and I emerged

unscathed, and Ruse wasn't anything like that prick. I couldn't imagine him harassing a child, even if he did let his sense of humor come out when it came to the real villains.

He watched the second guard amble off with a mischievous glint in his eyes. "I could have them marching through the halls singing Christmas carols if I wanted to."

I elbowed him again. "As much as I'd like to see that, it won't get Snap out. You can start your carol group once the cages are open."

"Oh, fine, you spoilsport."

He gave me a fond peck on the temple with a tenderness I hadn't been expecting. The incubus and I had gotten about as intimate as any two beings could be, but lately he'd had more standoffish days than not. Even after last night's celebrations, he hadn't made a single come-on to prompt an invitation into my bed.

I wasn't totally sure what was going on with that or with this brief PDA, but puzzling over it could wait for later too.

It was just five minutes to noon now. We sauntered back toward the door to the inner sanctum, and at twelve on the dot, Ruse knocked with a one, one-two, one beat. A signal he'd arranged with his new friend he'd been calling the Tiger King, the ropey-limbed guy who opened the door with a rasp of its lock a moment later. He wasn't wearing his own armor—Ruse had instructed him to shed it before he let us in.

"I haven't said a word to anyone," he murmured as he ushered us into a brightly lit, white-washed room packed with glass desks and computer equipment. Ruse gave a restrained shudder, now surrounded by the silver and iron embedded in the walls. "A couple of the guys might give you some trouble—I don't think they're in on the bigger picture. I'll bring them over like you asked, and you can decide—"

What he thought we were going to decide was lost with the click of the door at the other end of the room. I caught a faint whiff of chemicals with the breeze that emerged, my body tensing with the understanding that the lab—the experiments, the captives, *Snap*—lay that way, and then the two figures who'd appeared in the doorway gave a shout of startled concern.

"What are you doing—who are these people?" one demanded, striding forward. Both of them were drawing their guns. Okay, then. Plan: Peaceful Intrusion had just gone down the drain.

"A hand with your colleagues?" Ruse said to his charmed guard, his voice thrumming with renewed energy.

The guy leapt at the guard who'd barreled toward us with some kind of karate chop that sent the other man's gun flying from his hand. The third guard's gun hand jerked up—and Thorn leapt from the shadows in full brawny glory, smashing his fist down on the man's arm so forcefully I heard the crunch as the bone shattered.

The charmed guard had wrestled his other colleague to the ground and was now shoving off the guy's protective helmet. "It's for your own good!" he was declaring. "There's so much they haven't told us—so much we haven't seen..."

Thankfully, he seemed to be too busy wrenching at the ties on the guy's vest to see the next swing of Thorn's fist, which drove the warrior's crystalline knuckles deep into the underside of the third guard's jaw. The man slumped with a bloody gurgle, no de-armoring necessary.

I leapt in to help remove the last of the second guard's protective gear. The second he was free of silver and iron, Ruse's cajoling voice rolled out again.

"There's so much at stake—we have to hurry. These monsters are toxic, but they'll burn away if we drive them out into the sunlight. Quickly, quickly, before the people who wish to keep them here and protect them can stop us from doing what is right."

The appeal to the man's hatred of the shadowkind worked so well it made my stomach turn. He sprang to his feet and dashed for the door to the lab area without another word from Ruse. The sight of the mangled flesh on the body Thorn had dragged out of the way didn't exactly inspire my appetite either, but in that moment it wasn't hard to remember why my qualms about taking the bashing-their-skulls approach had worn thin.

We pushed into a larger room full of steel tables, shelves of lab equipment—and a full wall of silver-and-iron cages. There had to be at least thirty smaller ones and then several larger enclosures at the end. They all blazed with artificial light, thin shapes of shadow jittering in its glare.

Snap had to be in one of those big ones. "Open them up!" I said to the guards. "Come on, let's go!"

"You heard her," Ruse added with more voodoo in his

tone. "All of the beasties out, and then we'll drive them into the daylight to vanquish them for good."

"We don't have the keys or the codes," the guard said with an anxious stammer, waving to the cages. The large ones had keycode panels—the small ones only little locks with holes.

Ruse spun on his original ally. "You said you had access."

"To the rooms! You didn't ask about the cages before."

He hadn't wanted too much detail in case one of the guards let our plans slip ahead of time. Shit.

Omen rippled out of the shadow. "Who has them, then?" he demanded, but a surge of fury and frustration seared up through me, burning all need for that question away.

"It doesn't matter," I said tightly, ignoring the prickle of pain that came with my power. "I can open them."

I grasped one of the little cages, fire flaring from my palm. The metal warped like the pop can melting the other night. With a yank, I opened a gaping hole in the interlocking bars.

With enough space now to pass by the toxic metals, the shadow within flitted past me without so much as a thank you. That was fine. I didn't need one. Gritting my teeth, I grabbed the next cage and poured more of my searing power into my grasp.

"I don't know if this is going to work on the big ones," I gritted out. Those had solid walls, no bars. I had no idea how thick the metal was there.

"The computers," Ruse said with a brisk gesture

toward the other room. "Both of you, get on those devices and see what you can find. And if there's nothing useful there, then—"

The door to the largest cage in the row swung open with a mechanical whir. None of us had been standing anywhere near it. I wrenched the cage I'd been holding open and jerked around, my hands rising to face some new threat, but the figure that emerged was completely the opposite.

A tall, slim blur of shadow solidified into Snap's golden-haired, green-eyed form. He stared around him in a daze. My heart leapt, the impulse to engulf him in a hug ringing through me—but he was out now and there were still dozens more creatures to save. I settled for shooting him a smile of pure gratitude and reached for another cage.

Omen swiveled around, his body tensed, his lips curled as being surrounded by so much of the aversive metals was wearing on even his vast stores of strength. "Someone did that on purpose—someone knows we're here. They're watching us." His head snapped around toward the guards. "Is there another room?"

"I... don't think so," the first guy said uncertainly.

Thorn frowned. "This space doesn't seem large enough to account for the dimensions I charted from the outside. There should be more... there." He pointed to the wall beyond the lab tables where a fridge and a couple of large cabinets stood. Clenching his jaw, he flexed his muscles—and charged straight at the wall.

I'd seen the warrior smash through concrete and brick before, but never anything quite like this. As his massive form crashed through not just plaster and beams but plates of silver and iron too, his flesh hissed. Smoke puffed up from the wounds. A groan escaped him, but he'd managed to bash a big enough hole for us to stare through into one more white room with desks, computers, charts and maps on the walls, and two figures in lab coats staring at us wide-eyed.

"You should leave here now," one of them spat out, her hands clenched at her sides. "We've notified the rest of the Company. There'll be dozens of people here ready to fight you off in a minute."

She only cared about saving herself, then, not capturing us? Was that why they'd freed Snap—in the hopes we'd take just him and leave before we found them? I could respect that sense of self-preservation, but that didn't mean I was going to cater to it.

"They'll have the keys," I said, with a wild motion to the guards. "Grab them, help me get these open."

The two charmed men charged through the smashed opening to comply. As the scientists yelped in protest, I heaved another cage open by my own power. A few moments later, I had two helpers scrambling to shove keys into as many locks as they could. Which was a good thing, because the heat blazing from my hands was starting to rush through the rest of me with unsettling intensity.

"What's this about?" I heard Omen ask. I glanced over my shoulder just long enough to see that he'd stepped into the hidden room and was peering at a map that showed the whole world. "What do these markings indicate?"

One of the scientists sucked in a shaky breath. "We can't—we're not supposed to—"

"To hell with that. Ruse, make them *want* to tell me."

The incubus clapped his hands. "My good friend Justin, I need your services for a moment."

The Tiger King guard shoved his key ring toward me —I reined in my power as quickly as I could so I wouldn't melt the thing—and hurried to help his new favorite person. The ripping of fabric told me someone's protective badge had been removed from their clothing in a violent fashion. I checked the numbers on the keys, jammed another into a lock, and hurled the cage open as quickly as I could.

Snap had lingered in the room, watching us, his expression still hazy. I glanced at him and offered as much reassurance as I could manage. "We'll get out of here with you as soon as we have all the other shadowkind free. Just hang tight."

"Hang tight," he echoed in a faint but curious voice.

Figurative language wasn't the devourer's strong point. "Stay there," I said. "You'll be safer leaving the building with the rest of us."

Ruse had been speaking in cajoling tones to the scientist his guard had disarmed. Omen spoke up again, his voice on the verge of a snarl. "Explain the map to me. What do these blue marks mean?"

"Oh, those are the locations of Company facilities," the woman replied in a much chirpier voice than before. "And the red dots indicate areas where we've detected recent shadowkind activity. It helps us quickly identify patterns and decide who should investigate."

"They're not just here in the US. You've got polka dots all over Europe as well."

"Yes. That's where the Company started, as I understand it. The president of operations runs everything from over there."

Wait, the Company of Light was run from someplace overseas? We'd thought we'd have to go all the way to San Francisco to deal with the ultimate head honcho... I hadn't bargained for a trip across the ocean.

Neither had Omen, clearly. His voice came out with a sharp edge of sarcasm. "Wonderful. *Where* 'over there'?"

"I don't know. I've never talked to him directly. I got the impression he travels around a lot. With a mission this crucial, how could he stick to just one place?"

Omen swore under his breath. I wrenched open the last of the smaller cages. "Are you done with her yet?" I called. "We need these bigger ones opened."

The scientist sprang into action before Ruse even needed to prod her. He must have done quite a job on her with his hocus pocus.

"I can control the locks from the computers," she said, bending over a keyboard. Her colleague made an incoherent sound where he was sprawled on the floor—under the charmed guard, who'd taken a seat on the guy's back.

One cage door whined open, and then another. Thorn cleared his throat. He swung his hand toward a row of monitors mounted higher on the wall. "These TVs, they show what's real—what's happening now?"

This time Omen swore louder. Whatever he'd seen

there, he didn't like it. "Unfortunately, yes. You, open those last two. Everyone else, let's go. We've got a lot more jackasses incoming from the Company than I'd like."

It was hard to tell whether all of the creatures had left or only retreated into the nearest shadows. "Out, out, all of you!" I called to them. More fire stirred in my chest at the thought of our enemies closing in on us.

Ruse hollered at his charmed allies. "Head out there in front of us—divert the attackers as well as you can!" He grabbed Snap's wrist, and they vanished into the shadows a moment later. They'd herd any creatures who'd lingered out, I had to assume.

The guards and the charmed scientist dashed for the entrance to the outer museum. I ran after them, Thorn and Omen alongside me. A fresh jab of guilt that I was the only one who couldn't slip away into the patches of darkness hit me.

"You can go," I said. "I might be able to dodge them."

"You didn't see the security footage," Omen muttered. "We're not leaving you behind, Disaster."

We burst out into the hall between the galleries. Shouts echoed off the walls as the onslaught of enemies shooed the visitors out of the museum. Footsteps pounded on the floors. Two squads of guards hurtled toward us from either side.

My pulse stuttered with a flare of adrenaline. I wasn't dying here, not after all this—not when I hadn't even gotten to welcome Snap back. Fuck these assholes and the shit-show they rode in on.

Without my even consciously willing it, flames

whooshed up over three of the figures racing our way. I tuned out their shrieks with a wince. Thorn threw himself toward the other attackers at our right, and my gaze stopped on a broad window that looked out onto the street just behind them.

"Thorn!" I said. "We can crash right through."

There'd been a time not that long ago when Thorn would have been too caught up in his own combat focus to pay attention to any suggestions I made. We'd established more of a mutual having-of-each-other's-backs since then. He followed my motion, made a quick nod of agreement, and swung both fists to gash open two of the guards' throats. Then he snatched up a couple of steel-toed shoes and hurled them at more distant opponents with a kick hard enough to break their noses.

Omen was slashing through the wave of guards coming from the other direction, but there were a lot of them. They all wore their protective armor, and a few carried the laser-like whips that raked through the shadowkind's bodies in ways most other weapons couldn't.

I gritted my teeth, and another two of our attackers vanished into an explosion of flame, along with a couple of displays that let off a whiff of charred leather. My skin tingled, but I didn't seem to have caught fire myself this time. Having clearer, more deserving targets seemed to help keep that scalding energy focused away from my own body, thank tasseled toe shoes.

The smell of burning flesh wafted through the smoke. Bile rose in my throat, but I ignored my queasiness. I just had to get to the window, and we could be done with this.

Let them all burn. Why the hell shouldn't they, when that was what they wanted to do to every shadowkind in existence?

Thorn battered a couple more guards and hurled himself past them to the window I'd pointed out. The slam of his fist brought down a hail of broken glass. I sprinted toward it.

A movement by one of the display cabinets next to the window brought my fury back to the surface. I whipped my hand out, and a pair of ancient miner's boots turned into a fireball that careened toward—

A little boy. It was one of the tourists' kids: a scrap of a thing all round eyes and flyaway hair, who couldn't have been more than seven years old. My boot-iful fireball flashed toward him where he'd crouched trembling beside the case. A look of pure terror took him over, and a cry broke from my lips. *No, no.* I hadn't meant to—

Something in me heaved with that shock of panic, and the flaming boots veered just enough that they skimmed the boy's legs rather than roaring right into his face. He squealed, slapping at his jeans.

I'd still hurt him. What if he—

I didn't get to find out whether I had enough conscience left to make sure I hadn't flambéed a child. Thorn caught me around the waist and hauled me through the broken window. The fresh outside air slapped me in the face, waking me out of my conflicted anguish.

Get to the RV. Get to Snap. Then it would all be over.

I dashed alongside the warrior around the corner. Omen flickered in and out of view, loping along in his hellhound form, just long enough to show he was with us. As we came into view of the Everymobile, Ruse flung the door open for me and then dove back into the driver's seat. Thorn vaulted into the shadows around the steps, I threw myself up them and jerked the door shut behind me, and the RV lurched forward with a screech of its tires.

My heart was still thudding. I swayed over to the sofa and collapsed onto it. "Where's—where's Snap?" I managed to ask.

The devourer blinked into sight at the other end of the sofa in response to my question. Relief choked me. I found enough energy to shove myself over to him and dragged him into an embrace. His delicately dark scent, like a sunny meadow hiding mossy depths, filled my nose, fantastically familiar. It sent a pang through my heart.

"I'm so glad we got you out," I said, pulling back so I could look him in the face.

Snap regarded me, cocking his gorgeous head. "So am I," he said brightly. "It was very kind of you." His gaze slid from me to Ruse and then Thorn and Omen, who'd stepped out of the shadows on the other side of the table. "You all went to so much trouble to help me... Who *are* you?"

7

Sorsha

Thorn brandished the fruit like it was a sword. "*This* is a banana."

Snap took the yellow crescent from him and brought it to his nose. He breathed in, and a dreamy smile crossed his lips. "It smells delicious. Is it for eating?"

Ruse chuckled where he was standing next to Thorn by the RV's kitchen, but the sound came out a bit strained. "Absolutely! You ate one of those when we made our first appearance in Sorsha's apartment. Jog any memories?"

Snap raised the banana to his lips, taking a bite right through the peel like he had that first time what felt like ages ago. Watching him, my breath caught in my throat. At this point, I didn't really expect a light of recognition to spark in his eyes—the way it *hadn't* after all the previous memory-jogging we'd attempted—but it was hard not to hope for it anyway.

He chewed thoughtfully, every motion like the shadowkind man I'd come to know and to care about a lot more than was typically my policy. Then he shook his head, regretful as always that he was letting us down in some way he didn't even understand. "I don't believe I've had one of these before. It's fantastic, though!"

My stomach clenched tighter into the ball it'd been forming since Snap had first shown that he had no recollection of who any of us were. He *was* the same person—monster—whatever. It was just as if months, possibly years, had been wiped from his mind.

As the devourer downed the rest of the banana with equal enthusiasm to the one he'd pilfered from my kitchen, Ruse and I exchanged a glance. His was as fraught as my inner state. Omen had been held prisoner by the Company for weeks longer than Snap had, and *his* memories hadn't been addled as far as any of us had noticed. But who knew what additional tortures the scientists might have devised? It could have been some new tactic in their scheme to infect all shadowkind with a deadly plague or an unintended side effect from one of their experiments.

I stroked Pickle's back where he'd hopped onto my lap and tried to ignore the growing gnawing of the question I least wanted to face: What if Snap had lost those memories for good? All the work he'd done toward taking down the Company... All the intimacies and affection we'd shared...

When I'd first met him, he hadn't even realized what physical pleasures his body was capable of. I wasn't sure he'd felt anything for me other than gratitude that I'd helped free him—and he didn't remember *that* now either. I was a total stranger who meant nothing to him, and there was no way to replicate the scenarios that had brought us to our unexpectedly passionate union.

"If our equine friends had left us behind some dish soap, I'd make you a bubble stew," Ruse joked. "You liked those last time too."

Snap's forked tongue flicked over his lips. "Is this 'bubble stew' as tasty as the banana?"

"Ah, no, it's not for eating—that one's just fun to look at. Little shiny globes floating through the air."

The devourer laughed. "For a place without magic, the mortal realm has a lot of marvelous things! So many different flavors and colors... So much vivid sound. This contraption that carries us great distances without us having to move our bodies at all." He patted the RV's table with an awed expression.

The Everymobile wasn't carrying us anywhere right now. We'd parked it in the lot by the derelict strip mall while we sorted out what to do next. Omen stepped up to the table, his arms folded over his chest.

"It's unfortunate that you don't remember anything about our cause or the rest, but we do have to get on with that mission. Our enemies know we're in Chicago now. When I first sought you out in the shadow realm, you agreed to help me investigate the disappearances of our people. Now we know who's behind it—the same people who locked you up. Are you going to stick with us and make them pay?"

A flicker of uneasiness passed through Snap's expression and vanished just as quickly. I hadn't been able to tell whether he remembered all the way back to his first devouring, the one that had made him so horrified with himself that he'd sworn never to use that power again. Hints like that suggested he might, but he hadn't mentioned it.

"Of course," he said now in his brightly eager voice. "The way those mortals treated the shadowkind in that place—it was awful. So much pain..." A shudder rippled through his slim frame.

I had to resist the urge to take his hand. Would the gesture comfort him from a woman he probably associated more with the mortal villains who'd captured him than his shadowkind comrades? A quiver of anger shot through the ball of my stomach.

Snap recovered himself with a set of his shoulders. "They should be stopped. I'll do my best to help with that. I don't know what I can tell you right now. With all the energy of the metals in that place, I couldn't bring out any of my powers to test their equipment."

"That's all right," Omen said, so brusquely I'd have liked to punch him. Too bad I was on the other side of the table with a tiny dragon on my lap. "I'll let you know when you can pitch in." He turned to take in the rest of us. "So. We have an even larger challenge than we anticipated ahead of us. It appears the Company of Light has been doing their wretched work not only all across this country but on the other side of the ocean as well."

"So bloody many of them," Thorn muttered.

"Exactly." Omen paused. "I think our mortal disaster here might have had the right idea in our past operations, recruiting whatever help we could get. I never expected us to be confronting an organization this widespread, and I don't think the five of us will be enough to shut them down once and for all. More skills, more insight, and simply more beings in play will allow us to put together a more complex strategy. We need to seek out more allies. We managed it before—I'll be optimistic and assume we can find others willing to lend a hand at least briefly."

I should have been gratified that he was admitting out loud that I'd been right about something. He'd groused enough about my ideas while I was putting them forward before. But any pleasure I might have gotten from his acknowledgement was swallowed up by the overwhelming sense of all those pockets of shadowkind-torturing psychos spread out across the planet. So many fucking mortals so determined to ruin everything in their path—maiming and killing and whatever they'd done to Snap—

There was so much they needed to pay for. And sweet shredded seashores, did I want to be there delivering that payback.

The fire inside me roared from a quiver to a blaze in an instant. A burning sensation flared through my limbs—and Pickle squeaked, flinching so violently he tumbled off my lap onto the sofa cushions.

My heart lurched. My palms were prickling with the heat that must have burst from them. Pickle nuzzled his side—oh, God, were his shiny green scales faintly singed?

"Hey," I said softly, reaching out to the little creature in the hopes of offering some sort of apology. He leapt back with a widening of his beady eyes. My throat constricted. "Pickle?"

He stared at me, his head weaving from side to side on his slender neck, and then he sprang off the sofa-bench completely and scurried down the hall toward the bedrooms.

Tightly as my stomach was balled, the bottom still managed to drop out of it. He'd been *scared* of me.

My hands clenched at my sides. Ruse and Thorn had been talking, sharing their ideas about who we might turn to for assistance first, but when I glanced up, Omen's gaze was trained on me, his ice-blue eyes as piercing as ever.

"They might at least contribute a few of their underlings," Ruse finished. "That Talon gent didn't seem like the type to want to leave his home base unsupervised for long."

Omen nodded. "Yes, we'll speak to him again and see if he's willing to offer anything." He made a beckoning gesture toward me. "Disaster, a word outside? You two, have another go at stirring loose a memory or two in our devourer's head."

Oh, this was obviously going to be a laugh riot of a conversation. Did the RV have an escape chute?

Even if it did, I wasn't going to give our leader the satisfaction of thinking he'd intimidated me into pulling a runner. I'd managed to coax the big bad hellhound onto the dance floor last night. I'd kissed him and survived to tell the tale.

And there wasn't anything he could say to me that would feel any worse than what was already going through my head.

Thorn shot me a look of mild concern, but I gave his arm a light squeeze in reassurance as I passed him. "Is this a super-secret meeting for discussing mortal strategies?" I said to Omen, following him out in the cooling evening air.

The hellhound shifter made a point of not only shutting the door but also stalking across the lot to give us distance as well. With more than a little trepidation, I walked after him to where he came to a stop outside a hair salon. Its broad front window was plastered with posters of individuals who, based on their 'dos, needed to re-evaluate their personal style. A long-squashed shampoo bottle lying on the concrete walk outside gave off a soured honeysuckle scent. Way to set the mood.

I crossed my arms in imitation of Omen's typical authoritarian stance. "What's up? Was I not joyful enough that you finally recognized my genius?"

Omen rolled his eyes. "I'm just glad not to have you crowing about how you told me so."

"Oh, don't worry, that might come later. I'm waiting for my moment."

"Sorsha."

Something about the way he said my name, crisp and solemn, put a cap on my snark. When did he *ever* address me by my name and not "mortal" or "Disaster" or when he was having a particularly uncreative day, "you"? A chill tickled over my skin, but honestly, that was better than the flames I couldn't seem to stop from leaking out.

"What?" I said, serious now. "I'm listening."

He studied me for a little longer with a cool gaze incisive enough to cut into my skull. "You really are losing your handle on your powers, aren't you? More than you've let on. It's not just when you're trying to use them.

Something happened that startled your dragon just now, didn't it?"

I couldn't stop the cross of my arms from turning into hugging myself as I dredged up the answer. "I didn't just startle him. I burned him—I hurt him. And no, I didn't mean to do anything at all. I've tried to tell you a bajillion times already. There's more fire in me than I know what to do with or how to contain, and sometimes it just bursts out. Even when I *am* fighting, it's getting ahead of me."

I hesitated, and Omen's gaze sharpened. "What?"

"I almost fried a little kid in the museum," I said, the words scraping my throat raw on the way up.

"That was a reaction in the middle of a battle. You can't expect to be able to take the same care there."

Oh, now he thought it was time to go easy on me? I raised my eyebrows at him. "Would you let yourself off the hook for messing up your control like that?"

But the shifter stayed impervious. "I wouldn't be worrying about which mortals I took down, whatever their age, to begin with."

"You know that's not what I meant." I let out a rough sigh. "I realize you find it hard to believe that I could have enough power to be a danger to anyone when I don't mean to be. You probably still find it hard to believe that any mortal has powers at all. But I do have them, and—I don't like the way it feels now. It isn't a wonderous talent I can bend to my will. Sometimes the flames come out of nowhere, and I can't shake the impression that they could totally explode. That I could flatten the whole city if I didn't catch the fire in time."

Omen didn't retract his previous skepticism, but at

least he didn't argue with me. "It's been hurting you when you're using it—how often?"

"Most of the time, lately. And when I'm not, when it has those surges, too. But at least I heal from the burns quickly." I rubbed my forearms where the skin had been blistered last night but was now only faintly pink. "That kid wouldn't have recovered. Pickle wouldn't if I burned him badly enough."

The hellhound shifter sucked in a breath. He started to pace the width of the walkway, his expression intent. "I don't like it," he said finally. "We have too much at stake to bring a destructive wild card into the mix."

My back stiffened. "If you're going to try to tell me to take a hike after all this—"

He held up his hand. "Cool your jets, Disaster. I pushed you into bringing this power out; I can take responsibility for that. And you still contribute more to the cause than I can dismiss. But before these unusual reactions take hold any further, I think we should see if you can get a handle on them so that you can use them to destroy our enemies and not yourself. For that, we need to understand them. Understand you and what you are. Do you know where you were supposedly born?"

That wasn't the direction I'd expected this conversation to go. "I'm not sure. I was three when Luna escaped with me, and she refused to tell me very much—she didn't want me going back there. I think she figured the hunters who murdered my parents might still be looking for me. But I remember a few things. We might be able to figure it out."

"Good. Then we can add that to our list of goals

alongside building our base of allies. There must be someone in that place who'd know more about this fae woman and your supposed parents, and therefore how you came to be. If we're going to get answers, I have to imagine they start there."

"Okay." A tingle shot through me, both exhilarated and uneasy at the thought of digging into my history. Even if I got answers, that didn't mean I was going to like them.

"I'm glad we're agreed," Omen said in a slightly wry tone. He'd actually been pretty... considerate about the whole thing. And that wasn't a word I'd ever thought I'd associate with the hellhound shifter, at least not when it came to his attitude toward me. But we had been through a lot, hadn't we? We'd found a pretty good rhythm for working together until my powers had started turning me into even more of a pyromaniac.

My gaze had drifted to his mouth: those perfect Cupid's bow lips. The lips that had branded mine with a heat that still made my knees weak remembering it.

He was turning away to head back to the Everymobile. "Omen," I said quickly. "About last night outside the club—"

His gaze shot back to me with a flash of orange fire that didn't look at all welcoming. Maybe that'd been designed to cut me off, but he should know by now that keeping my mouth shut wasn't a particular skill of mine.

"I take it you want to pretend it never happened," I went on.

He spun the rest of the way to face me again. His eyes had settled back into their usual cool hue, but a heat wafted over me that I was pretty sure had come from his well-built body. If he wanted me to believe he had no emotions at all about our split-second encounter, he was being about as convincing as a dog drooling over a forbidden bone.

Except I wasn't forbidden, definitely not where boning was concerned. So what exactly was the issue?

"Do you have any alternate suggestions?" he asked. "Because if you think you're going to reel me in like you somehow did my associates, you can incinerate that idea. Even if anything *did* happen between us—which it won't—it isn't going to buy you any special favors."

I blinked. "Hold on. Why would you figure I was looking for favors, special or otherwise?"

He shrugged. "You do seem to be making a habit of seducing some rather powerful shadowkind. Do you really need one more just for the hell of it?"

He was lucky I didn't incinerate *him* for what he was implying. I glowered at him. "I didn't kiss you—or do all the *many* things I've done with the others—for some kind of personal gain, unless you count the gaining of fine times between the sheets. It isn't part of any plan. It just... happened. And I liked that it happened, so I didn't see any reason to stop more happening when the occasion arose. This situation is already crazy enough. Is there really something wrong with taking part of that craziness in an enjoyable direction now and then?"

"I suppose not. What was last night about, then?"

"I don't know. Sometimes you're appealing in a very annoying way. Sorry if that bothers you. I kissed you because I wanted to, plain and simple. If you're looking for a huge conspiracy, you're not going to find it there. But if it was so distasteful to you, I'm sure I can restrain myself in the future. As you've pointed out, I have plenty of other supernatural beings to kiss if the urge strikes."

Omen's mouth twitched. There I went, staring at those damn lips again. When I met his eyes instead, a hint of their orange glow had come back.

"I didn't say it was distasteful," he said, in a carefully restrained voice that spoke of so many emotions he might be tamping down. "But if you're concerned about how many blazes you set off, perhaps you should pick your dance partners more carefully. Let's have it end where we left it last night."

"Fine," I said. I definitely wasn't disappointed about that. All right, all right, maybe a teensy weensy bit. "I just thought we should clear the air. Look! Clear as crystal. Now back to our regularly scheduled programming."

That twitch of his mouth was in the direction of a smile. And maybe it would have gotten all the way there if Ruse hadn't hurried over to us from the RV right then. The fire in Omen's eyes went out as swiftly as a doused campfire.

"No luck with Snap?" he said, taking in the incubus's expression.

"Not exactly." Ruse ran a hand through his already rumpled hair. "I didn't want to say this in front of him in case it made things worse."

My pulse hiccupped. Was there more wrong with Snap beyond just his memory?

Ruse looked at me and then back at Omen. "I took as good a read as I could on his inner state. It's not easy picking up emotions and the rest from shadowkind—most of us keep our minds too guarded. But you know our devourer is pretty much an open book. I think... I think he's in there. All of him. The Company jackasses didn't burn those memories out of them. He's just buried them so deep even he can't dredge them up again, for whatever reason."

"Why would he do that?" I asked.

"I don't know. Maybe he was trying to pull his consciousness away from the torment and he overshot by a couple of miles?" Ruse let out a short laugh that had no real humor in it. "In essence, you could say he devoured himself."

8

Thorn

If Talon's fidgety comrade didn't stop sneering at Sorsha, I was going to have to apply my fist to his skull and enjoy the billow of his essence escaping. Our lady wouldn't like it, but I was starting to feel it'd be worth weathering her disappointment.

The syndicate boss himself wasn't cultivating my good favor either. He'd grimaced and sighed through Omen's explanation of our need, and now he was working his jaw in thought with his basilisk eyes still hidden behind those dark-paned glasses.

You couldn't trust a being who wouldn't look you in the eyes—even if it was a look that could kill. He'd have been thinking rather highly of himself if he believed he could fell any of us shadowkind in attendance.

But of course one of our number was not shadowkind and thus not of the same bodily durability. And Jinx—

who, based on his frenetic movements and the quivers of energy that rippled off him with a faint lemony tang, I'd become increasingly sure was a poltergeist—absolutely delighted in reminding us of that.

"Not sure what you need allies like us for when you've got this one already," he mocked, waving his hand toward Sorsha. "Interesting strategy, bringing a human along to fight enemies who can topple even higher shadowkind. Makes me wonder what other screws you've got loose up there."

Now he'd managed to insult both my commander and my lady in one go. We could discover how amusing he'd find the situation when he was leaking smoke all over his clubhouse.

I took a step forward, my hand clenching, and Sorsha caught my arm. She gave me a little smile with a sharpness I suspected was intended for the other shadowkind. "Leave him be. He doesn't know how much he doesn't know."

Jinx squirmed at the affront to his intelligence and shut his mouth, which satisfied me enough for the moment, even if it was mostly because of the stern glance Talon sent his way. Omen might not be terribly pleased if I thrashed one of our potential allies in the middle of negotiations either.

Or perhaps we were already at the end of those negotiations. The basilisk turned back to us, his mouth still twisted at a not-at-all-promising angle.

"I hear your concerns," he said. "But I've already offered plenty of assistance within the city bounds. My base of power is here—I can't say I have any resources on the other side of the ocean. I'm not about to leave my operations here untended, and I'm hardly going to ask even the employees I can spare to traipse off across the world on some potentially suicidal quest."

"*Not* tackling the Company of Light as soon as we're able to could be even more suicidal," Omen said, but I could tell from the weary edge to his tone that he was even less optimistic now than he'd been going into this place.

When he'd first brought us together, my old associate had said the four of us would be enough to see through his mission, that the shadowkind who refused to recognize the impending catastrophe would only slow us down. The urge gripped me to say we didn't need any of these buffoons, that we should continue as we had been after all. Suggesting otherwise had made me uneasy to begin with, as much as Sorsha had proven her case before. I'd chosen to follow Omen on this path because I trusted he would lead us well.

And I knew far too well the consequences of questioning one's superiors. It was because I'd gone to seek out another possible solution to the conflict—against the orders of the wingéd generals—that I hadn't been there for the final slaughter in the wars that had demolished my wingéd brethren. I'd chased a hope of a better way rather than standing by my comrades, and they had died without me standing by them while I'd lived with fewer scars than I'd deserved. If I'd been dedicated enough to stay the course, would it have gone differently?

I'd thought that if this time I devoted myself completely to a figure smart and strong enough to be worthy of that faith, it would be my redemption. But this course had turned out to be much more complicated than I'd expected.

"You could at least tell your underlings about the problem and see if any of them would be willing to pitch in without being ordered to," Sorsha said. "Or is your grip on your operations so shaky you couldn't spare even a few shadowkind to make sure you don't all end up in cages?"

"*No one* is going to cage me," Talon retorted, a threatening hint of a hiss creeping into his voice. "You can make your own invitations. I have better things to do than cater to your crusade."

"Fine," Omen said flatly. "Can you at least answer one question before we leave you to your oh-so-important business? I hear the Highest were making inquiries with the mortal-side shadowkind some twenty or thirty years ago, looking for a powerful and potentially dangerous being. Possibly by the name of Jasper or Garnet or similar? Did you catch wind of any of that?"

Talon frowned as he appeared to consider. "That does ring a bell of some sort. I remember the word going out... I seem to have gotten the impression the search was mostly to the south."

"Do you remember if you heard that the being was apprehended?"

"No, nothing more after the initial questioning. What do you want with that one anyway?"

Omen's lips curled with the subtlest of sneers. "I'm wondering if he'd have the balls to go up against a conglomerate of mortals, unlike some others I won't mention."

He turned on his heel and stalked out without another word. Sorsha and I followed, my lady shooting a derisive glare Talon's way for good measure. As we headed back to the vehicle where Ruse had stayed with our befuddled Snap, she gave herself a little shake as if to release the tension of the encounter, the sunlight flashing in her lovely hair.

The stresses of our mission had appeared to weigh on our lady more than usual these last few days, even before we'd discovered the devourer's unexpected predicament. I hadn't wanted to impinge on her honor by revealing that I'd noticed when she clearly was attempting to master those concerns on her own. Still, I was glad that she'd seemed more settled since her talk with Omen earlier today.

"Who—or what—is the Highest?" she asked him now.

"The oldest of the shadowkind," he replied. "Some say they were the first ones, the only ones that have existed from the beginning. There aren't many of them, and they don't have much to do with the rest of us, generally speaking. They only intervene from time to time when they get the idea someone's making quite a bit more trouble than they'd prefer."

"I've never even encountered one of the Highest," I said. We all knew, perhaps by some instinct, that it was best not to venture too far into the deepest depths of our natural realm. The ancient beings there preferred not to be disturbed.

"And you should be glad for it," the hellhound shifter said darkly.

Sorsha hummed to herself. "So why are you really interested in this shadowkind they were looking for?"

"Essentially the same reason I gave that trumped up lizard. If the Highest take issue with this being's behavior, he's got to be something of a rebel. Maybe that means he won't care about our cause either, but at the very least, I doubt he'd beg off out of fear of disrupting the status quo." Omen let out a huff of breath. "As we've witnessed yet again, most of our kind are useless when it comes to paying attention to anything other than their own self-interest."

"We found allies before," Sorsha insisted. "There'll have to be others who'll care enough."

She always challenged him so easily, without the slightest fear. And she *had* been right. I didn't know if we'd have managed to destroy the main facility in that last city without the assistance she'd worked to obtain, often against Omen's direct command.

I hadn't tended to question my own capacity for bravery, but this mortal lady sometimes put me to shame. Watching her was making me start to wonder if the problem all those centuries ago hadn't been that I'd ventured to question what we were doing but that more of my comrades *hadn't* questioned it. Which I supposed was why when I opened my mouth, the remark that fell most easily from my lips was, "I believe there are potential allies out there, as difficult as it may be to find them."

Omen gave me a sideways glance as if in askance, but

he'd clearly come around to agreeing with our lady's perspective on this matter, even if he still muttered about it now and then. He didn't bother to argue. "Then it's a good thing we'll have plenty of time to ask around while we're dealing with our diversion. We need to work out exactly where we're going next to unravel your mysterious history, Disaster. Let's hope it won't be too catastrophic."

Sorsha made a face at him as she climbed onto the RV. "You obviously wouldn't have any frame of reference for this, but a three-year-old human's memories are pretty vague. We can go over the bits and pieces I do remember, and—"

She stopped in her tracks in the space between the driver's seat and the living area. Ruse had just emerged from the shadows farther down the hall, Snap popping into view behind him, but Sorsha wasn't looking at them.

I peered over her shoulder to observe three pairs of shoes lined up on the floor beside the cupboards. From their size and their neon hues, I guessed they were possessions the unicorn shifter had left behind.

I was about to ask Sorsha what had disturbed her about them when two of those shoes leapt up in the air and switched places. Then three of them started hopping around in a little dance. They flipped over each other, smacked the floor in a rhythmic beat, and suddenly all six of them flew up two at a time to stack into a wobbly tower. It held, swaying, for a few seconds before the shoes tumbled back to the ground.

A figure about the size of a partly-grown human child blinked into view beside them, spiky orange hair sticking up from her rounded head and skinny arms flung out to grab at the shoes. Her voice came out thin and squeaky. "Darn it, darn it. Never get the balance right." She glanced up at us—at Sorsha, mostly—and gave a grin that stretched far into her cheeks. "I hope you were a little entertained by the trick anyway."

"Um," Sorsha said, apparently at a loss for words.

I wasn't going to brandish my fists at a figure this pathetic, but security was my job. Stepping up beside my lady, I cleared my throat. "Who are you, and what are you doing on our vehicle?"

"Oh, I—" The figure fumbled with the shoes and then shoved them all into one of the cupboards with an exaggerated sigh of resignation. She sprang up to her full height, which only brought her about level with Sorsha's waist. Still grinning, she gave us both a brisk salute. "Antic, at your service. Here to help in whatever ways I can."

"An imp," Omen said from behind me with a note of distaste.

Ugh. Imps were mischief-makers, always seeking human attention in the most obnoxious ways. Since they liked to scamper around mortal-side and I'd rarely crossed the divide in centuries, I'd thankfully had few dealings with them.

"You didn't entirely answer the second question," I said. "Why are you here? Our human doesn't need your version of 'entertaining'."

The imp raised her pointed chin. "I did answer. I'm here to help. You're looking for help, aren't you? I heard you talking about it. And you obviously know what you're doing, the way you marched into that awful room where they had me shut up behind bars. If you're going to stick it to more of *those* kinds of humans, count me totally on board."

"I don't think your sort of helping is exactly—" Omen started.

Sorsha held up her hand. "Wait a second. Weren't you just complaining about how few shadowkind want to get their hands dirty? She just proved she can move things around invisibly, even if her shoe towers need a little work in the steadiness department. There's got to be *some* way she could contribute."

Ruse had ambled closer. He peered down at the little being with a smirk. "I don't get any sense that she has motives beyond what she's offering."

"The question is whether she'll contribute more than she'll make us long for a quick sword to the chest," Omen said, echoing my own reservations.

"Hush, you," the imp said, as if she wasn't speaking to a hellhound shifter more than twice her size and approximately a thousand times more powerful than she was. She bounded up onto the sofa and sat there with her scrawny legs dangling. "The human wants me to stay, and that's good enough for me."

"No one asked your opinion," Omen muttered. "Really, Disaster?"

Sorsha gave him a firm look. "Really. You can't moan about not getting enough help and then moan that the help we get isn't in the perfect package." She turned back to the imp. "Thank you. *I* really appreciate it."

The imp beamed at her. "How are we sticking it to 'em first?"

Sorsha sank down on the sofa across from her. "Well, we need to figure out where we're going next—for a sort of side mission. Maybe you can even help with that. I'll mention all the things I can remember about the place, and if it sounds like anywhere any of you have been mortal-side, speak up."

As I propped myself against the counter by the sink, keeping one eye on the imp in case she turned out to have more malicious intentions—you could never be too sure—Sorsha rubbed her mouth.

"All right. There was someplace we got ice cream at least a couple of times—there was always a line-up and I'd get impatient, and it had a bright red sign. I remember things about the inside of our house, but that won't help anything. Um... there was a park near the house, with a slide my mom said was too tall for me to go on yet. Some kind of festival we went to with lots of music, in the summer I think—my hair got all sweaty. And there was a big bridge I loved... something about it at night, like smoke rising across the sky?" She knit her brow. "I know that's all incredibly vague. I do have the box with the note my parents left me, too."

She reached for her purse, but Omen brushed past me to touch her shoulder. "Hold on. Say what you did about the bridge again. As much as you can remember."

Sorsha frowned in concentration. "It was definitely big—although hard to say how much of that impression is relative to when I was a preschooler. I only remember it when it was dark. Maybe not full night but evening. And that smokiness moving toward the sky—"

"That." His fingers tightened where he was gripping her. "There's a glamour on your memory. I can feel it coming through when you try to verbalize the scene. Your fae must have put it there."

"Why would Luna have messed with *that* memory?"

"That's the question, isn't it? Maybe to make sure you didn't go back. All the more reason I should break it. A nearly twenty-five-year-old bit of fae flim-flam shouldn't be too difficult to dispel. Keep focusing on that image."

Sorsha tensed. "What are you going to do? Is this some kind of mind-reading trick you never mentioned?"

Omen shook his head. "Don't worry, Disaster. I've got no interest in unraveling the entire contents of your head. I can simply sense the magic there when you're concentrating on the information it's clouding. And I can break it, if you'll let me."

She exhaled slowly. "All right then."

Her eyes closed as she must have brought the memory back up, and Omen's did too. The rest of us watched silently—even the damned imp, though she was squirming in excited anticipation.

Our commander's hand gave a little tug on Sorsha's shoulder, and her eyes widened. Then she laughed. "It wasn't smoke. It was *bats*. A whole cloud of them, soaring up past the bridge."

Ruse snapped his fingers. "I know where that is. It figures you'd have come from a city with plenty of shadowkind." He nudged the devourer. "Sounds like we're heading down to Austin."

"Austin," Sorsha repeated as if trying out the word. She smiled, but hesitantly. Maybe wondering the same thing I was.

If her fae guardian had taken steps to meddle with that memory, what else might she have hidden in our lady's mind?

9

Sorsha

It was going to be a long drive from Chicago to Austin, so I figured I might as well find something useful to do with the time. Only because I was such a hard worker, and not at all to distract myself from the fact that the woman who'd raised me had distorted my memories without telling me, of course.

Why had Luna been so adamant that I never return to the city of my birth? She'd never given me reasons, just obscured that key image so I had no choice, no way of knowing where to go. Would she *ever* have talked about it with me if she'd lived to see me all the way to adulthood, or had she planned to take that secret to her grave regardless?

I couldn't ask her now, and I didn't think Omen would appreciate it if I asked him to listen to my entire life story up until age sixteen to find out if she'd glamoured other blanks into my memories. So I just wouldn't think about it. Piece of cake. Ha.

I wasn't really looking forward to the call I was about to make either. Vivi had told me that Ellen was home from the hospital, so I should be able to contact her at her regular number, but that didn't mean the co-leader of my local branch of the Shadowkind Defense Fund would be happy to hear from me. Being attacked by Company goons as a warning would tend to sour a person to the gal who'd drawn that attention in the first place.

But Ellen had gone to the trouble of reaching out to me when she'd realized I was in danger, even while she was still in the hospital. I couldn't be totally out of my mind to think she might help us again.

I pulled my legs up where I'd tucked myself into one corner of the sofa-bench and brought my phone to my ear. At the other side of the sofa, Snap was examining a coffee mug Ruse had handed him in the game of Let's See If You Remember This that had been going on without any wins all day. Rather than remind myself of the innocent bemusement so often in the devourer's expression now, I gazed out the window. The lights along the freeway flashed by through the thickening dusk.

To my relief, Ellen picked up on the second ring. "Hello?" she said with an unusual tentativeness that made me wince inwardly.

"Hey, Ellen," I said, suddenly tentative myself. "It's Sorsha. I'm sorry I haven't checked in on you sooner—hell, I'm sorry about all of it. Things have gotten pretty... crazy."

Understatement of the century.

Ellen made a dismissive noise. "I know you hadn't expected any of us to get hurt. This group you've clashed with—they're obviously much more of a menace than we've dealt with before. *None* of us expected that." She paused. "Did you get my warning about Leland in time? He didn't turn up at the last meeting. I'm not sure if he's sided with this Company of Light completely now."

I *hadn't* gotten her warning soon enough—not in time to save us from getting T-boned by an armored truck, anyway. And my ex-FWB hadn't shown up because he must still be staked out in his townhouse wearing boxers on his head and drinking cold, stale coffee as Ruse had instructed him to do for his "protection." It seemed better not to mention either of those facts, the former for Ellen's benefit and the latter for mine.

"Who knows, with him?" I said with a stilted chuckle. "I really appreciate you looking out for me, especially considering the state you were in. Are you doing okay?"

"Oh, yes, no permanent damage here. I'm made of stronger stuff than those criminals realized."

A sporadic crackling sound carried from the background. Was that... popcorn popping? A smile tugged at my lips despite my guilt. If Ellen was experimenting with popcorn flavors again, she couldn't be feeling too bad.

Lord only knew when I'd get to sample any of her new combos again. When would I be welcome at another Fund meeting? Assuming I made it back home in the first place...

I shook off the gloom of that thought and focused on

my main objective. "About those criminals—we've found out that their operations are spread out much farther than we'd guessed: across the country and even overseas. I know a lot of the Fund members aren't feeling all that friendly toward me or that cause right now, but if *any* of you would be willing to lend a hand even in some teeny tiny way... We'd make sure you stayed out of the line of fire, of course."

The moment the words came out of my mouth, I felt like a shit heel. She'd just been beaten to bits, and here I was suggesting she might do me another favor. What had I been thinking when I'd come up with this ridiculous plan?

Well, I'd been thinking that Ellen was just about the only ally with much in the way of resources that I still had that I could call on, but that didn't make it an act of compassionate genius.

Ellen was silent for a moment. I was debating asking Ruse if he could take a break from shoving assorted paraphernalia in front of Snap to charm the Fund leader into forgetting I'd ever brought up the subject when she finally cleared her throat. "Something needs to be done about them. I don't know what we'd be able to offer on our end, but—I'll give it some thought and make some discreet inquiries."

"*Very* discreet," I emphasized. "I don't want anything else happening to you. Don't—don't mention the Company or take any action against them, not right now. Just let me know when you know if you've got anyone who still *wants* to take action, and I'll work out the details from there."

Even with that cautioning and Ellen's willingness, I ended the call with a lump of nausea in my stomach.

Ruse was now dipping his fingers into a cup of water and sprinkling droplets over Snap's head. "There was this time it started raining while we were scouting out one of the disappearances, and you were so surprised you stayed right in it instead of vanishing into the shadows like a sensible being."

Snap laughed, shaking his head as the drops hit his curls. "I wish I could remember that. The water falls right from the sky?"

"Unfortunately," Thorn muttered. I couldn't tell whether his grimness was due to the devourer's continued forgetfulness or his distaste for mortal realm weather. Maybe a little of both.

Past him, near the driver's seat where Omen was at the wheel, Antic the imp was hopping from one foot to the other like a kid trying to avoid the urge to pee. She turned a map in her hands. "The next exit," she said determinedly in her squeaky voice. "You want to get on the 24. Oh, it's a pretty one."

"I don't care what it looks like as long as it's going to get us to Austin," Omen said.

I didn't know where Pickle had gotten to. He hadn't come scampering to me for pets since the accidental burning this afternoon. So much for two years of back rubs and bacon.

My phone, still in my hand, pinged with an incoming text. Another one from Vivi. *I know you're probably very busy saving the world, but could you shoot me a quick message letting me know you're okay? Ditto!* Kissy-face emoji.

As I looked at the words, my throat tightened. My best friend's effortless cheer felt leagues removed from anything my life resembled at this moment. What might I inadvertently do to *her* if we ever hung out again? The image of one of her trademark all-white outfits singed to brown and black flashed through my mind, and the constricting sensation ran down to my chest.

This was what my life had become: monsters and mayhem... and maybe this was what it should have been all along. I didn't know what to say to her anymore.

Still alive, I forced myself to write back, because a reassured Vivi would be much safer than a panicked one. *Reasonably okay. Not much to report yet. You hang in there. Ditto.* The sign-off was our homage to one of our favorite cheesy romance flicks, and I couldn't *not* say it when she did. You could consider that a sacred pact, no matter how far I veered into monsterdom.

"And then we make a right at those shiny lights," Antic said to Omen's wordless grumble.

Ruse slid onto the sofa beside Snap and gave the devourer's hair an affectionate ruffle. "You know you're all right now, don't you? We'll make sure those assholes never get their hands on you again. There's no need to be hiding away."

Snap blinked at him with one of those puzzled looks that wrenched at my heart. "Is someone hiding? I'm right here." He spread his arms as if in demonstration.

My dear, sweet shadowkind. If Ruse was right that Snap had essentially devoured everything about himself from the past however many months, was it even possible for him to spit himself back up, so to speak? What would it take? If I needed to put on a full-blown musical production or sacrifice a crow or some other hocus pocus, someone had better fill me in quick.

The incubus glanced across the table and caught my look. Whatever my expression showed, it turned him as grim as our warrior companion. He opened his mouth as if to speak, but at the same moment, Omen's voice barked from up front.

"That sign says we're heading toward Atlanta. I might not be a geography expert, but I'm pretty sure that's a hell of a lot more east than we want to be going to get to Texas."

Antic let out a squeal of apology and fumbled with the map. "I think—I think—*Texas*. Yes. Right. I had it turned the wrong way. We don't want to be on *this* road at all."

Omen's next growl suggested that if the imp gave him one more direction, he'd be picking her bones out of his teeth in a minute. Ruse arched his eyebrows at me, his expression still more solemn than usual, and sauntered over to lend a hand.

"We're not too far off track," he said, and grabbed Omen's phone from the dashboard. "But you know, even if we don't need sleep, we could use a break from the highway. Let that road rage simmer down and all. It's been a stressful day. I'll charm us a space in a hotel so luxurious it'll mellow even *you* out, Luce."

He flashed a grin at his boss, who bared his teeth in a much more menacing fashion in response. The incubus retorted with some gesture I couldn't quite make out but knowing him was probably obscene.

The hellhound shifter sighed. "Fine. But mainly because *Darlene* could probably use a break. I expect us to be up and on the road again at sunrise." He glanced over his shoulder at me. "If *you* had ever bothered to learn how to drive, the rest of us could have slipped in and out of a rift and been there already."

I stuck my tongue out at him, although sadly he didn't get to see my show of immense maturity because he'd already returned his gaze to the road. "As if you'd leave 'Darlene' in my disastrous hands anyway."

"Good point," he said, in a tone I chose to believe was more amused than annoyed. "Work your magic, incubus. If you can shock our mortal speechless for a minute or two, I'll consider that a victory."

10

Sorsha

I wouldn't say I was struck speechless, but Ruse hadn't been lying when he'd said he would aim for luxury. The place he led us into a half hour later boasted sweeping velvet-carpeted staircases around marble pillars so wide the ancient redwoods would have been envious. I resisted asking the concierge if they'd stolen their lobby furniture from the Palace of Versailles.

The penthouse suite the incubus had charmed our way into wasn't any model of restraint either. The main lounge area stretched wider than my entire apartment back home—before, y'know, I'd burned it down and all—with leather furniture so buttery soft a person could melt right into the cushions. The bathroom sported a small, marble-tiled swimming pool I couldn't imagine anyone in their right mind calling a "bathtub." And the bedroom...

"Where the magic happens," Ruse said with his typical smirk, sweeping his arm toward the king-sized canopy bed draped with gauzy silk on the other side of a Persian rug so thick I was in danger of drowning in it. Holy mother of majesty, we were living like the crustiest of upper crusters tonight.

Pickle, who'd accepted being carted in via my purse, charged across that red-and-gold expanse and promptly tumbled head over heels as his tiny feet sank deeper than he'd anticipated. With an indignant snort, he changed course and trotted off to the bathroom, where he had designer towels to shred into a very high-class nest.

"Good night!" I called after him, but the little dragon didn't glance back. Apparently we still weren't on speaking terms.

Snap took the whole place in, beaming with wonder. "What a fantastic building. Mortals do make things so much more bright and colorful than anything in our realm. I think I'll explore the rest of this... 'hotel' from the shadows." He paused and looked at the rest of us with evident concern. "Unless there's something you need from me."

Always thinking of how he could help everyone else first. A renewed ache woke up in my heart.

"No, no, you've done plenty, whether you remember it or not," Omen said, more gently than I was used to. Sometimes I forgot that underneath his preferred cold exterior, he really did care about the members of the team he'd assembled. He gave the devourer an awkward pat on the shoulder and walked with him toward the door. "But since we don't want to lose you again, maybe I should make the rounds with you. It wouldn't hurt to keep an eye out for any suspicious activity."

"Yes, we can do both! Explore and investigate." Snap beamed even brighter.

My heart might as well have been broken into pieces and fed to a pond of koi. "You be careful," I said, unable to stop myself.

"Of course," Snap replied cheerfully, and vanished into the shadows.

Maybe forgetting everything that had happened since he'd first ventured among mortals—not just forgetting me and his original companions but the way he'd used his power too—made things easier for him. With the pang in my chest, a lyric swam up and twisted in my mind. It came out mournful when I sang it. "You were always in a bind. You were always far too kind."

Antic had leapt onto the bed and was now bouncing on the mattress, the satin sheets rustling beneath her feet. She grabbed the silk drapes of the canopy. "What shall I make for you? A clown on a surfboard? A fish falling from a skyscraper?" She vanished behind the fabric while swinging it into a shape that did somehow resemble that second offering.

"Er, I think I'd like to just relax, like we planned," I said. "I don't need a show."

The imp harrumphed and popped back into view. "I'll go see if someone else in this place would enjoy some antics from Antic, then." She jabbed her finger in Thorn's direction as she skipped past us. "I *will* be back at dawn when we ride again!"

Thorn managed not to grimace until she'd slipped out of sight. He gave me a baleful look. "And you think she'll be a valuable addition to our plans?"

I threw my hands in the air. "I haven't got a clue. If worse comes to worst, we can tell her building shoe towers is an essential component and let her occupy herself in the mall while we do the real work, right?"

"With allies like these, who needs enemies," Ruse teased. His gaze had lingered on the bed. A thread of heat ran through my body at the thought of all the ways he could help me, ahem, "relax" between those sheets, but he turned as if to leave the room.

"Ruse," I said. When he met my eyes, his were warm and maybe even intrigued, but something in his face struck me as uncertain. I found I didn't know how to follow that up, and not only because his gorgeous face could steal my breath.

A deeper, sweeter emotion than desire welled up inside me. Even without peeking inside my head, I doubted it'd escaped his notice that my mood had gotten pretty dour during the drive. None of the shadowkind really needed pit stops. He'd come up with this scheme as much for my benefit as the fun he'd planned for my birthday last night. Why?

I wasn't really sure, but I did know how badly I wanted to show him I'd noticed and what it meant to me. How much *he* was coming to mean to me. I could have invited him into my bed, but that was just a night's work for an incubus, wasn't it? He'd indicated before that no other mortal woman had ever wanted anything from him *other* than his talent for pleasure.

So maybe it was time he got to experience what it was like to be at the receiving end of that kind of attention. I could invite him into bed after all.

I held out my hand to him. "Come here. You arranged all this—I think you should get to enjoy it as much as anyone."

He cocked his head. "What exactly did you have in mind, Miss Blaze?"

The suggestive lilt he gave the nickname sent a tingle all the way down to my toes. Even if I was focusing on him, I was still going to enjoy this a hell of a lot myself. "Get over here already, and you'll find out."

Thorn coughed. "In that case, perhaps I should—"

Ruse gave the warrior's arm a tug as he ambled over. "I don't see any reason for you to go anywhere, my friend. Our mortal here has been known to require, shall we say, additional servicing." He winked at me.

He seemed more at ease saying that—like he'd relaxed more when I'd asked him to join me and Snap last week. If he preferred the company, I sure as sugar wasn't going to say no. I peeked at Thorn through my eyelashes as coyly as I was capable of. "The more, the merrier?"

The warrior's tan complexion flushed slightly pinkish. He glanced between us as if waiting for one of us to laugh and say it was all a joke. When we didn't, he took a step closer. His voice came out with a roughness that got any part of my body that hadn't already been tingling on board. "If m'lady wishes it..."

Ruse did laugh at that. "Just get your medieval ass over here, my friend."

I poked the incubus in his deliciously sculpted chest, prodding him toward the bed. "I'm starting with you. Now strip."

"Oh, getting bossy, are we?" He raised his hands to the buttons of his shirt, the glint in his eyes turning more heated.

He didn't move fast enough for my liking. Before he'd finished unbuttoning his shirt, I was reaching for the fly of his slacks. Ruse let me undo it and stepped out of his slacks gamely, finally shedding that shirt so nearly all the well-muscled planes of his body were on display.

"This doesn't seem quite fair," he remarked as I pushed him the last few steps to the bed, but when he reached for my blouse, I shook my head. He glanced past me to his comrade for assistance. "Thorn, are you going to get to work on her or what?"

Thorn let out a low rumble of a chuckle from where he was standing behind me. I rarely heard a laugh out of him—it turned my earlier tingling into an eager flare of desire.

"I don't believe you're in command of this encounter, incubus," the warrior said.

I smiled. Indeed he was not. "Down you go," I instructed Ruse.

The incubus sprawled back on the bed, everything on display other than the bulge hidden behind those briefs, so languidly sensual in his pose I practically orgasmed just looking at him. He shot another remark at Thorn. "But don't you *want* to see that lovely form on full display? I doubt you're in this to ogle *me*."

That much was true too. Thorn rested his broad hands on my waist, grasping the hem of my shirt. "May I?" he murmured, his gravelly voice full of promise. Who was I to argue?

I raised my arms so he could pluck the blouse off me and then squirmed out of my undershirt with its silver-and-iron badge before he had to deal with that. I stayed put just long enough for Thorn to cup my breasts through my bra and press a kiss to my shoulder, soaking in the strength that emanated from his brawny form with an encouraging hum, but I had another lover I'd meant to attend to.

I crawled onto the bed next to Ruse, and Thorn sank down at my other side. The incubus teased his fingers into my hair as if to draw me to him, but I knew how easy it was to get lost in his skillful kisses. I diverted my mouth to the edge of his jaw, then the side of his neck. The bittersweet cacao scent of his skin flooded my senses.

As I charted a path across Ruse's drool-worthy chest, Thorn unhooked my bra and palmed my breasts skin to skin, the roughness of his calloused hands adding a spark of friction to the caress. I sighed happily against the incubus's toned stomach and raised my head to tug at his briefs. "These need to go too."

Ruse lifted his hips to help me peel the undergarment off. He pushed himself up on his elbows and reached for my jeans, but I brushed his hand away, doing some ogling of my own. His cock had come to attention, jutting at its eager angle like a glorious leaning tower of pleasure. I couldn't wait to be the one generating that pleasure tonight.

The incubus peered at me with what looked like genuine puzzlement. "Where are you taking this, Miss Blaze?"

I lowered my mouth to his hip, then his thigh, and ran

my fingers up the straining length of his erection. "I'm taking care of *you* like you've always been taking care of me. About time we did a little role reversal, don't you think?"

Before he could respond, I skimmed my fingertips back down his cock and wrapped my lips around its head. The cacao flavor of him was even more intense on that sensitive flesh, with a tang of salt when I teased my tongue over the tip.

He sucked in a ragged breath. "You don't owe me this."

I looked up at him, slicking my saliva and a bead of his precum down his cock with my hand. "I know. I want to do it. And even if I'm not the most talented gal you've ever been with, I'd imagine I can make it reasonably satisfying."

"That's not—" His mouth twisted into a crooked grin. "You don't have to worry about being compared. Not many of the women I've been with would have thought to offer this. But why should you forego your own pleasure?" He beckoned to me, his eyes glinting slyly. "Turn around, and we can at least make this a mutual love-fest."

The fact that so many of his past lovers wouldn't have thought beyond getting their own rocks off only made me more sure of my intentions. I didn't budge, giving his cock a firm pump that made it twitch against my hand. "I'm getting off plenty just knowing how good I'm making you feel. And I'm sure Thorn can add to that as he'd like. For once, *you* are going to do nothing except lie back and enjoy yourself."

I bent over him again, taking him into my mouth as deeply as I could. Thorn had eased back to give me room, caressing my naked back with rhythmic strokes, but at my invocation, he leaned closer. He followed my spine with scorching kisses, one hand fondling my breasts again and the other sliding over my belly. The pleasure he stirred fueled my desire into headier flames.

I swiveled my tongue around Ruse's cock, cupping his balls, and he groaned. When I glanced at his face, his eyes were flashing between their hazel guise and their natural glowing gold. Faint shimmers of that same sheen flickered over his skin as if he was struggling to hold himself back.

"Go ahead," I said. "Let your shine out. You know I like it."

His body flared in response, his incubus glow lighting up every part of him, even the cock I sucked down again. It curved at its sharper shadowkind angle in my mouth, the bump of his pubic bone protruding, all designed to give his partners the most possible satisfaction. But he'd fed plenty from me in that way in the last few weeks. He'd had his sustenance—now he deserved a treat.

His supernatural glow brought a giddying warmth with it. The sensation spread through my mouth and all through my limbs as I bobbed over Ruse's thighs. Thorn fanned the flames higher with the pressure of his hands and mouth. His fingers trailed lower to tease right between my legs. I gasped against the incubus's cock and reached back to caress the warrior's arm in return.

As I sped up my rhythm, Ruse bucked into my mouth. I tightened my lips around him and sucked harder, and he came with a flood of bittersweet heat that I swallowed down. Before I could do more than give his cock one last swipe of my tongue, he'd sat up to tug me to him, his mouth claiming mine at long last.

Thorn was undoing my jeans. Melting into the kiss, I kicked them and my panties off, but my warrior seemed to think his work was done there. I snatched at his arm before he could withdraw and pulled him back. My lips left Ruse's so I could twist around and capture the wingéd's mouth for myself, my fingers tangling in his white-blond hair.

"I want you," I said with a stutter of breath as Ruse pinched one of my nipples. "I *need* you." My core was throbbing now, aching to be filled—and no one could fill me like Thorn.

"I think you'd better attend to our lady," Ruse said, his amusement coming through the smokiness of his shadowkind voice.

Thorn dipped his fingers right between my legs from behind and groaned approvingly at the slickness of my arousal. He jerked at his trousers. "As m'lady desires."

I did desire—oh, I desired every bit of his massive form. He bent over my back, easing his thick cock into me with that incredible searing stretch, and the bliss of it radiated through me. I moaned.

One of these days I was going to have to take him in *his* full form, even more massive as that was, but I knew he didn't want Ruse seeing what he was.

As Thorn began to thrust into me, Ruse's mouth crashed into mine. I arched to meet the warrior, my fingers slipping up to grip one of the incubus's horns. I was locked between them, all that immense power looming over me and the giddy glow beneath, and yet I couldn't imagine feeling more free. The pulsing rush of pleasure swept me higher and higher—

I tipped over the peak with an even sharper surge of ecstasy and a cry I couldn't contain. My sex clenched around Thorn, and his arm tightened where he'd looped it around my waist. He drove into me again. Ruse's tongue tangled with mine, and I came apart all over again as the warrior found his own heated release.

As Thorn sagged down beside me, I rolled over to kiss him properly. He stroked his fingers down the side of my face, the gentleness of that touch a perfect contrast to the force of his mouth on mine.

Ruse slung his arm around me and kissed my shoulder. I snuggled in between my two lovers and clung to this moment of contentment before the thought of the lover I'd lost could creep back in.

11

Snap

From the short while I'd gotten to enjoy the mortal realm, I had to say it was a spectacular place. Why did anyone return shadow-side when they could have all this? The bright colors and soft textures of the expansive room the incubus had gotten for us... The intoxicating mix of scents from the platters of items something called "room service" had delivered just moments ago... It was nothing short of its own sort of magic.

I'd admit the first experiences here I remembered, being shut away under brilliant lights with a prickle of poisonous metals all around, had been rather disturbing. But if I hadn't endured that, I'd never have gotten to taste this miraculous object Thorn informed me was a breakfast sausage.

I chewed on the meaty bite, salt and savory juices mingling on my tongue, and my smile stretched wider. Yes, this world was a paradise for a devourer.

A cool quiver shot down my back at that thought, there and then gone so quickly I couldn't have examined it even if I'd wanted to. Why should I bother with that discomfort, though? It didn't feel as if the impression wanted to be prodded. And I had a great deal more breakfast to eat.

"And this?" I asked, tapping a heap of lumpy yellow stuff that smelled much more appealing than it looked.

Ruse glanced over and chuckled. "Scrambled eggs. I think you'll like those too."

The little imp we'd picked up before we'd left that last city bounded around the table. "Is there anything he *doesn't* like? He'll be having the table next!"

"And he may have it, if that's what he'd like," the incubus declared.

The mortal woman came over, still tugging at her red hair, which always drew my eye. It was more vibrant than even the furnishings in this extravagant room. She was tugging at it, I'd gathered, because she'd woken up to find the imp had woven it all into a mass of little braids while she'd slept.

Antic watched her work at untangling the strands with a huff. "*I* thought it looked nice that way."

"It's just—not my style," Sorsha said. I got the impression she was trying to spare the imp's feelings, which she seemed to do rather often, although I wasn't sure why. The two of them hadn't appeared to know each other already. The mortal obviously had a certain kindness to her. I liked that—and I liked her hair down in its loose waves best too.

She let go of the strands long enough to paw through

the offerings on the table. "Didn't we get a fruit salad? There it is. You can't skip this, Snap."

She pushed the shiny bowl with its glistening rainbow of chunks toward me, an emotion coming into her eyes that I saw quite a bit when she fixed them on me. Something hesitant but also hopeful, as if she were waiting for something she didn't actually expect to happen. I hadn't figured out what, but it made her sad, and that didn't seem right.

All of them wanted more from me than I'd been able to give. They knew me from a long while before this, and I hadn't known them until they'd pulled me from that prison.

I furrowed my brow as if that might push the memories to the surface, but I had nothing. Nothing except the journey on the large, sparkly vehicle and before that, the harsh lights in the uncomfortable cage—and before *that*, the stretch of hazy gloom in the shadow realm that I'd wandered through not knowing all the delights I was missing.

There must have been more experiences that I simply couldn't remember. Ruse and Thorn had shown and told me so many fascinating things I couldn't have imagined but had apparently encountered before. I supposed I'd have to seek out those they couldn't immediately supply all over again. That didn't sound like a horrible burden.

I popped a piece of banana into my mouth and reveled at the soft sweetness of it, even better with the peel removed. Oh, yes, I was looking forward to rediscovering everything that had slipped my mind. Even if this physical body had its quirks. A tiny itch had woken up in my forearm again. I scratched at it absently and reached for a perfect grape.

A small green shape launched itself onto the table with a warble of ineffective wings and a scrabbling of little claws against the polished wood. "Pickle!" Sorsha cried, leaping at the little dragon. He snapped up a piece of bacon before she managed to grab him. "You've had plenty already. Leave some for the rest of us."

The shadowkind creature gave a snort of disagreement and scuttled away under the table as soon as she'd set him down. That made her appear sad too. No, I didn't like that look on her at all.

"Are you going to have some eggs?" I asked. I was never sure how much I should say to her, since it seemed to both cheer and dishearten her when I spoke. I thought she might have grabbed a morsel or two in the midst of her work on her hair, but I'd been too absorbed in my own meal most of that time to pay attention.

"Nah, I'm more of a sausage gal myself," she said, spearing one of those with a fork, and shot a grin at Ruse. The incubus guffawed as if she'd said something funny, which didn't make much sense to me.

"I prefer the sausages too," I offered, and suddenly Ruse was laughing so hard his breath sputtered, and Sorsha swiped her hand across her mouth as if she were holding back a snicker as well.

I turned my gaze to Thorn, who shrugged with a resigned shake of his head. I couldn't tell whether that meant he didn't understand the joke either or he simply didn't approve of it. There appeared to be a fairly large number of things the large shadowkind didn't approve of, from what I'd seen so far.

"Sausages, sausages!" the imp started to sing in her chirpy voice, and the dragon let out a sort of bugling noise from under the table, and I could laugh at that.

Omen stalked into the room in the midst of the mirth and surveyed us with his mouth flat. His aura of power and authority filled every space he entered. I quieted out of respect. I hadn't determined yet what sort of a shifter he was, although I could tell he was one—it felt rude to outright ask—but whatever it was, there was clearly a reason the others looked to him as the leader.

And he had wanted *me* to join this team of his. I couldn't say how I'd be of much use, but I hoped I'd figure that out. It must have been an honor to be chosen by a being so formidable.

"The sun's rising," he barked. "Let's get a move on. You've lounged about long enough."

"I don't imagine Austin is going anywhere while we eat breakfast," Ruse replied in a teasing tone, but I noticed he got up quickly all the same.

Sorsha sighed and grabbed her purse. She knelt down by the table, clucking her tongue to coax Pickle into it. Not wanting any of the precious refreshments to go to waste, I snatched up the bowl of fruit salad and tipped its contents into my mouth.

I was just gulping down the last of that riot of flavor when the door crashed open with an explosive *bang*.

A horde of figures in shiny helmets and vests charged into the room, tools glittering in their hands. The metals sent a wash of vibrations through the air that dug through my skin down to my bones. Pain prickled through the sensation.

I sprang to my feet with a jerk, some instinct in me rearing its head with a vicious shudder—and another impulse yanked me backward. A chill gripped me even more potent than the poisonous energies of those metals.

I flung myself into the nearest shadows and away—away from the clang and crackle of the battle, away from the beings who'd acted like my friends, *away*... Because deep down in some cold, dark place in the center of me lay the certainty that my presence would only mean a far greater pain for those around me.

They all were safer with me off in the distant darkness than they were if I stayed among them.

12

Sorsha

The second the Company mercenaries burst into the hotel room, my fighting instincts took over. Heart thudding, I snatched up two of the brass platters our breakfast had been delivered on, briefly lamented the waste of delicious food, and slammed them into the faces of the men who'd lunged my way.

Metal clanged and eggs squelched. An invisible force I assumed was Antic followed my example and started hurling more dishes off the table at our attackers. Delicate china cups smashed left and right. Tea and butter splattered the ornate rug.

Well, what do you expect when you open up a penthouse to a bunch of monsters?

An instant later, the tea and butter was joined by a gush of blood. Thorn gouged one crystalline fist through one soldier's neck and bashed the other into a second man's face. Omen tore through the room in a maelstrom of hellhound brutality, raking his claws across thighs and calves, sinking his jaws into one woman's belly. The magma-like streaks that seared through his dark gray fur blazed with fury.

Our efforts might not be enough, though. As I ducked down and knocked the feet out from a gunman with a sweep of my leg, the sight of more figures charging through the doorway made my gut lurch. One of them was already hefting a silver-and-iron net to toss over the fighting shadowkind.

A crackle of fire rushed through me in response. I hadn't meant to risk burning the place—and all the other, perfectly innocent guests—down, but flames spurted across the guy's shirt before I had any chance to rein them in. His colleagues shoved him to the floor to drop and roll, one snatching the net from him as they did.

Shit. If I let out more than that, a lot more than just the Company assholes might end up incinerated on this fine morning.

As I swung the brass plates again, willing down the vicious heat inside as well as I could, my gaze darted across the room. At the other end, the gauzy curtains drifted in the cool breeze where we'd left the balcony door ajar. Inspiration shot through me like a bolt of lightning.

Just this once, I didn't need my supernatural allies to ensure my mortal self made it out of this alive.

"Get out of here!" I shouted. "You don't need to wait for me. I've got my own escape route; I'll meet you at Darlene."

Not that I approved of the Everymobile's new name,

just to be clear—it was only a way to avoid tipping our enemies off to where we were heading.

"M'lady," Thorn called out in protest, apparently unwilling to take my word for it. Time to get a move on anyway.

"Just *go*!" I said, snatching up my purse with a sputtering Pickle in it, and dashed toward the balcony.

It helped that our attackers had entered from the main door and were opting for a "mow them down" approach rather than "surround them." I only had to dodge a couple of fists and one gleaming whip before I was springing past the curtains into the crisp dawn air. My devoted shadowkind defenders had better take the hint and escape into the shadows now that I'd exited the room.

Leaving the balcony looked to be slightly more difficult than reaching it. Our lovely penthouse stood twelve stories above the sidewalk I'd like to end up on, and I hadn't brought my grappling hook and rope. Note to self: All occasions are good occasions to have the cat burglar gear on hand.

The thunder of impending footsteps told me I'd better get going one way or another. I glanced down, ignored the flip of my stomach—I was no chicken when it came to heights, but I generally wasn't prancing around on buildings *quite* this tall—and vaulted over the balcony's railing.

With a grasp of the bars and a swing of my legs, I launched myself onto the smaller balcony below. One floor down, eleven more to go. Too bad the rest of the windows below me only featured Juliets—who in their right mind called that little stub a balcony anyway?

The inhabitants of the sub-penthouse had left their balcony door locked, but even in a hotel this fancy, those things weren't really built for keeping people out. Who expected robbers to descend from the sky? I gave the handle a well-practice kick, grinned at the snap of the lock, and shoved the door wide just as shouts hailed down from above.

I sprinted through the room of some hotel goer who was lucky enough to still be sleeping at this hour—at least, until my pursuers crashed in—and down the hall to the stairs, not wanting to risk the elevator. My feet had never flown faster. On the ground floor, I peeked out through the window, spotted the metal-helmed figures by the front doors getting stares from the desk clerks, and eased the door open just far enough to make a run for the kitchen.

The staff who'd provided our delightful breakfast were clattering around fulfilling other room service requests. "Thanks for the lovely meal!" I hollered to them as I sprinted past. As I'd hoped, a door at the far end of the room offered an exit into an alley that held a dumpster and exactly zero Company assholes. For now.

Thankfully, we'd taken the precaution of parking the Everymobile—in cargo van guise—a few blocks away from the hotel. I loped over there before our attackers could get their act together and figure out where I'd snuck off to.

As our vehicle came into view, tension prickled through my muscles. The shadowkind *had* all hoofed it out of the penthouse when I'd left, hadn't they? I couldn't remember even seeing Snap in the fray. If we'd lost him again, or any of the others...

The door flung open to admit me, Thorn standing on the other side with an urgent beckoning. I spotted Ruse in the driver's seat behind him, foot poised over the gas.

Neither of them looked at all concerned about getting anyone on board other than me. Thank holy hamburgers. I accepted Thorn's hand, he yanked me on board, and the RV peeled away from the curb the second the door had thumped shut behind me.

"We all made it?" I asked, just in case.

"All present and accounted for," Omen said tersely from where he was standing by the kitchen. Snap was sitting on the sofa-bench with a vaguely bewildered expression, and Antic... was bouncing on her heels right on the table.

She shot me an eager smirk when she saw me look her way. "I gave them a good lesson with those teacups, didn't I?"

"You were great," I said. No need to pick apart exactly how much each of us had contributed to the skirmish. I dropped onto the sofa across from Snap and released Pickle from my purse.

Omen was frowning. "Hey," I said, aiming a teasing kick at his calf. "We just escaped a vicious ambush with all lives and even body parts intact. What more could you ask for?"

He swiped his hand across his narrow jaw. "I'm more concerned about how those pricks found us in the first place. There's no way they should have been able to determine that we'd head to Austin from Chicago, and even if they had, we weren't on the right course." He aimed a particularly icy glance at the imp.

I hadn't had enough time to recover from the whole fleeing for my life bit to consider the implications of the attack. "That's true. I didn't mention where we were headed to Ellen or Vivi, so it couldn't have come from them."

Ruse glanced back toward us. "The hotel was the first place we've been in one spot for any significant length of time since we stormed the museum and then hit the road. Could the Company have tracked your phone, Sorsha?"

I shook my head. "I've had it off except when I was using it while we were on the road, just in case."

"It's possible they were tracking something else." Omen's gaze settled on Snap. "Didn't any of you find it odd that our devourer's cage opened on its own to release him when we came for him? The Company's scientists had already called in back-up. Why would they *want* us to leave with him rather than be caught?"

"I figured they got scared that we'd find them before back-up arrived," I said. "But yeah... They didn't have any reason to worry at that point. It was *because* his cage opened that we got suspicious."

Snap had stiffened against the leather seat. "I wouldn't have helped the people who locked up me and Antic and the others in those metal boxes."

"Of course you wouldn't have, not on purpose," Omen said in the same unexpectedly gentle tone he'd used with Snap before. He stepped closer to the devourer, studying Snap's lean frame from head to toe.

"But you might have without even realizing it. There's a trick I've seen hunters use when they want to collect a lot of little shadowkind at once. Some of the lesser creatures tend to congregate together. They catch one and fix a tracking mark of some sort on it, then release it and let it lead them to the others."

I'd heard of that too. They marked the creatures' bodies with a little silver ink that wouldn't vanish even if the creatures slipped in and out of the shadows and that created a resonance they could detect with a specialized device. A shiver tickled through me. "You think the Company scientists put a tracker mark on Snap? Wouldn't he have noticed?" The lesser shadowkind might ignore a little discomfort in their relief at being freed, but Snap was more aware than that.

"Possibly not, if it was small enough. He hasn't used a physical body long enough to be all that aware of what's normal in the first place." The hellhound shifter motioned for Snap to stand up. "Let me check you over. We don't want them tracking us any farther than they already have."

Snap got to his feet, his eyes wide. "They attacked us because of me? I never thought—if I'd realized—"

"We know." I scooted close enough to take his hand, although I didn't know how much real comfort that would give him. Still, I ran my thumb over his knuckles in as soothing a gesture as I could offer while Omen leaned in, practically sniffing the devourer with his houndish senses.

"Here," he said abruptly, grasping Snap's other arm and turning it to tap a spot just below his elbow. "There's just the faintest hint of it..." He grimaced. "Not on the flesh, but there's a bit of a regular scar here. They must have cut you open and etched it right on the bone."

A shudder ran through Snap's body. "There is something there—a bit of an itch. I thought that must be normal." His head jerked up. "I can't stay. You'll have to go on without me. I could return to the shadow realm—they won't be able to follow me there. Then you'll all be safe."

Like when he'd run from us when he'd been afraid of how we—how *I*—would see him after he'd devoured that man in front of us? Panic jabbed through my chest, and my grip on his hand tightened. "No. There has to be a way to get it off." I just didn't like thinking about how bloody those ways might be.

Omen glanced at Thorn. "You know your way around a blade."

The warrior bowed his head. As he opened the drawers beneath the kitchen counter, I tugged Snap down beside me. He turned to me. "I had a feeling, in the hotel room—I *knew* it was dangerous for me to be with you. You all could have been captured or killed, and it would have been my fault."

"Not your fault," I said firmly. When his gaze started to slip away from me, I touched the side of his face to bring his attention back. "Hey. It'd be the fault of the assholes who put that mark on you. I know you don't remember it, but you've helped us so much. We need you. Don't you want the chance to see them totally shut down?"

"I don't know how much more I can do."

"I do." I kept all my focus on his moss-green eyes. "And even if you weren't going to stay with us, would you really want them to be able to track you down any time you came mortal-side again? *You'd* never be safe here again." I couldn't imagine Snap having to give up everything he'd taken wonder from in this world. He'd make that sacrifice if he thought it would protect us, because that was how he was, but he'd never stop missing the color and flavor his home realm lacked.

Just like I wasn't sure I'd ever stop missing the passionate devotion he'd brought into *my* life.

That thought brought a lump into my throat, but I kept holding his gaze. "If we can get the mark off you, do you think you can handle the pain?"

He hesitated, his forked tongue flicking across his lips. "Yes," he said softly. "Yes—to be able to stay here. To keep up with the mission. To have all the fantastic things I haven't gotten to experience yet."

"Good. Then think about all the fantastic things you *have* had already, and I'll keep holding your hand, and we'll pretend Thorn isn't even there."

Snap drew in a breath and squeezed my hand in return. His eyes became distant as he must have thought back to some favorite of the new memories he'd accumulated in the past day—the grandeur of the hotel? The rush of the RV's speed? Or maybe the simple pleasure of his fruit salad, knowing him.

As I watched his face, I could see Thorn applying a carving knife to the devourer's forearm at the edge of my vision. I restrained a wince at the smoke that unfurled from the cut. Snap blinked, and his jaw tensed—the only sign that he'd felt it. He could be as stoic as the warrior when he needed to be.

"Tell me your favorite things here," he said abruptly.

Recently? *Lying on a cramped bunk bed with your arms around me. Seeing your face light up at a taste of honey.* I swallowed hard. There were plenty of other things too.

"Listening to music," I said. "Letting the beat move through me. Singing along, finding ways to play with the words. You haven't gotten to do any of that yet. Opening those cages and watching the beasties big and small leap free. Burning the places that belong to the assholes who built those cages down to the ground."

Thorn had opened up a gash wide enough that the smoke was billowing now. His expression was as pained as I felt seeing it.

"There's the mark," he said. "Barely larger than the head of a pin. I think I can scrape the silver off with the edge of the blade."

He braced himself, and a flinch ran all through Snap's body. The devourer closed his eyes with a hiss. His fingers clutched mine so hard my hand ached, but not half as much as my heart did.

Then the warrior was tossing the knife into the sink. Omen stood ready with the roll of gauze they'd procured for *my* injuries days ago. He'd smeared a little of the green paste that helped contain shadowkind essence on the pale fabric.

As he bandaged Snap's arm, the devourer's shoulders sank down. His head dipped toward me. "Thank you," he murmured.

I wished I could kiss him. I wished that was still something he'd take joy from. "Any time," I said with forced cheer.

"You should rest," Thorn said gruffly. "After losing some of your essence..."

"Yes." Snap stood, took a step, and wavered. I followed him, ushering him down the hall to the RV's main bedroom.

He sat down on the edge of the bed and then didn't seem to know quite what to do with himself. An impulse gripped me, so insistent I couldn't ignore it.

I sat down next to him and wrapped my arms around him, tucking my legs over his lap. Almost like that time in the back of our long-ago borrowed SUV when the friction of me jostling against him during a getaway had woken up his sense of carnal desire. His fresh yet mossy scent filled my nose.

Fruit and flattery hadn't unearthed his memories. Would something about this embrace do the trick?

Snap gazed down at me, stroking my hair, but the gesture felt more absent than affectionate. "Are *you* all right?" he asked me.

So much for that idea. I'd stop throwing myself at him now.

I pulled back and gave his hand one last squeeze. "Just making sure you are. Lie down—it's easier to rest that way. And don't you dare go anywhere."

"I wouldn't," he said, with a determined assurance that killed me. "Whatever I can do here, it's so much more than I could ever offer where I came from."

I didn't really want to go back to the others just yet.

Thorn would probably look at me pityingly, and the devil only knew what Omen was thinking about my soppiness. I retreated into the second bedroom that had almost become my own and flopped down on top of the purple cloud-print comforter. It didn't *feel* all that cloud-like. After the heavenly linens in the hotel, this fabric was scratchy against my skin.

Damn. Penthouse life had ruined me for the plebeian existence in a matter of hours.

Someone rapped on the door. "Still alive in there, Disaster?"

I rolled my eyes at the ceiling. "Yes, *Luce*, as much as you might hope otherwise."

Omen didn't bother with opening the door—he slipped in through the shadows, his well-built form solidifying at the edge of the bed. I supposed I should be glad he'd bothered to knock at all. I looked at him without raising my head from the pillows, which to be honest strained my eyeballs, but I didn't feel like giving him the satisfaction of sitting up at attention.

"I thought we'd established that I don't particularly want to see you dead," he remarked with a coolly casual air.

"More like that you think I'm too useful to get rid of, regardless of what you'd personally prefer."

He let out a soft huff at that but, I noticed, didn't put up an argument. Then he just stood there, as if waiting for *me* to figure out why the hell he'd come in.

"Was there something you wanted?" I asked.

He folded his arms over his chest. I braced myself for whatever criticism he had for me now, but what he actually said was, "You handled yourself well in the ambush. And—with Snap. You know how to... settle him down. Keep his head on straight."

At that admission, I couldn't help propping myself up on my elbows so I could look at the hellhound shifter without giving myself a headache. "It's easier when your first priority isn't being the most ice-cold bastard in the room."

Was that a wince he'd suppressed with the tightening of his lips? "That may be true," he said evenly.

It might not have been totally fair, though. I'd seen him making an effort to be kinder with the devourer in his uncertain mental state. "You haven't been quite as much of a bastard to Snap as you generally are to everyone else," I conceded. "And I appreciate the recognition of my many talents."

That time I could tell it was a smile he'd caught. "Ice-cold bastards get things done, you know. Better to have one than none." He turned to leave.

"Omen," I said before I was sure what I was going to ask. He paused, and I pushed myself all the way up, tucking my feet under me to sit cross-legged.

He'd come in here for a reason. Just to pay me a compliment? I didn't completely understand, but the moment felt vital yet tenuous, like a chance I shouldn't let slip through my fingers.

What did I most *want* to ask? I turned the possibilities over in my head before settling on a topic.

"Why did you decide you needed to become all ice-cold anyway? You obviously don't take to the chill naturally—the other day, you talked about how hard you worked at it. And I know from some of the things the others have said that you were a lot more laissez faire with your abilities however many eons ago."

"The incubus and his loose tongue."

I couldn't hold back a smirk that would have made Ruse proud. "Oh, don't complain about his tongue. He puts it to all sorts of wonderful uses."

Omen glowered at me, but he stepped away from the door to prop himself against the bed's footboard. "I didn't come to the decision lightly," he said. "I *did* use to be much more careless with my powers, playing with mortals for entertainment." He paused, looking toward the wall with a distant gaze. "I had a lot of power to work with and an associate who enjoyed the revelry of horrors even more than I did, always encouraging fresh intrigues."

"Not Thorn." The warrior was the only shadowkind I knew Omen had associated with ages ago, but I couldn't imagine the stalwart wingéd instigating mayhem.

Omen snorted. "No. And you don't have to worry about meeting her. In the end, Tempest was too caught up in her cleverness for her own good. She was a sphinx, but taunting mortals with riddles wasn't thrilling enough—she shifted her form I don't know how many times, riding humans to their deaths as a night mare, riding doom through their towns when she led what they called the Wild Hunt, and the Highest only know what else. Which was the problem. The Highest caught on to how much hell she was raising and sent a pack of wingéd to take her down, back when there still were enough wingéd around for them to form packs."

"And you decided you'd rather not end up bashed open by a hail of crystal knuckles, so you committed to changing your ways?"

"Not exactly. I wasn't quite as flamboyant as her. I thought I could stay beneath their notice. But there was a night—"

He halted as if grappling with the memory. I gave him a good long stretch before impatience got the better of me and I prompted, "A night?"

"I'd messed with a lot of the mortals in one settlement, and they came to get retribution. Instead of finding me, they stumbled on a cluster of lesser shadowkind who'd been drawn by my energies. The humans slaughtered every creature there without a moment's hesitation. And I realized the Highest were right in the little bit of enforcement they do enact across the divide."

His gaze was still fixed on the wall, his tone as even as ever, but his hand had come to rest on the bed frame, the knuckles paling where he'd clenched his fingers. I waited another moment before asking, "How so?"

"It was my doing," Omen said. "The mortals were brazen fools like so many of them are, and they deserved all the havoc I brought into their lives, but in wreaking that havoc I stirred up their distrust and hatred of all shadowkind. How many hunters took up hunting because I hurt them or theirs? How many humans simply blundered into causing massacres like the one I witnessed that night in fits of rage? So many lesser creatures and no doubt some higher ones as well paid for my crimes more than I ever have."

Ah. I tried to imagine what it would have been like, arriving at a personal revelation on that scale, and couldn't. His voice had only gotten flatter as he spoke, but I'd been around Omen well enough to know that meant he was clamping down even more control over emotions threatening to leak out.

"So this is your penance?" I said. "Making yourself a model of self-restraint and ordering everyone around while you save the shadowkind you can?"

"Something like that." Omen's gaze finally slid to me. "I was selfish and undisciplined and foolhardy—all the worst qualities mortals have in abundance. By provoking them, I was sinking to their level. Yes, I have plenty to make up for, but mainly I want to be as little like those pricks as I possibly can be."

I guessed that could explain why so many parts of my mortal self—impossible supernatural powers aside—irritated the hell out of him. Or the hell *into* him?

Whatever. I glanced down at my hands and then back at him. He hadn't needed to tell me any of his history. Maybe he was already regretting that he had. I could avoid driving that regret home.

"I see your point," I said. "For what it's worth, the being I've seen when you let the ice crack isn't *anything* like the worst human beings I've met. Do you ever think you could ease up on yourself a little after all this time?"

A gleam lit in his eyes. "And ease up on the rest of you as a natural consequence?"

I spread my hands. "You said it, not me."

He did smile then, a gesture that only curled one side of his mouth but that I'd take as a victory anyway. In that moment, the vibe between us felt almost companionable. Then he straightened up.

"Get some rest. I got the impression you didn't spend all that much time in that big hotel bed *sleeping* last night."

The thought that he'd been paying any attention at all to my interlude with Ruse and Thorn sent a flicker of heat through me that wasn't exactly comfortable but not totally unpleasant either. "Spying on us, were you?"

He scoffed. "It isn't exactly difficult to put the pieces together with certain scenarios."

I leaned back on my elbows again with a tingling awareness of my body laid out on the bed. "Next time, maybe you should join in."

I was mostly joking—but a little part of me wasn't. And there was no joke in the flash of orange that lit in Omen's eyes before he jerked his gaze away.

"Less snarking and more napping," he said in a definitive tone. "We'll want you sharp when we get to Austin."

13

Ruse

If the chaotic events of the past twenty-four hours had made anything clear, it was that no matter how much of himself Snap had swallowed into the deepest depths of his being, the devourer still had a puzzling but valiant habit of caring about everyone else's welfare more than his own. This despite the fact that as far as he could remember, he'd only known the bunch of us for those twenty-four hours.

That observation led me to a spark of inspiration. None of the items I'd offered him so far had jogged any familiarity loose. My reassurances that he was among friends hadn't cajoled his old self free. But maybe if he believed our lives depended on him dredging up times past, whatever force was holding them down in his gullet would shatter.

It was worth a try, anyway. Every time Sorsha looked at him with the loss shining in her eyes, I wanted to shake him until he snapped out of it. I would have if I'd thought there was any chance of that tactic working. I'd always liked the devourer well enough, but starting over from scratch with his naively precocious self was getting rather irritating.

I got my chance to try out my new strategy when we stopped at a gas station-slash-burger joint just past the Texas border to fill up both the RV and our mortal. My job, of course, was to persuade the establishment that they didn't need any money for their trouble. Snap stepped out of the Everymobile with Sorsha and me and tipped back his head to bask in the midday sun.

"Wait right there," I told him. "I'll find a tasty snack for you too."

He beamed at me so brightly you'd have thought I'd offered him a ten-course banquet on a week-long tropical cruise. He had always been easy to please.

It wasn't pleasing him I was after, though. I had a little chat with the man at the counter, watched him call out our order eagerly to the cook staff, and left Sorsha to collect the goods. As I reached the restaurant door, I threw myself forward, bursting out into the parking lot as if I'd run all the way to the entrance.

At the sight of me dashing over, Snap straightened up with a jerk, his body tensing. "What's wrong?" he asked, buying into my gambit before I'd even had to really sell it.

"Sorsha," I said in a breathless voice. "The Company goons were waiting for us—they've grabbed her, and they'll be coming for the rest of us any minute now."

The devourer turned even more rigid. "What should we do?"

I waved at him frantically. “Quick! There was something you picked up about a guy named Meriden before—I think if we could show we knew him we could get them to back down—”

It had to be a real fact, or it wouldn’t connect with his smothered memories. A fraught expression crossed the devourer’s pretty face. He opened his mouth and closed it again, his hands moving at his sides as if groping for an answer in the air.

I almost thought I had him, that something was jostling loose, when he let out a choked sound of dismay. “I don’t know. Meriden, Meriden—there’s nothing.”

“Just give yourself more of a chance. It’s got to be in there somewhere.”

“I don’t know.” The furrows in his brow dug deeper as the seconds slipped by. He shook his head and spun toward the RV. “We have to tell Thorn and Omen. They’ll know how to push those people back and get Sorsha away from them.”

Throwing the whole group into a panic wouldn’t solve anything. I grabbed Snap’s arm before he could reach the door. “There isn’t time. Even if you have the slightest sense—tell me anything that comes to you. It could make all the difference in saving her.”

“Saving who from what?”

The restaurant had worked faster than I’d anticipated. Sorsha was walking over, a paper bag dangling from her hand and a crease forming in her own brow as she looked from me to Snap. Her grip on the bag tightened. “What’s happened? Do we have to get out of here?”

Snap brightened with such intensity the brilliance of his smile stung my eyes. "You're all right! Did the Company people let you go? You have the food..." He trailed off and then looked at me uncertainly.

I made a living out of lying, but I had to admit the hint of betrayal in his expression provoked a prick of guilt. I gave him a tentative pat on the arm. "Just a little... prank. I was hoping it would jumpstart your memory. She's been perfectly fine the whole time."

"Of course I'm fine." Sorsha grimaced at me. "All you did was freak him out. The last thing he needs is more stress after this morning."

The prick of guilt expanded into a sword-like stabbing. Although the wound where Thorn had scraped out the silver mark on Snap's arm hadn't leaked any smoke since being bandaged, it was true that this morning's events had been far from a pleasant stroll in the park for the devourer. And the look our fiery mortal was giving me was the exact opposite of the sort I'd have wanted to elicit.

She didn't need more stress in her life either.

I dipped into an apologetic little bow. "I'm sorry. I only wanted to give every possibility a shot, and we seem to be running low on them." I glanced at Snap. "We'd all like to have you back with full history intact."

"I'm sure we'll have plenty of other chances that don't involve giving him a panic attack," Sorsha said, and shot Snap the soft smile that seemed reserved just for him.

Snap's head drooped. "I'm not sure whatever you've

been looking for is still there to be found. I've tried... I truly have."

"I know." She swallowed audibly and then made an attempt at cheerfulness. "Good thing I'm not the kind of girl who gives up just like that." Her gaze came back to me. "No more staging supposed attacks. We've had enough of the real thing."

"What's the hold up?" Omen barked from inside the RV. "Let's get a move on!"

"All right, all right," Sorsha hollered back—and a little flame licked from her palm to her elbow.

She suppressed her flinch so quickly I might not have noticed it if I hadn't been watching her already. She pulled her arm to her torso, snuffing out the flame, and all that remained was a thin pink line over the sensitive skin. I might have offered to kiss it better if the clenching of her jaw hadn't warded me off from any teasing remarks.

"Just—just behave yourself for a little while," she grumbled at me, and handed Snap his bacon cheeseburger before clambering on board.

The devourer and I followed, Snap gulping down his lunch in a few swift bites and then looking mournful that somehow the meal was already gone. He licked his lips. "The different types of meat do make an excellent combination, especially with the cheese and the fluffiness of that bread."

I clapped him on the shoulder. "A little more practice and we'll get you writing a food blog."

"Blog? Is that some kind of fallen tree? Why would someone write on one?"

Good old Snap. "Don't worry yourself about that."

We stopped in the kitchen area. Sorsha had kept going, disappearing now into her bedroom with a flash of her scarlet hair. I suppressed a fresh jab of guilt. If my gambit *had* worked, she'd have been overjoyed. It'd been worth the chance. Snap clearly wasn't traumatized in any lingering way.

Snap was watching *me*. "You like her," he said in his direct, well-meaning way. "Quite a bit."

I yanked my gaze back to him. "You did too," I felt the need to point out. "You and her..." I didn't know how to describe the bond that had appeared to be forming between the two of them, partly because those sorts of tender feelings weren't my domain... and partly because remembering that fact sent an uneasy twinge through me.

"Come on," I said to distract him. "Let me show you the best view we can get from this thing." I motioned to him and leapt into the shadows. The least I could do after my trick was give him a more enjoyable experience to make up for it.

Snap trailed after me into the shadow around the small sunroof positioned over the hall. From the top of the RV, the suburban landscape we were passing through sprawled out on all sides, every bit of it visible without us needing to move an inch. The clear blue sky and the warble of the wind faded as they reached our senses through the patch of darkness, but I'd take that dulled view over risking a tumble in my physical body at the speeds Omen drove at.

A serpentinely slim presence beside me, Snap made a sound of approval. For a few minutes, we simply crouched there, taking in the sights of the mortal world with the colors of early fall whipping past us and the faint tang of gasoline rising from the freeway.

"It's too bad the mortal can't join us up here," Snap said. I felt his attention shift to me. "Why is she particularly important to you?"

I suspected he was really asking why she'd mattered so much to *him*. Was that the way to get through to him—to remind him of the devotion she'd enflamed?

"She's proven herself to be a—how would you put it?—a particularly fantastic being of any sort," I said. "She's been standing up to and sticking it to the people who collect shadowkind for years. Even when we turned up in her home out of nowhere, she held her own and refused to be intimidated. You saw just now that she doesn't put up with any crap from me."

Snap nodded. "She protects all of us in every way she can."

"That's one way of putting it. But she's hardly all severity like Thorn. She has a playful spirit to her, a bountiful capacity for amusement and enjoyment..." I had to smile, thinking of her absurdly switched-up songs, all the banter we'd exchanged. Of the passion that radiated from her in the bedroom, so eager both to give and receive pleasure...

Maybe I'd answered the question he'd actually spoken as well.

"It's hard not to care about her, even when it's not the wisest idea," I finished.

Snap was silent for a moment. "What's unwise about it? Everything you've said makes her sound like a worthy mate, if you wanted one. Is it not accepted for shadowkind to have relations with mortals? I thought I'd heard of others forming bonds, from talk in the shadow realm—maybe I misunderstood."

"It's not that," I said automatically. "*I'm* just not made for that sort of connection. My nature is to focus on bodily gratification."

"Well, I don't know anything about that, but you seem to be affected by her words and feelings as well."

"That doesn't matter. What matters is *she* wouldn't want a being like me."

I had the sense of Snap blinking at me in confusion. "Why would you say that? I haven't noticed her treating you differently. Did she say that to you?"

"Well, no, I just—"

I cut myself off, feeling vaguely ridiculous that I wasn't managing to hold my own in a debate with *Snap* of all beings. I could even play out his counterarguments in my head. *There was another woman,* I'd say, and he'd reply, *What does that have to do with Sorsha? Do they share the same mind?* And I would point out—

I didn't even know what else I'd point out. The truth was that Sorsha *hadn't* ever treated me as anything less or different because of my inclinations. Last night... She'd offered up an experience that was all about pleasuring me without a second's hesitation. She'd seemed to revel in the bliss she'd provoked.

Remembering sent a flare of heat through me that wasn't entirely lust.

How could I say she was yet another mortal woman who'd see me as little more than an extremely extravagant vibrator when she'd already proven she cared about me so much more than that? It wasn't ridiculous that I couldn't convince Snap to believe me. It was ridiculous that I'd convinced myself to suppress all the tenderness that had been growing in me with every passing hour I spent in her presence.

Was I really such a coward that I'd push away the one woman who'd enjoyed my company at least as much outside the bedroom as in it—all because of some harlot more than a century ago who couldn't have held a candle to Sorsha anyway? Why was I so intent on throwing away the exact thing I'd wanted so badly all those years ago now that I had it for real?

What a relief it would be to stop reining those unexpected feelings in and... and simply love her.

A sense of release was already spreading through me, loosening more tension than I'd realized had tangled up inside me. Yes. Screw anyone who thought they could decide what an incubus was capable of or deserved. If she wasn't going to be governed by the rules of what made mortals mortal and shadowkind of the shadows, then I could sure as hell take a slight deviation from the typical cubi path. It'd simply be in the name of a different sort of satisfaction.

"You know," I said, with a broader smile, "you might actually have a point."

Now if only we could get the devourer to remember how deeply he'd fallen for this woman too.

14

Sorsha

"Remind me again what *possible* use these pathetic attempts at heroes could be?" Omen said as I checked myself over in the RV's narrow hallway mirror.

As far as I could tell, I looked reasonably civilized in the clean blouse and jeans Ruse had obtained for me, but I couldn't say I totally trusted my ability to judge these days. Not that I could ask Omen—I'd have even less faith in his assessment.

I swiped at my hair one last time, smoothing an unruly wave, and turned to face our leader. "I get that you don't like mortals, and we had some issues with my usual branch of the Fund—but my friends there *did* help us. Heck, even my asshole ex turned up information that helped us decimate the Company's operations. All I'm going to be asking these people is whether they know anything about my parents."

"And you're so sure they'll have something to tell rather than just screwing us over?"

"They've got no reason to screw us over," I said. "Since thankfully I haven't *screwed* anyone in this bunch. Even if they're not superheroes, I think we can assume they generally want to avoid outright hurting shadowkind, or they wouldn't be in the Fund. And yeah, this is the best shot we have at finding out anything about my parents. They wouldn't have been murdered by hunters if they hadn't been working against the douches, and that sounds like Fund work. They probably met there."

Assuming the two people who'd raised me for the first few years of my life really had been my parents. But even if they hadn't been, I still needed to know who the Mom and Dad from my vague memories and the note in my trinket box were. That should lead us on the path to discovering where I'd actually come from—and how I'd ended up with magic powers and blood that turned to smoke when my adrenaline blared.

Ruse came up behind me. He gave my ponytail a flirtatious tug. "Woe betide anyone who fails to give you answers. I've seen how quickly you can dig up the truth, Miss Blaze. And I'll be right there in the shadows to hear if any secrets come out behind your back."

"Just restrain yourself from tripping anyone," I said, not that I'd really minded seeing him knock my treacherous ex on his ass at the first Fund meeting my shadowkind companions had followed me to.

"I'll do my best to behave... while we're there, at least." Smirking, he set his hands on my waist and leaned in to press a kiss to the crook of my jaw. Sweet silky champagne, the incubus did know how to light up every inch of my body with one small touch.

The tenderness of the gesture sent a flutter of warmth through my chest that wasn't just lust. Our interlude with Thorn at the hotel hadn't seemed to change anything at the time, but today Ruse had been back to his affectionate and demonstrative self—the man I remembered from the early days of our... association.

Maybe even more affectionate, or simply in a way that felt more like an expression of his own happiness rather than an attempt to work his charms. I wasn't sure what had made the difference, but I wasn't going to complain.

"I'll keep an eye on the incubus," Thorn said in a rumble, a note of amusement emerging in his usual somber tone. "And make sure none of the mortals cause any trouble for Sorsha."

"There you go," I said to Omen, folding my arms over my chest—and maybe leaning just a *little* into Ruse's embrace to stretch out the enjoyment. "I'm well-protected."

"One might even say... in good hands," Ruse murmured, trailing his fingers up my sides to set off a wave of heat to join the earlier warmth. He kissed me once more, on the side of my neck, before easing back. "But of course I shouldn't let those hands distract you from your mission."

I shot him a look through my eyelashes. "Save that for later."

Antic skipped down the hall between us, flickering in

and out of her invisible state. "I want to meet this bunch of mortals too! So many new humans to play with. If I entertain them, maybe they'll feel more friendly?"

"Er..."

I was saved from needing to answer by Omen, although he took a harsher approach than I would have. He fixed the imp with his cool stare. "Has your 'playing' *ever* put its recipients in a better mood? Think hard now."

She pouted at him. "I do my best. Sometimes they simply don't appreciate a good joke."

"I think we should save the jokes for when I've gotten to know them a little," I said, jumping on that excuse. "So we can make sure you cater to their specific sense of humor."

Omen raised an eyebrow at me as if to ask why I was even bothering to humor the shadowkind he saw as a pest, but he didn't argue with my framing.

Antic sighed and plopped down in the middle of the floor. "I suppose you're right. I just feel my talents aren't being put to full use."

A glimmer of inspiration lit in my head. "Why don't you spend some time exploring town, chat up the local shadowkind you meet—see if you can find anyone who was around twenty-five years ago and might have heard about the murders?"

"I could do that!" She jumped up again and gave me a sharp salute. "I won't let you down."

The hellhound shifter's gaze followed her as she flitted away. "Are you sure you want *her* making our first impressions for us?"

"At least the shadowkind won't flee in terror at the sight of her like they should with you, right?" I knuckled his bicep teasingly as I headed past him to the door. "I'll try to keep this short."

Nothing about the city beyond the Everymobile was exactly familiar. I only had those few wavery fragments of memory from my childhood to go by, and no doubt the place had changed plenty in the twenty-five years since I'd last set foot here. But still, walking down the bustling street past café patios and various vibrant stores gave me a sense of homecoming, as if my body knew I belonged here. Maybe it was all a delusion because I knew I'd started my mortal life here, but there was something enjoyable about it all the same.

After our business with the Company of Light was done, maybe I'd have to spend some time getting to know the city of my supposed birth all over again.

I'd gotten the contact information for someone in the Austin branch of the Shadowkind Defense Fund from a list all Fund members received once they'd participated in the organization for long enough to show their dedication. When I'd reached out last night as we'd approached the city, the woman had told me their next meeting would be in the gaming shop I was walking up to now. The plastic figures of orcs and trolls poised in the windows looked like caricatures of the actual "monsters" living among us.

I walked up to the counter as if I belonged in the place and smiled at the guy behind the counter, who was buff enough to have wielded a sword in real life as well as with a roll of a die. "I'm here for the 4pm gaming session. The password is Dragonlance."

The dude gave me a thumbs up and motioned to a door behind a rack of LARPing instruction manuals behind him. "Head on in. Most of the usuals are already here."

I braced myself and pushed open the door. I hadn't told my contact—just "Monica," since the contact sheet didn't include last names—anything about myself other than that I thought my parents might have been involved in the Austin Fund a while back. My branch back home didn't have any reason to believe I'd left the city, let alone that I'd come here. I didn't *think* anyone would have sent out a general warning when as far as anyone there knew, the worst I'd done was get mixed up with some brutal local shadowkind. But if our experiences with the Company had taught me anything, it was that I was better off being careful than not.

From the size of the room and the—small—number of "usuals" who looked up at my entrance, this branch wasn't as active as the one I'd left behind. The space held two tables, one like a dining table with eight chairs around it and a small card table off to the side that right now held assorted pop cans and a couple of bowls of chips that laced the air with a salty potato scent. Only four of the chairs at the larger table were occupied.

The woman at the head of the table had to be Monica... because she was the only woman in the bunch. She squinted at me through owlish glasses and then leapt up with a grin. Relieved at the thought that she might get a respite from testosterone dominating the room?

"You must be Sorsha!" she said eagerly. "Come in, come in, no need to be shy."

You could tell she hadn't met me before.

The three guys who got up more slowly might as well have been the personifications of a few of the more current mortal legends. The first had on a black suit and shades with a grim expression like he was auditioning to join the Men in Black. Across from him, a short, stout dude with wild, curly hair could have passed for one of Santa's elves in that ruffled green shirt... which was especially noticeable because the burly man next to him was doing an excellent impression of Father Christmas himself with that bushy white moustache and beard.

My hopes sank before I'd said one word. Everyone here except Saint Nick looked to be under forty—too young to have been active in the Fund when my parents would have been.

I gave them a little wave. "Hey. Nice to meet you. Is this the whole group?"

Monica's hands twisted where she'd clasped them in front of her. "I know our branch isn't super impressive. There are a couple other people who come around maybe once a month, but they're not quite as dedicated. Things have been pretty quiet around here lately, I guess. Not many humans stumbling on the shadowkind and ending up connecting with us these days."

The man with the beard let out a low chuckle. "Back in the day, we'd have ten people show up and that was a small turnout. No accounting for how things change." He dipped his balding head to me. "Welcome to our humble abode. My name's Klaus."

Of course it was. I could picture Ruse snickering in the shadows. I managed to keep my own smile friendly rather than incredulous.

"If anyone here can help me, it's probably you," I said. "I don't know how much Monica told all of you—I think my parents were part of the Fund before I was born. Maybe for a little while after too. That'd have been almost thirty years ago. Were you working with the branch that far back?"

"I've been a member since I was twenty-two—which, I'll thank you not to tell anyone else, was a whole forty-five years ago now." He stroked his beard thoughtfully, only amplifying the Santa Claus look. "What were their names?"

I bit my lip. "I'm actually not sure... They died when I was three. From what I understand, they were murdered by hunters, presumably as revenge. I don't know much about them other than that, but that's why I thought they must have been working with the Fund. Why would hunters come after them unless they'd been getting in their way to help the shadowkind?"

For a few seconds, the four humans just stared at me. I guessed colleagues being murdered wasn't a subject that came up a whole lot. To be fair, no one in the Fund back home had died for the cause in the eleven years I'd worked with them—I'd never even heard of anyone there getting hurt in the line of duty until the Company of Light had come for Ellen.

Then Klaus's eyes widened. "*That* must be what happened to Philip. My God. It never occurred to me—maybe I'm naïve."

My pulse stuttered. "You knew them?"

"I knew *him.*" He leaned his weight against the table as if he couldn't hold himself all the way up while he thought back. "He was with the Fund for about five years, if I remember right. Near the end he stopped coming all that much—mentioned something about a woman he'd met, getting serious with her. I saw her once, at a distance, when she came to pick him up after a fundraising event. She had red hair like yours. You don't see many with that color. She must have been your mother."

"So, she wasn't part of the Fund?"

He shook his head. "And from what you've said, it must have been around the time you were born that he stopped coming to meetings altogether. We kept in touch a little over the phone, but the last time I called him, his number was out of service. That was back when we still used landlines for most things... I assumed he'd just moved out of town. If I'd had any idea—*murdered*—"

There mustn't have been any major coverage of the slaughter on the news, then. Maybe no one had realized what had happened. The hunters could have covered their tracks. The Company's employees did so very effectively on a regular basis.

And for all I knew, it hadn't been random hunters but the Company themselves who'd come for my parents. Luna had been afraid that whoever had killed them would target us next, and it'd appeared to be Company mercenaries who'd attacked her.

"Do you have any idea what they might have gotten into outside of the Fund that would have pissed off hunters or other people out to harm shadowkind?" I asked.

"Can't think of it. Philip definitely wasn't the type to go for violence... I remember how much he'd grouse when he had to deal with even a little blood from a papercut. He was more about the research, so papercuts were a fairly common thing. But I don't know what your mother might have gotten up to. And maybe he developed a stronger stomach for direct confrontations after he left us."

Well, that answered another question I might have asked—whether the guy had definitely been human. If Kris Kringle here had seen my dad bleed, he couldn't have been any typical shadowkind, anyway.

"Papercuts are about the most painful injury known to mankind," I said.

"He'd have said that, I'm sure." Klaus squinted at me. "I can see him in you now. You might have your mother's coloring, but that nose and jaw... I'll have to see if I have any photos I can give you. We don't record our activities in all that much detail, as I'm sure you understand."

"Right, of course not." A sensation squeezed my lungs, thrilled and yet uncertain. I'd found a lead already—I knew my father's name now. But where did that actually get me? Klaus clearly didn't know anything about the circumstances of my birth. He hadn't even known I existed.

And if I took after my mother *and* this Philip guy... then I really was human. Or I'd started that way, at least. Well, I had already realized I couldn't be a shadowkind, what with being able to handle silver and iron and generally bleeding human blood myself.

Had one of my parents or someone else done something to create the power in me?

Jolly old Saint Nick here wouldn't have a clue. I sure as hell wasn't going to go spilling the beans about my fiery voodoo to this bunch. Some first impression that would make.

Monica glanced at Klaus. "Is there anyone from that generation you're still in touch with? Maybe someone else stayed in closer contact with Philip and could tell Sorsha more about what happened after he left the Fund."

"I can't think of anyone. He always kept his life outside of our business to himself. Like I said, I didn't even know he was still working on behalf of the shadowkind after he left, but if hunters came after him, he must have been. We never carried out any operations that would have provoked them that much. No one still with the Fund was hassled."

Maybe that was why Dad had left. He'd had a bold side under his bookishness and had gone vigilante, knowing the Fund wouldn't approve of pushing back harder against the people who threatened the shadowkind. Just like I'd always kept my breaking-and-entering to free collectors' menageries secret from the rest of my branch. Like father, like daughter?

I swallowed hard. "What if I told you that I think the people who murdered him and my mother might still be around? That they've hurt a whole lot more people—and shadowkind—since then?"

The Man in Black straightened up. "Well, then we'd have to do something about them, obviously. We haven't seen anything major happening here, though. You think they've managed to keep it hidden?"

"I'm not sure how much they're doing in Austin right now," I said, measuring out how much I told them with an eye to caution. "The people I think are responsible have built up quite a network across a bunch of different cities. I think I know where they're the most active here in the US—there are a few of us who're going to travel there and see if we can stop them from continuing."

The green-shirted elf-guy frowned. "Stop them how? If they're that entrenched..."

"Clearly we'd have to try!" Klaus drew himself up straighter. "We haven't had more than minor incidents to deal with in years, and not many of those. We could make a trip for a greater cause, couldn't we, Monica?"

The woman blinked, her eagerness fading, but then she lifted her chin. "I suppose I don't see any reason we couldn't... in one way or another. There have to be steps we can take without making a commotion out of it."

Right. Because here just like back home, avoiding a commotion took precedence over actually protecting the shadowkind from murderous psychos.

The tension in my chest condensed into a lump that settled into my gut. I was human—and right now all I could see was how right Omen was to disparage my kind. They hadn't even noticed when one of their own members was *murdered* right under their noses. And now that they did know, they'd gone straight to figuring out how they could address the issue with as little disturbance to their own lives or the villains' as possible.

I'd accomplished more in defense of the shadowkind in the past month than these people would in a lifetime.

But they were willing to pitch in somehow or other, and if that was good enough to bring Antic on board, it was good enough with our human allies too. I had to look at this glass as half full.

"Great," I said. "I'm going to do some more poking around in the city to see what else I can find out about my parents, but when we have a plan for tackling their killers, you'll hear from me."

And maybe once the idea had sunk in, they'd care a little less about commotions and a little more about justice.

15

Sorsha

All the questions still hanging over me cast an unsettling gloom. Still, I put on my best upbeat front when Omen demanded a report of the meeting and through the other conversations that followed, both with my shadowkind companions and the various mortals I encountered as I made what I could of Klaus's information.

Unfortunately, none of that talk got me anywhere. Klaus sent me snapshots of a couple of old photos he'd found that included a skinny guy around the age I was now with shaggy blond hair and copious freckles, but seeing my dad didn't tell me all that much about him, let alone myself. My Saint Nick couldn't even recall Philip's last name.

I checked the public records I could find through the city's administration, but there'd been no Sorsha born or any kid at all born to a Philip on or around the day I'd always believed was my birthday. Was that a lie, or had my parents simply refused to document my birth?

Given what I was, the latter didn't seem totally unbelievable. But it did mean I had nowhere to go from here—no way of tracking down other relatives or even having good questions to ask.

By the time we'd had dinner, the weight of the uncertainty was wearing on me. I retreated to my bedroom to gather myself.

Pickle might have forgiven me a little since I'd accidentally toasted his scales, but we weren't back to best buds just yet. When I scooped him up for a cuddle, he squirmed out of my arms, scampered across the bed and around the room a few times, and finally darted under the bed where he'd been building a nest out of a heap of gauzy curtain fabric the equines had left stashed down there.

I lay back and tried to clear my head, but the dragon's restlessness had infected me. After several minutes of shifting around and not finding any position that felt relaxing, I got up and went back out into the RV's common area.

Ruse and Snap were sitting at the table, both with a handful of playing cards. The incubus had decided that since his attempts at unearthing Snap's memories hadn't panned out, his next project should be teaching the devourer poker. They were placing their bets with blueberries from little bowls by their elbow. Snap probably preferred winning those over money anyway.

"I see your three and raise you five," Ruse said, waggling his cards, and glanced up at me.

"Where'd everyone go?" I asked. "Or are they just lurking?" Even after all the time I'd spent in shadowkind company, knowing they could be around and watching without my having any way of telling was a bit unnerving.

The incubus shook his head. "Thorn went to conduct a wide patrol, because of course he would. The imp set off to search for shadowkind in the suburb we passed on the way out here, and Omen got it into his head that he needed to make some kind of inquiries of his own. I'm not sure where he headed—he wasn't very loquacious about the decision."

"That is generally his style."

"Indeed." Ruse motioned to the table. "Want to join a friendly game?"

I wavered, but I wasn't sure I was in the mood to exchange banter right now. "I think I'll just take a walk. I won't go far."

"Don't be gone too long, or Thorn'll have a conniption."

The corner of my lips quirked up. "I'll do my best to avoid that."

We'd parked on the outskirts of the city in a secluded treed area not far from the river. I ambled past a picnic bench, which from its splintering edges and dirt-crusted boards hadn't been used in years, and followed an overgrown trail down to the water's edge.

The breeze murmured through the leafy branches and licked cool air across my face. The crisp, earthy scent of autumn was starting to emerge through the last whiffs of summer. It was all very peaceful until a chorus of frogs that somehow sounded both wheezy and hoarse started up. Excellent mood music.

The sun had nearly descended behind the distant buildings to the west. I walked in the other direction, dodging fallen branches and clumps of bushes, which gave me plenty to focus on other than how exactly I'd come to be the impossible being I was. When the breeze turned chilly enough that I wished I'd worn a jacket over my thin tee, I turned and headed back the way I'd come.

I'd nearly made it to the path when the last rays of sunlight caught on a head of golden curls moving toward me. Snap's face brightened when he saw me, but there was something tentative in his expression too. Not a typical look on the being who liked to throw himself headlong into anything that caught his interest.

Keeping up the breezy, nonchalant front was harder with him than with the others. Every time I pretended we were just casual associates, my stomach knotted all over again. But that wasn't his fault.

"Felt like stretching your legs?" I said with my best offhandedly friendly smile.

The devourer smiled back, but the tentativeness lingered. He came to a stop just a few feet away from me. "I wanted to see how you're doing. You'd been gone for some time."

"Oh." I wouldn't have thought this Snap paid enough attention to me to be concerned, but maybe I'd been unfair. I held out my arms in demonstration. "I'm fine. Just needed some air."

"Are you going back to the Everymobile, then?"

I'd thought I was, but my legs balked. The gloom

didn't weigh as heavy out here. I wasn't in a hurry to return to it. "I might just sit by the river for a little while longer."

Snap paused. "I could sit with you if you'd like company."

His presence brought a different sort of weight, but I found I couldn't send him off when he'd offered so sweetly. "All right. Thank you."

We settled in on a grassy patch by the remains of a concrete wall, just a few saplings between us and the rippling water. I leaned against the crumbling surface. Snap fingered a spiky flower that had sprouted nearby, careful not to detach it from its stem.

"I guess you must need a break from the rest of us sometimes, huh?" I said when the silence started to itch at me. "Always badgering you about things you can't remember."

"I would like to remember," Snap said. "I don't resent you for trying to help me. It bothers all of you too." He glanced up at me. "Especially you, I think."

It wasn't a question, but I felt the need to address it anyway. "We'd... gotten to know each other pretty well before all this. You're still *you*, but the way it happened—I don't know if that can be replicated. Maybe we'll never end up in the same place. But that's okay. It isn't your fault. If anything, it's mine."

He blinked. "What do you mean?"

"Well, I..." I drew my gaze away and tugged at a few tufts of grass near my knee. "The worst part we can obviously blame on the Company assholes. I know that. But they only captured you because you'd gone off on your own, and I think if I'd handled certain things better, you might not have."

"I'm sure if I left it was for reasons completely my own. You couldn't have forced me."

"Of course not, but— It's hard to explain." How could he understand how emotionally entangled we'd gotten when the being he was now had reverted back to having no concept of intimate relations? "But, you know, we've got bigger problems to worry about. It'll be however it'll be."

Snap considered me for a long moment. "I don't know what I would have done or said before, but I do know that I don't like seeing you upset." He scooted a little nearer to me. With a deliberateness that made me suspect he was bringing to mind a memory of seeing Ruse or Thorn taking the same action and was afraid of getting it wrong, he took my hand in his.

The simple gesture that would have meant so much more a week ago brought a lump into my throat. I swallowed thickly. Maybe it was okay if I just tipped my head slightly to the side so it could rest against his shoulder.

Snap didn't pull away, but he didn't tug me closer the way he would have done before. I closed my eyes, breathing in the smell of him, clover sweet with its mossy dark undertone. An ache filled my chest. Was this making things better or worse?

"I miss you," I couldn't help saying. The words were too true to hold down.

I supposed Snap with his literal mind couldn't help his answer either. "I'm here."

Yes, the most essential parts of him were here: the gentleness, the wonder, and the compassion. Just not the man who'd wanted to claim me as his own, who'd seen me as a shining hero, who'd been both so fierce and so tender in his devotion. The man I'd started to imagine building some kind of life with when all this was over, regardless of what realm he came from.

I'd woken up lust and passion in him, sure, but hadn't he woken up plenty in me at the same time? I'd started seeing things, enjoying things, wanting things I'd never have thought of before... or maybe that I just wouldn't have *let* myself think of.

The ache expanded down to my gut and up to the base of my throat with a more wrenching truth that could have followed my first admission. But what was the point in saying that? This was my chance, from here onward, to pretend it wasn't true. To step back from the path I'd been hurtling down where my life would have been entwined with my shadowkind lovers far beyond the mission we were on.

Wouldn't it be better to sever that connection here and go back to some kind of normal human existence as soon as I could?

The question passed through my head, and all of me tensed in rejection of it. I *wasn't* a normal human—and whatever I was, it was okay. I'd rather be that than one of the people so afraid of risks and consequences.

I could admit this much: Even if I couldn't have Snap the way we'd once been together, I wished I could.

I opened my mouth, but the words stuck in my throat. I hadn't said them to anyone since Malachi, years ago—since the man who'd decided I wasn't even worthy of a conversation had erased himself from our shared life. A sliver of a lyric came easier, twisted to almost the thing I meant to say.

"Somehow I've stayed like glue-ue-ue," I sang softly, gazing through the trees toward the river. "Full of snow and frost I was until I found you."

"Sorsha?" Snap said without moving to dislodge me. Moonlight glimmered across the ripples in the water, and my chest constricted.

Mangled lyrics didn't cut it. Just say it. Once, out loud. He deserved to know, even if he couldn't really understand it.

My fingers tightened around his. My lips parted, and the words fell out. "I love you. Just as you are, with everything that makes you a devourer too. I should have told you back then, when it mattered a whole lot more, but—this is the best I can do. I love you."

Snap had gone rigidly still beside me. Shit, I'd probably terrified him with the seemingly random declaration. His hand released mine, and I lifted my head to give him space—should I apologize? How did I apologize for *that*?—but before I'd had a chance to say anything, his arms were wrapping right around me, tugging me into a full embrace.

My heart skipped a beat. I wanted to look up at him and take in his expression, but I was afraid of shifting in his hold and breaking the moment.

His chin had settled in a familiar position on the top of my head. A faint shudder ran through his body, and his arms squeezed tighter. His next breath came with a hitch.

Then he spoke, his bright voice so faint it sounded as if it were coming from a deep, dark hollow inside him.

"My peach?"

My pulse hiccupped. Had I heard that right? He couldn't have—unless someone had told him about the nickname he'd given me?

There was only one possible answer. "My devourer?"

Another shudder passed through him, and then all at once he was pulling me right onto his lap, turning me at the same time to face him. "Sorsha," he said, still strained but with a ferocity of emotion I hadn't heard from him since we'd rescued him. Like a demand. Like a claim.

A burn crept into my eyes. "Snap? Do you—?"

I forced myself to raise my head despite my fears of shattering the moment. Snap stared back at me with a look so fraught yet full of longing that the hope I hadn't quite dared to let loose before flooded me.

I touched his cheek, and he leaned into my caress, the edge of his jaw coming to rest against my temple. His breath stuttered in a warm wash down the side of my face. His embrace tightened.

"The look on your face," he murmured. "I—" He jerked back with a flinch. His arms fell to his sides, his expression tensing with a neon glow flaring in his moss-green eyes. "I'm a monster."

The admission cut through me. I swiveled around in his lap, gripping his face when he made to move even farther away. That was why, after all—not the Company's torments, although no doubt they'd contributed.

He hadn't devoured himself just to escape their

experiments. He'd devoured the moment he'd become the thing he'd hated about himself and accidentally taken everything else about the last few months with it.

"Yes," I said, looking straight into his eyes. "You're a monster. So are Ruse and Thorn and Omen. Some days, so am I. I love you with all the monstrousness included. I didn't—I was just startled. I hadn't known what to expect. It didn't change how much you matter to me, not one bit."

"I didn't just kill that man," Snap said. "I shredded apart his soul bit by bit, and every moment of it was agony for him."

I gave him a grim smile. "And I've burned alive more people than I can currently count. I don't imagine they enjoyed that experience very much before it killed them."

"I *liked* doing it. I reveled in it, in all the pieces of his life I got to consume. I—" His voice dropped. "For a moment, I wanted to devour *you*."

That would be the ultimate act of making me his, wouldn't it? I wasn't going to volunteer, but the admission didn't stir any of the horror he'd obviously expected it to.

I stroked my fingertips over his cheek again and into his golden hair. "But you didn't. Do you have any idea how many awful things *I've* wanted to do in my entire lifetime? No one has control over what ideas or feelings pop into their head. We are the things we say and do, not the things we don't. The fact that you wanted to and didn't shows what really matters to you, more than if you'd never wanted to in the first place."

"It could happen again. I thought I could make sure I never gave in to that hunger again, but I was wrong. That's why... The things I gleaned from that man's memories—I thought maybe the Company knew how to destroy the dangerous parts of me. I went to ask them, to show— But they didn't give me a chance to say anything."

I bristled on his behalf even as my heart wrenched for him. "Of course they wouldn't. They don't *want* to believe any of you could be anything other than a total beast."

"I know that now. They wrapped me in one of those jabbing nets and shut me in that glaring box, and when they took me out there was only more pain, and more, and..." He flinched just at the memory. "I wanted so much to get away from that, from what I'd done before, all of it. I didn't mean to forget that completely. I'm not sure what I even did. It just... happened."

"I don't blame you for doing whatever you could to get through their torture. And I don't blame you for what you did to that asshole either. If some prick is on the verge of gutting me again, I hope you *do* shred his fucking soul into as many little bits as you can manage."

The neon flare returned to Snap's eyes. His forked tongue flicked between his lips. He still didn't look completely convinced, though.

I pushed myself off his lap and tugged him with me. With his slender frame and heavenly beauty, it was easy to forget just how impressively tall he was until he was standing right over me, his chin hovering above my forehead. But he was here. My devourer. He was with me completely like I'd started to believe I'd never have him again, and that felt like nothing short of a miracle.

I took a step back so I could catch his gaze again. "You saw how I looked at you when the change surprised me. Why don't you see how I'll react to you now? Bring out your devourer form. I know you won't hurt me."

"Sorsha..."

I walked my fingers up his lean chest. "Please, my devourer?"

I didn't know whether it was the plea or the claiming that decided him, but he inhaled sharply and eased backward to give himself room. His shoulders stiffened. For a second, he looked so uneasy that I almost took back the request. Then the eerie green light that had glinted in his eyes shimmered over the rest of him.

His body stretched upward the way I remembered until he towered a good two feet over me. His face lengthened to accommodate that monstrous jaw that could unhinge to encompass an entire human head. His pupils had narrowed into slits around the neon glow in his eyes, and his fingers stirred restlessly at his sides, long and spidery.

Maybe I should have been horrified. But he hadn't lost his golden curls, and the planes of his face still reminded me of a stunning sun god, if a more vicious version. I could see Snap all through the form that was his more natural state, even though he'd rather have shunned this side of himself. He looked brutal and unsettling and unnervingly but undeniably gorgeous.

Not your type? Not a problem. He was all mine. Just let anyone try to take this monster away from me.

Reaching up, I could just trace my fingers along his treacherous jaw. "*My* devourer," I said again. And then, softer, because somehow it was still hard to say it, "My love."

The light in Snap's eyes blazed. He contracted in on himself with a rush of air, his body barely returned to its more human-like state before he'd caught me up in his lithe arms.

He kissed me like he'd been suffocating and I was his only air. In all the passion he'd shown me before, he'd never been quite this intense. As I kissed him back, I tangled my fingers in his soft hair and held on for the ride.

"My peach," he said against my lips. "My Sorsha." Then he dove back in to capture my mouth just as utterly a second time.

I let one of my hands trail down his chest, and a savage sound reverberated up his throat. Still kissing me, he swept me around. I found myself pressed up against a tree trunk, the bark rough through my shirt and my legs splayed around the devourer's waist.

Snap adjusted me against him, his hands on my thighs, as he dropped his mouth to the side of my neck. The flick of his forked tongue seared across my sensitive skin. His groin pressed against my sex with an unmistakable bulge that sent a wave of heat tingling up from my core.

"Too long," he muttered. "Too many days I lost with you in that awful prison and then forgetting. I want to taste you everywhere again and make you gasp in so many ways, but for now I simply need to be inside you."

"Please," I said, with a perfectly good gasp just from the friction of his erection pressing between my legs through the layers of fabric.

His nimble hands made short work of my pants. He

had to ease away to let me kick off those and my panties, but the second the clothes dropped to the ground, he hefted me up against the tree again. As he gripped my ass on one side, he delved the slender fingers of his other hand inside my slit. They curved into my slick channel to find the point of deepest pleasure within. When they stroked against that spot, I moaned at the flood of bliss.

Snap rocked his hand inside me and swallowed whatever other sounds I'd have made with another scorching kiss. It felt so fucking good, but it wasn't what he'd promised me.

"Snap," I said when he released my lips, a whine of need creeping into my voice.

He understood. With a blink, his clothes vanished—he formed them with his shadowkind magic and could dismiss them just as easily. He grasped my hips and plowed his rigid cock into me, not slow and lingering like the first time we'd fucked but all the way to the hilt in one go, thank all that was firm and fanged. The thrust set off a fresh surge of pleasure that knocked my head back against the tree trunk.

Once we were joined, though, the devourer's urgency seemed momentarily quelled. He hummed happily, the sound carrying from his chest into mine, and traced a giddy path along my jaw with his tongue.

"My Sorsha. I love you too. More than any peach."

A laugh tumbled out of me, even though my body was aching for him to ravage me to my release. "That's pretty impressive, but only peaches? What about bananas? Strawberries? Mang—"

He let out a rough noise that was almost a growl and

plunged deeper into me, exactly the way I'd wanted. "More than any fruit. More than anything. You are mine, and I am yours."

"Mmm." As he thrust again, more pleasure seared through me, and I couldn't find the concentration to tease him any more. But one other point that I needed to make swam up through the ecstatic haze clouding my mind. "You don't leave again. No matter how worried you are. You'll stay and talk. Promise me."

"I won't leave," he agreed. "I swear it." Then his mouth descended on mine, our breaths and tongues mingling, and we were both completely done with conversation.

My hips bucked to match Snap's thrusts, and if my backside was getting rubbed raw by the tree bark, I didn't give a damn. I couldn't feel anything but the bliss spiraling through my body with each pulse of his cock inside me. As I clutched his shoulders, I sped toward my peak faster than a hurricane.

My whole body quivered as I came, an electric shock of the most exhilarating kind jolting through me. The cry that broke from my throat probably carried all the way back to the RV. What the hell. Let them know our devourer was himself again.

Himself and mine.

Snap followed me over the edge to release with a groan of satisfaction. His fingers clenched around my thighs as he poured himself into me. He held me there against the tree for a minute longer, nuzzling the side of my face, as gentle now as he'd been ravenous moments ago.

"I suppose we should return," he said regretfully as he lowered me so my feet could touch the ground. "The others will worry."

"About you as much as me." I bobbed up to give him one last quick kiss and groped for my pants. "We wouldn't want to cause them any panic attacks. Anyway, I do have a room in the RV, and we haven't got any plans for the rest of the night, so..."

Snap beamed at me with a slyer slant to his mouth than usual. "We have a lot of time to make up for."

"We do." Struck by a wave of gratitude and affection too powerful to ignore, I wrapped my arms around him in another embrace. Tears that were mostly joyful this time formed behind my eyes. "In case I haven't made it clear enough, I'm so glad to have you back."

And who knew how much time we'd get to make up what we'd lost before the Company or some new catastrophe came hailing down on us.

16

Omen

After spending much time mortal-side, it became obvious just how dreary and amorphous most areas of the shadow realm were. How could any setting have the same impact as even the mortal world's more mundane sites in a world where our interactions were reduced to vague impressions and ephemeral sensations?

So, it said something that the deep, sprawling hollow of the place where the Highest dwelled still managed to strike me as imposing. The shades of darkness lay somehow thicker and blacker there than in any other part of the realm. The shadowy planes seemed to loom over you and simultaneously threaten to suck you down. If I'd been mortal side, the scent that drifted through the filmy air here would have made me think I'd stumbled onto a rotting old ocean-liner: a combination of salt and rust and wet loam that spoke of the immensity of the sea.

Had this area arisen this way naturally, or had the

shadows collected more densely and pungently because of the ancient nature of the beings that dwelled here? Or maybe the Highest had constructed the atmosphere in some purposeful way. They did enjoy wallowing in their self-importance.

I waited at the edge of the depths, the innate scorching heat of my shadowkind form holding off what might have otherwise been a chill in the darkness. The scrap of a demon lackey who'd run off to inform the Highest of my arrival was taking so long I was considering eating him for dinner if he ever returned. The Highest drew in enough fawners that they weren't likely to notice one minor being missing.

I was equally tempted to turn around and head back to the rift I'd leapt through—to return to the crisper air and the vivid colors and sounds that I had to admit I often preferred to this place even if I wasn't terribly fond of most of the mortal beings that inhabited that world. But if Sorsha could swallow her pride and turn back to her Fund for as many answers as she could get, and even the damned *imp* was willing to spend hours scouring the streets for a shadowkind who might have information, how could I shy away from making at least this one attempt to support my greatest cause?

It was a matter of dignity.

The unimpressive demon didn't return after all. Perhaps one of the Highest had decided he'd make a nice snack. Instead of a lackey coming to usher me in, the call arrived in an echoing swell of a voice that I felt wash through me more than heard.

"Hellhound, you may come."

So kind of them to allow this meeting. As I traveled forward, I suppressed the snarky remarks my old self would have liked to make. I wasn't sure I *would* have made them, even back when I'd had a hard-on for making trouble. Not after my first meeting with the Highest, anyway. I'd been smart enough even back then to prefer toying with beings who couldn't turn around and bite me in two.

The attitude that came over me when I sensed the massive, ponderous presence of the Highest ahead of me was more than shrewd caution, though. There wasn't much dignity in it at all.

I'd heard one of the humans I'd conned long ago speak about how he reverted into the postures of his childhood when he visited his parents, as if their expired authority over him could reduce him from his current status as an adult. While I'd never been a child in the same way as mortals, and the Highest had nothing to do with my existence, confronting their enormity made me contract inside myself instinctively, as if I wasn't one of the oldest beings in the realms besides them. My hellish heat shrank back beneath my skin; my fingers curled their claws against my palms. I didn't quite tuck my tail between my legs, but an embarrassingly large part of me wanted to.

I couldn't help imagining the choice remarks Sorsha would have made about that. Which annoyed me even though she wasn't around to actually make them, doubly so because of the other emotions that stirred at the memory of the glint that lit in her bright eyes with her teasing.

Our mortal ally had tangled herself up far too much in my thoughts.

"You return, hellhound," one of the other Highest rumbled. They towered so close together I'd never been entirely sure how many of them there were. "Have you tired of your quest?"

I drew myself up with as much confidence as I could exude without crossing the line into insubordination. "Not at all. Actually, that's what I came to talk to you about."

There was a general rumbling between more than one of the beings—a chorus of disgruntledness. I thought it was a different one who spoke up next.

"When we permitted you to take your leave on this endeavour you requested to pursue, it was with the understanding that we had no interest in it ourselves."

The "permitted" remark rankled, even if it was technically accurate. "I know," I said. "But I thought you might be interested now that I've discovered more. The harm I thought was being done to our kind—it's much more serious and widespread than I ever suspected."

Another of the Highest let out a sound that could only be described as a grunt, which even the echoing quality of their voices couldn't make portentous. "Are there rabble-rousers like yourself fanning the flames of ire again? We can send a host to bring them in line—"

"No," I cut in, instinctively bracing myself. For good reason, because an instant after my failure of manners, a jab of pain coursed across my throat like the jerk of a choke chain—if that choke chain had been buried within my flesh.

I barrelled onward. "I haven't seen any of our kind inciting the conflict at all. The offense is all on the mortals' side. There's a large collective of humans spread out across the mortal realm, determined to destroy not just every being of our sort on their side but the entire shadow realm as well."

"Hrmph. Not surprising after all the work you and your ilk did to stir up those hostilities in the past."

My jaw clenched. I didn't need them to remind me of my complicity in the problem. That was exactly why I couldn't back down now and let the Company do their vicious work unimpeded. I'd helped set the stage for them, and I'd damn well yank it out from under them if I possibly could.

"What these mortals are attempting goes far beyond any damage the shadowkind ever caused them. They're attempting an outright extermination. And from what we've uncovered, they're close to achieving it. They're even working on ways to extend their influence through the rifts. They want *all* of us dead."

And that includes you, I thought but kept in. The Highest could read between the lines. The last thing they'd appreciate was a being beneath them suggesting they were in any way vulnerable.

One let out a bellowing sort of chuckle. "They could never penetrate our home. You may disdain the creatures, hellhound, but you give them too much respect at the same time. They are frail, waning beings who barely breathe before they're gasping their last."

It would seem like that to the Highest when they'd

been around who knew how many millennia. As if a human lifetime wasn't plenty long enough to wreak all kinds of havoc.

Some part of me abruptly wished that Sorsha *were* here, just to see what she'd say to these lumbering ancients. Better that she wasn't, though, if it'd even been possible. I'd get to admire her brashness and the flare of that flaming hair for about two seconds before she was down one of these leviathans' gullets.

I hadn't really expected any other answer. But for the sake of being at least as intrepid as that one mortal, I gave it a final go. "I think they might come up with a way. But even if they don't, they're tormenting and killing all sorts of mortal-side shadowkind."

The sublime presences of the Highest loomed even larger over me. "That is not our concern. We regulate the rest of *you* when we must, but we don't trouble ourselves with mortals. If one of our kind has been intensifying the problem, then perhaps we would step in, as we did with you... and your associates. Otherwise those who choose to pass through the rifts must own that risk themselves."

Naturally. They would police and even slaughter their own kind if other creatures complained about the turmoil we were stirring up, protecting the mortals from *us* as much as those creatures from the mortals, but ask them to shield us from a direct, organized onslaught of maliciousness from those same mortals...

What did these ancient goliaths know about any of this anyway? None of them had ever ventured mortal-side, as far as I knew. They laid down laws and punishments about a world they'd never even experienced.

I would simply be thankful that they'd provided a convenient opening for the other topic I'd wanted to raise with them, one I thought I might get a smidge farther with.

I picked my words carefully. "On the subject of our kind causing problems... I've heard a few beings mention one you were searching for not that long ago. A shadowkind you wanted reports of but warned others to stay away from because of the danger—the name might have been Jasper or Garnet... some sort of red stone?"

That question elicited a much more energetic rumbling. My throat prickled as several sets of senses focused intently on me. Their voices blurred together.

"What have you heard? Has someone located that being? What destruction has it already wrought?"

They were definitely worked up about this rebel shadowkind—and obviously their minions hadn't located it yet.

"Nothing that I'm aware of," I said quickly. "And no one I spoke to had any idea of that one's current whereabouts. I simply wanted more information so that if I saw evidence that might point you in the right direction, I'd recognize it to pass it on."

There was a moment of silence I couldn't help feeling had a skeptical edge to it. Then one of the Highest responded. "It was in the region the mortals call 'America' when last we heard, but that was some span ago by mortal time. The name you must watch for is Ruby.

And even you should not challenge this one. If you catch any sign, bring the matter to us at once."

"As you request. I want nothing to do with anyone who's raised so much of your ire. What has this one done, if I might ask, so I can be particularly wary?"

"That is none of your concern." The attention on me shifted, with another pinch of pain around my neck. "*You* haven't been disturbing the mortals again during your quest, have you, hellhound?"

Darkness save my soul if they ever found out just how much mortal blood had already spilled at my hands—and claws and fangs—in the past few weeks. Not enough that it would have mattered to them if it wasn't for my history, but with that hanging over me...

I forced a smile I wasn't sure they'd notice and lied through my teeth. "Of course not, oh Highest ones. I'm keeping within my bounds. I'll return to my quest, then—and do my best to ensure none of the shadowkind affected by these treacherous operations ever need to call on your help."

"Very well. That is satisfactory."

I had the impression of them turning their backs on me, and the tension that had coiled through my chest released. Breathing more steadily again, I loped out of their hollow as quickly as I could move without looking as if I were fleeing.

Despite all their power, that was the only thing the Highest really cared about in their old age: being left alone. Even telling their lackeys how to carry out their orders was an imposition to them. All the better for me that they'd let much of their surveillance of the mortal realm dwindle over the past century.

But it was clear we wouldn't find more allies against the Company of Light among them. We'd just have to hope we could track down this "Ruby"—and that the enemy of my enemies would turn out to be a friend to us.

17

Sorsha

I didn't think I'd ever seen Antic quite so invigorated, which was saying a lot considering she was the most excitable being I'd ever met. She bounced up and down on her little feet as she led us through the thinly forested area that bordered a post golf course. The teenage son of one of the players blasted a jaunty ska tune from his phone for a minute or so before the employees hustled over to scold him, and the rollicking tune matched the imp's exuberance perfectly.

"The gnome said he's been living in this city for almost fifty years," she exclaimed breathlessly. "He must have been here when you were born, Sorsha. Maybe he knows about the hunters who killed your parents!"

I'd also never heard anyone speak quite that cheerfully about a double homicide. "Maybe," I said, tugging at the hem of the starchy button-up blouse I'd had to wear for this adventure. My shadowkind companions had been able to slip across the grounds to the shelter of the trees invisibly, of course, but I'd needed to disguise myself as one of the staff to avoid questioning. As long as no one asked me to distinguish between a putter and a driver, we were good.

Under the canopy of leaves, this section of the grounds was cooler and dimmer than the grassy stretch under the morning sun I'd left behind. I eased aside a low branch blocking my way and continued that thought. "Or at least he might have known my guardian. Luna could have told him something about them or me, or…"

Or how I'd come to be the only human being I'd ever heard of with magical powers.

"If he has any answers, we'll get them out of him," Omen said. The words could have been menacing—they usually would have been, coming from him—but his tone was mild, almost as if he was trying to reassure me. Hold the presses! The ice-cold hellhound might be softening up after all.

It didn't seem totally fair to think about him in those joking terms anymore, though. He *had* accepted this substantial detour in his quest to let me investigate my heritage. Now, that might be in large part because he didn't want his secret weapon incinerating herself before we were done destroying the baddies, but I'd take the generosity anyway.

"Are gnomes dangerous?" Snap asked by my other side. "I don't think I've ever met one." His grip on my hand adjusted to twine our fingers more tightly together. As pleased as all our companions had been to find out he'd come back to himself, he'd stuck like glue to me since last night—and I couldn't say I minded. I was still wrapping my mind around the fact that I had my devourer back and that the intimacy we'd shared might not be so fleeting after all.

"The worst he's likely to do is bite her knees," Omen said with a crooked smile.

Snap squeezed my hand. "I won't let him do that!"

The hellhound shifter shook his head in exasperation. "I don't think we really need to worry about that unless our mortal here decides to start using *him* as a soccer ball. But if he's a particularly rabid one, I think we can manage to save her."

"I'll restrain myself from playing any contact sports with our informant," I said.

We'd decided not to bring the full group on this excursion-slash-interrogation so as not to intimidate the gnome too much, but naturally Bossypants couldn't allow anything to happen without being there to oversee, and Snap had refused to let me out of his sight. Thorn and Ruse were patrolling the edges of the golf course at a greater distance. I definitely didn't feel in any danger from the being we intended to meet.

Antic halted by an aged stump about the height of my waist and knocked on it. From the thump, the thing was hollow. "Hello there!" she chirped. "I'm back with my friends that I told you about."

Omen couldn't manage to stop his lips from curling in disdain at being referred to as one of the imp's "friends," but he schooled his expression into something if not friendly than at least emotionless rather than openly hostile.

A little man wavered out of the shadows around the stump. And by "little," we're talking *little*. Like, the dude barely came up to my knees. Although I guessed that did put him in the perfect position to bite them if he decided that was a fun way to pass the time after all.

Other than the absence of a pointed cap, he looked disturbingly like the garden gnomes—you know, the ceramic kind—I was more familiar with than the real deal. His chubby cheeks were rosy above a tuft of silvery beard, his eyes twinkled, and his diminutive body was stout and plump beneath his bright blue jacket and emerald trousers.

Despite the twinkle in his eyes, which I guessed was a permanent feature and not an expression of joy, he was frowning. "What's this all about?" he muttered in a reedy voice. "I don't like showing myself when there are mortals around."

Unlikely he'd been fast friends with my parents, then. I crouched down so I wasn't towering over him quite so much and flashed him a smile. "I'm really sorry. We just wanted to ask a few questions about things that happened quite a long time ago. There aren't very many shadowkind who've stuck with this city with as much dedication as you have."

The flattery got me somewhere. The little man puffed up his chest, and his frown faded even though it didn't disappear completely. "I know when I've got a good thing. What is it you wanted to know?"

"There was a fae woman who lived around here about thirty years ago. Her name was Luna. In her shadowkind form, she had filmy wings and she was pretty sparkly... well, like faeries are. I don't suppose you ever ran into her?"

The gnome rubbed his chin. "Luna. Luna. I can't say that name sounds at all familiar."

As my heart sank, he waved a finger in the air. "I know who you might ask, though. She's rather fickle, as faeries are too, but they do often gravitate to their own kind. There's a fae by the name of Daisy that hangs around out back of the lighting store over that-a-ways. It's been a time since I went that way, but she's been in this city almost as long as I have, I think, so I don't see why she'd have left. You could try her."

He motioned to the east toward this lighting store. Well, that was the start of a trail, at least.

As I straightened up, Omen cleared his throat. *He* didn't bother lowering himself to the gnome's level. "One more thing. At least a couple of decades ago, powerful shadowkind might have come through the city asking about a being they'd have said was dangerous—one named Ruby."

The gnome paused, and then his eyes widened. The recollection made him quiver on his feet. "Oh, yes, I didn't like those ones that asked about it. Three times they badgered me—a lot less politely than you lot."

"Three times?" Omen repeated. "Did you know something about Ruby?"

"Not at all. But they seemed to be making the rounds over and over thinking they'd turn something new up. I can't say why. It must have been over the course of at least a month they kept coming around."

"How long ago was that?"

"Like you said, years and years ago." The little man grimaced. "I'd put it out of my mind."

"All right. That's helpful to know." Omen gave the gnome a slight but definite tip of his head in thanks.

"I guess we'll have to hope this fae who might or might not be at the lighting store will have more dirt to dish," I said as we headed in the direction he'd pointed us.

Snap cocked his head to one side. "How do humans sell *light*?"

I wasn't going to get into the extent that we actually did, or I'd end up needing to explain the entire science of electricity. "They just sell fancy ways of generating that light for inside our houses. Lamps and ceiling fixtures and all that."

"Ah, yes! They had many glowing things like that in the hotel that were lovely to look at." The devourer beamed so brightly at the memory that we probably could have put him up for sale in the store.

Omen, on the other hand, was frowning now as if the gnome's expression had been contagious. "We do know more than we did before. There must have been a reason the Highest's minions would have focused on this city more than others. If there was a definite sighting of 'Ruby' here, or more than just a sighting—we might be able to pick up that trail while we're here too."

I didn't know why he'd frown about getting closer to this shadowkind he figured might help us, but with Omen, sometimes it was better not to ask.

The lighting store was easy to spot: a big building with massive amounts of crystal fixtures glittering in its broad windows. Snap re-emerged from the shadows in time to take in the view in all its splendor with an awed inhalation, careful to hold his forked tongue out of sight.

Antic had vanished from view with the others while we'd headed out of the golf course. As we came around the back of the store, she sprang into sight again, pointing at a little house that was really more of a hut, wedged between the rear end of two neighboring shops. The paint on its clapboard front and slanted roof had dulled and faded, but I could tell it'd once been a vibrant pink and blue. That looked like a fae's design sense, all right.

"Is she around?" I asked without thinking the question through.

"I can pop in and check!" the imp offered, and sprang toward the closed door.

"Hold on!" I said quickly. I should have remembered she didn't have much sense of boundaries. "I'd imagine it'll give a better impression if we're polite enough to knock rather than barging right in."

Antic shrugged as if it was all the same to her and rapped her small fist against the door. "Daisy?"

Omen stepped closer. No visible hint of his shadowkind form showed, but his aura of power intensified enough that the energy tickled over my skin. "We know you're here, and you know we're shadowkind," he said to the patches of darkness around the house. "We only want to ask a few questions. I'd rather not have to get more insistent about that."

I smacked his arm. "What did I just say about politeness?"

He gave me a baleful look. "I phrased that threat very

politely." He turned his gaze back to the house. "To be clear, I'd much rather keep things peaceful."

What was he going to do if the fae woman didn't emerge—dive into the shadows and wrench her out by force? She'd be just overjoyed to answer our questions then.

I made a face at him and attempted my own plea. "We wouldn't be asking—or being assholes about it, in the case of someone I won't name—if it wasn't important. It's about a fae named Luna who used to live in Austin a long time back. A gnome suggested you might have known her."

For a moment, nothing happened. Then a form shimmered into being in front of us.

The fae woman wasn't Luna's twin or anything, but she had enough of the same fae features that I could have believed they were cousins. Her pale hair sparkled in the pigtails she'd wrapped with shiny pink ribbons; actual glitter gleamed all over her frilly dress. She'd draped several strands of crystalline glass that looked as though she might have stolen them from the store's chandeliers over her shoulders as an opulent sort-of necklace. Her features were delicate except for her eyes, which were just a little too large to look comfortably human. Those eyes fixed on me.

"You know Luna?" she said in a tinkling voice that reminded me of my guardian too, so much that my lungs constricted. "It's been so long—I kept hoping she might come back."

The constricting sensation deepened. She didn't know that Luna couldn't ever come back. "Luna... looked after me when I was a kid. But she was taken down by hunters several years ago. I'm sorry. Were you close when we lived here?"

"Oh, no. She's gone?" The woman's face fell for a moment before she seemed to recover. Her makeshift finery tinkled as she shifted on her feet. "I couldn't say we were *really* close, but, you know..."

She tipped her head to the side and gave me a dreamy smile that sent another wave of recognition through me. I hadn't really talked to any fae women other than Luna—I hadn't realized how much she simply represented her kind rather than her own unique approach to life. Apparently coyness was another common trait.

"I always wished we could be better friends," the fae went on. "She had so much energy; it was lovely to be around her. But she was so busy too..."

I fought past the eerie resemblance to focus on my search for answers. "Do you know who else she spent time with? Was there anyone in particular?"

"Let me see, let me see... It was so long ago!" She tapped her lips with another cutesy tip of her head to send her pigtails bobbing. "She mostly stuck to the downtown area. I can't think of anyone still around who'd —oh. There was the elf. I always wondered why she bothered with *him*. But I saw them together a bunch of times."

I'd take whatever leads I could get. "And this elf is still in the city? Where we could find him?"

"Oh, he came from the worst place. I don't go out that way anymore, but he never moved that I knew of. He might still be there."

"*Where*?" Omen demanded, the threatening edge coming back into his voice.

The fae woman let out a faint huff, and I was afraid she'd vanish rather than tolerate his tone. But she wanted to dish her gossip more. "He lived in the *sewer* of all places. Near the spot where the busy road crosses the river." She shuddered. "The one time I talked to him, he said no mortals would ever oust him there, but *I* could never tolerate it."

"Thank you," I said, and then, since the hellhound shifter had at least tried to support me in his overbearing way, added, "I don't suppose you know about anyone named Ruby? Shadowkind might have come around asking about that name a while back too."

"Ruby... Ruby... That does sound familiar. I thought if it'd been an actual ruby, I'd have cared more." She tittered. "They were so insistent about it, but I don't keep track of every being in this place."

Nothing more than the gnome had told us about that one, then. Even less, really. "Thank you," I said again anyway.

She bobbed her head and blinked away, shooting a hint of a glare at Omen just before she vanished. He simply rolled his eyes.

"I wonder why anyone was so interested in this Ruby shadowkind," Snap said as we headed to the Everymobile. "It doesn't sound as if the local beings even knew about them before the Highest sent their underlings around to ask."

I knit my brow. "That's a good point. If—she?—did something so offensive that the Highest shadowkind wanted to bring her in, wouldn't someone have heard about what she actually *did*?"

"I think you're missing the obvious," Omen said in a dark tone.

"What do you mean?"

He looked over at me, his expression grim but not cold. "The search for this Ruby happened somewhere around the same time as your birth. We haven't determined yet how you got your powers, which no mortal should have. Maybe Ruby was in the habit of imbuing shadowkind skills on beings that weren't meant to have them."

A chill pooled in my gut. "You're saying—"

"I'm saying our two mysteries might almost be the same one. It's starting to seem like an awfully big coincidence otherwise. Whoever this Ruby is, maybe it's because of *her* that you are as you are."

18

Sorsha

We figured the "busy road" the fae woman had mentioned was probably the highway that cut through the city—at least, it'd better be, because otherwise we'd be down in the channels of excrement for days. As Ruse drove along it toward the river, I peered out the window for promising-looking manholes. A mix of nervousness and excitement gripped me as tight as a toddler clutching her blankie.

We were going to talk to a shadowkind who might have been Luna's closest friend, as shadowkind went. If anyone would know more about her history here and what had gone on with my parents, it'd be him.

Which also meant that if he *didn't* know, the trail might run totally cold.

I drummed my fingers against the top of the sofa-bench and sang to settle my nerves. "Drive it by, we'll watch for you, don't plead or even move."

Ruse let out a chuckle from the driver's seat. "Are we going to ask this elf some questions or hold him up?"

"If we let Omen do the talking, it might end up being a combination of both."

Antic smothered a giggle where she was perched on the edge of the table.

Omen bared his teeth at me, but only a little. Progress! "You're assuming I'm coming with you into that dank place."

I raised my eyebrows. "You'd actually let me off the leash to handle things on my own?" I teased. "Not afraid of all the catastrophes I might cause down there?"

"You have occasionally managed to handle yourself acceptably."

"I think you mispronounced 'amazingly.' Anyway, you'll miss an excellent opportunity to show off your authority and all."

"Perhaps I'd rather use that authority to avoid treading through sewage." A glint lit in his eyes that was uncharacteristically playful. "I'd almost think you're afraid to go down there by yourself, with all these attempts to badger me into coming along."

Oh, he thought he could turn the tables on me that way, did he? I resisted the urge to stick out my tongue at him. I could be slightly more mature than that, this once.

"I won't be alone. I'll be accompanied by the shadowkind who think getting answers that could help us take down the Company is more important than steering clear of shit." I patted Snap's thigh where he was sitting next to me and Thorn's elbow where he was standing beside the sofa at my other side. "Maybe 'boss' doesn't mean the same thing it used to."

"I'm pretty sure delegation has always been part of the job description." He glanced toward the front of the RV as Ruse slowed to a stop. "But don't worry, Disaster. Since you're so keen on having my protection, I'll sacrifice a few minutes to the stench."

"That's not what I was saying," I groused—and holy heretic hounds, was that a hint of a *grin* from the hellhound shifter, despite our argument?

"I *could* hang back then," he said as he pushed himself away from the counter across from the table. "Darlene needs protection more than you do while you're around."

"Oh, no." I gave him a light shove toward the door. "You said you'd come, and you've got to be a man of your word. Come on. You'll get to do so much glowering and growling. Probably mostly at me. It'll be fun."

He caught my hand before it'd even finished grazing his back and pushed it back toward me—not roughly, but firmly. The heat of his fingers blazed over my skin, making the banter suddenly feel electrically charged. "You won't want to misplace this where we're going."

"A gentleman would offer his elbow," I informed him.

"Good thing I've never pretended to be one of those, then."

"M'lady," Thorn said, offering me *his* elbow and looking as if he took the whole gentleman thing as seriously as he did most other subjects.

I smiled up at him and rose on my toes to kiss his cheek. "I already know you're perfectly chivalrous. But you'd better stick to the shadows unless we need defending—it's going to be hard enough getting down there without anyone asking why we're messing around with city property."

Ruse appeared on the steps by the door, apparently having already scoped out the area. "There's an opening to the sewer down one of the quieter streets," he said. "We can go through the shadows and push it up for you, and if you're quick about it, there aren't too many people around to notice."

"Sounds like a plan."

The other shadowkind vanished, except for Snap, who rested his hand on my hip with his arm around me. I tipped my head back to put my face at the perfect angle to receive a kiss, and he didn't disappoint me.

"I'll be fine," I told him. "You'll all be right there—and I'm just walking down the street." And disappearing into a manhole of some sort, but I'd rather not dwell on that too much ahead of the stink. Slipping stealthily through the gap shouldn't be any trouble after all my thieving practice.

"Of course you will," Snap said with automatic confidence. "I only wondered..."

When his pause stretched on, I poked his arm. "What? You've wondered a lot of things, and I'm always happy to answer."

He wet his lips with that tempting tongue. "Have you and Omen become closer? The way we are, and how you are with Ruse and Thorn?"

The memory of the hellhound shifter's hot fingers just now—and of the moment days ago when he'd responded to my kiss—tingled through me. "Not like that," I said. "Why?"

"It's only—there are times when the two of you have that energy between you, for what Ruse calls mating." The devourer looked abruptly, adorably awkward. "I wouldn't be upset. He is... very different from me, and very powerful, and he's doing so much for all shadowkind. I couldn't say I'm worthy of your affection and he isn't."

I gave him a wry smile. "I think it's more whether he thinks *I'm* worthy of his. That's all right. The three of you are plenty to keep me occupied. And he's a jerk at least as often as he's tempting."

Snap hummed. "He carries a lot of weight on his shoulders. It's made him hard. But he's been good to me." He pressed a peck to the top of my head. "I'd better catch up. Hurry to meet us."

I shut the door of the RV—currently in tour bus form—carefully behind me and made for the ridged metal surface that stood out against the asphalt just down the street. As I reached the manhole, the heavy cover lifted to show an inch of darkness and the faint gleam of Thorn's white-blond hair.

A couple of teens were ambling down the street toward me. I gestured for the warrior to wait a moment, became fascinated by the closed storefront next to me until the teens had passed by, and then made an upward motion with my hand.

The second he'd raised the cover higher, I squeezed through the gap and found myself wrapped in Thorn's free arm, pressed to his brawny torso. He lowered the metal disc, his body braced between the tunnel's walls with his back and feet at opposite sides, and adjusted me against him.

"I'll convey you down, m'lady."

"Thank you ever so much," I said with a grin.

It was hard to keep that good mood intact as the sewer smells closed in around me in the dimness. Only a few thin streaks of light fell from the little holes in the manhole cover. Thorn set me down on a stretch of dingy concrete, his mouth set as if he were restraining a grimace at the stench. "It is very dark from here on. The others have gone ahead to search for our elf."

"Let's hope they find him soon." I had no qualms about wrinkling my nose. Breathing through my mouth to dilute the stench, I pulled out my phone and switched it to flashlight mode. I wasn't afraid to go tramping around in these tunnels, but if I could avoid taking a wrong turn into a trench full of literal crap, I'd prefer that.

Up ahead, one of those trenches held a turgid flow of murky water. Well, water and lots of other things much less appealing than H2O. Was that the swish of a crocodile's tail?

Better not to look too closely.

I crept along the walkway beside it, my stomach starting to churn for reasons that had nothing to do with my nerves. After what felt like a hundred and one years, a figure emerged into view up ahead: Omen, a hint of his hellhound magma glow making him stand out against the darkness. "Here he is," he said in a dry tone that didn't give me much idea of what to expect.

The skinny man who stepped out beside him could

best be described as "sullen." Everything about him seemed to droop, from the fall of his black hair, the bags under his eyes, and the slope of his jaw, all the way down to the floppy tongues of his miraculously spotless sneakers. True to elvish form, his ears had sharp tips aimed toward the ceiling. If we had to take this meeting out in public, maybe Ruse could give him some hat pointers.

"He says his name's Gloam," Ruse said, materializing just behind me. He rested his hand on my waist with the sweep of his thumb in a fond caress. "I asked to make sure, and surprisingly enough, it's definitely not 'Gloom'."

I held back a snicker with a twitch of my lips. "A fae woman by the lighting store told us you were good friends with Luna."

The elf sighed, the sound heavy with disillusionment. You'd have thought we'd just told him his house had burned down and his car exploded. Although given where he was living, maybe that had already happened.

"Luna," he said in a dour voice. "I thought I mattered more to her than to be *abandoned* without a second thought. But off she went to who knows where and left me all alone."

Antic popped out of the darkness with a tsk of her tongue. "She's dead now, elf. So maybe it's better you didn't go with her, huh?" She tweaked his sagging shirt sleeve and shot me a smile as if seeking my approval of the point she'd made.

Gloam appeared so depressed already it was hard to tell whether that news affected him. "Some mortals say to die is to go to a better place. It could be that's true."

"Let's hope it is," I said, aiming to speed things along. "And she left in a rush because she thought she was about to get murdered *right then* by hunters who were in the process of murdering other friends of hers. I take it that you did know her pretty well?"

"We explored the human nightlife together. She said I was the only one she could talk to who wouldn't think she was strange." He sighed again. "Everyone thinks *I'm* strange. Who am I to judge anyone else? Not that it stops them."

I wasn't sure "strange" was the right word for the impression he gave off, but getting into a debate about it didn't strike me as a good use of my time. "I'm sorry to hear that. You don't happen to know about other people she was friendly with in the city, do you? Maybe a man named Philip... a human man?"

"Oh, yes," Gloam said, as if this were common knowledge, so why was I bothering to ask him? "The human man. She talked about him. One of her daytime companions, since my company isn't good enough then."

His head drooped farther. How had perky Luna ever ended up friends with *this* dude?

Omen looked as though he were restraining himself from grabbing the elf's shoulder and shaking the answers out of him. "What did she say about him? Did she mention anything to do with his wife?"

"That's the only reason she knew him—his wife. Not that she was his wife to begin with. Who would have thought? But these things—sometimes it's strange..." The elf shook his head dejectedly. "Luna made it sound like the most wonderful experience, not that I'll ever have it."

Antic gave him a jab in the belly with her finger. "What experience?" She made a face at me. "I think he's trying to make us all just as miserable as he is."

"No. No, no one should ever have to feel as I do right now." He rubbed his mouth. "Ember was Luna's *best* friend, really. How could I compete with an ifrit? And then she goes and has this romance with some human man—Luna found that so fascinating—but she stopped talking to me all that much, she got so wrapped up in helping *them*..."

My heart stopped. "Wait, you're saying the guy named Philip that Luna knew—he married an ifrit? A shadowkind woman?"

"It does happen from time to time," Gloam said, as if he couldn't imagine any fate more tragic. Or maybe he thought the tragedy was his own lack of romance? It was difficult to tell through the general haze of melancholy. "All hush hush, of course. Luna barely let it slip even to me. Augh, maybe I shouldn't even have told you." He dropped his head into his hands.

My pulse started up again, but its beat kept stuttering. Naturally it was Snap, ever curious, who asked the question we must all have been thinking in that moment. He might not even have realized how ridiculous it would sound to anyone more familiar with shadowkind-human relations. He set his hand on my shoulder and leaned past me toward the elf. "Could the human man and the ifrit have had a child?"

Gloam laughed, but somehow he turned even that noise despondent. "Everyone knows shadowkind don't produce children. But it's funny that you ask. Luna said something once—looking up legends of when fae and the like had supposedly mingled with mortals to that extent—I suppose they might have been looking for a way. I doubt they found one, though."

I swallowed hard, staring at him, not yet ready to look at my companions and see what they made of that revelation. No doubt rose up in me. What he'd said wasn't definitive proof, but the pieces fit together in a way I couldn't deny.

I bled both blood and smoke. I could hold iron and silver, and I could generate fire by will alone. I was human, and I was also shadowkind.

My parents and Luna had found a way.

There was my answer—and it was just as much a puzzle as it'd been before I'd started this quest. How could anyone tell me what being a hybrid of human and shadowkind would mean or how to handle my powers? Even this elf, who was apparently the only being still alive who'd known that secret, had dismissed it as utterly impossible.

19

Snap

How could I ever have forgotten the tempting spicy sweetness of Sorsha's skin? Thinking back to those days when everyone and everything I'd known in the mortal world had felt so unfamiliar sent a jarring sensation through my mind.

So I put the thoughts out of my mind and focused on the much more enjoyable sensation of slicking my tongue across the nub of my beloved's breast.

Sorsha's breath caught with the hitch I loved to provoke, her fingers tightening where they'd twined with my hair. I gave the risen nipple a little nip I'd discovered could bring out even more delightful sounds and eased up to claim her mouth again.

My hand delved through the tangle of sheets on her bed to tease between her thighs. The slit where we both found so much pleasure met my touch slick and ready.

Mmm, I would have to start our mornings off this way more often.

Sorsha's knee rose against my hip, but she pulled her face slightly back from mine with a rough inhalation. "Snap—I think we're going to need to be more careful from now on."

I couldn't resist dipping one of my fingers into that hot slickness within her. The way she bit her lip made me want to kiss her all over again, but I wasn't sure what she'd meant. "Careful how?"

"Well—what we found out about me. That from the sounds of things, my parents discovered some way that my mother could have a kid even though she was a shadowkind. It sounds like it must have been pretty difficult to manage, but—we don't know whether I could get pregnant. So probably better not to risk it."

Right. This act of merging bodies was how humans created life. Could what we did here, what we'd already done mingling so closely and passionately, bring about a being that was somehow both her and me?

The idea sent a quivering thrill through me. She *was* my beloved, in every sense of the word I understood. She'd told me she loved me even when faced with my most monstrous form, even after I'd admitted how harsh and selfish the hunger inside me could be. And I didn't know what else this other hunger—tender and selfless instead, wanting to possess her but only as much as the act would please her too—could be.

Love barely seemed a big enough word to encompass the feeling that lit me up with a warm glow whenever I looked at her.

I kissed her temple and eased my lips down until I could nibble her tender earlobe. "Would having a child be so awful, Peach?"

Sorsha laughed and tugged my mouth to hers so she could kiss me back. "Maybe not, someday *way* down the line," she said. "You have no concept of what babies are like, do you? They take a lot of work, and they need a lot of attention and security. Not really a good fit for our current lifestyle."

"Hmm. But perhaps later. When there's no more Company of Light to worry about?"

"We'll see. I never really saw myself starting a family, at least not… not recently. But it's starting to feel a little more possible. I mean, assuming we all survive this war we've ended up in."

"We will," I said, wishing I felt as certain about that as I did about my adoration of the woman beside me. I worked another finger inside her, testing the sensitive inner flesh for the spot that sent the greatest flush of bliss over her skin. "How do we be 'careful' in the meantime?"

Sorsha arched into my touch. When she managed to speak, her voice was thick with desire. "For now, we'd better stick to hands or mouths. Which you're doing a *very* good job of, by the way. And I'll have to pick up some condoms—we put those over you"—she stroked her hand across my erection, drawing it even stiffer with a surge of delight—"and then no worries about babies."

I could follow those rules—and perhaps adapt them to my purposes to even more enjoyable effect. I pulled myself down her body, still stroking her between her legs. "How about hands *and* mouths, then?"

"I'm sure as hell not going to argue—"

I flicked my tongue over that other responsive nub just above her slit, and her agreement cut off with a gasp. I transformed the gasp into a moan by adding the pressure of my lips.

Her taste filled my mouth, even more fiery down here. The most delicious thing I'd ever tasted.

Something clanged from the kitchen area down the hall. Ruse's voice filtered through the wall. "I come bearing breakfast! Who's ready to eat?"

I was too busy savoring this delicacy to be tempted by whatever he was offering. But Sorsha would need to fill her stomach simply to keep her strength up. I wouldn't keep her from her sustenance very long, then.

I suckled harder, pumping my fingers in and out of her while adding a third. Sorsha let out a guttural sound. Her body clenched around me and then sagged with a shudder of release. More wetness seeped over my fingers as I withdrew them. I licked it off and smiled. "All the breakfast I need."

Sorsha laughed again and tugged me down next to her. Her hand trailed over my chest to my still-rigid cock. When she wrapped her fingers around it, a groan tumbled from my lips. I would so much have liked to delve that wondrous part of my physical body right inside her. Perhaps Ruse had some of these 'condoms' around, given that sexual intimacies were his specialty?

But that thought led me back to the reasons we needed that protection and the possibilities of how Sorsha herself had been conceived. Even through the expanding swell of pleasure, my mind latched onto a memory from before we'd ever become so intimate.

I stilled her hand before I could lose the thought in my distraction. Sorsha looked up into my face with a question in her expression.

"It makes sense now," I said.

"I'm glad my hand job came with bonus enlightenment. What does?"

"The impressions I gleaned from that pretty box that your parents left for you." I might not have known just how much I'd come to value Sorsha's existence at the time, but I'd still been honored that she'd trusted me with the treasures of her past. "The strongest sense was that they'd taken a lot of risks to bring you into their lives—that it almost hadn't been possible at all. Because of how difficult it must have been for the two of them to conceive you at all."

"That's true. I'd forgotten you took your reading of the box." She paused. "You didn't get any sense of someone else being involved in that process—someone they owed a debt to or wished I could have met or anything like that?"

"You mean if the Ruby shadowkind was connected to them and helped them somehow?" I shook my head. "It was all focused on you and their bond with you. But that doesn't mean Ruby wasn't involved. It was so long ago, the impressions were quite vague."

"I get it." She grimaced. "I remember that you also told me there was someone from Luna's past that she missed. I wonder if that was the lighting store fae or our gloomy elf. I never thought to ask her about the things she left behind—somehow I always took it for granted that her whole life should be dedicated to me."

I stroked my hand over Sorsha's hair. "From what I know of shadowkind, I don't think she'd have made the sacrifice if you weren't *much* more important to her than anything she gave up."

Thinking about her losses had dampened my desire. I could fulfill it to greater effect once she'd gathered her protections anyway. I sat up, tugging her with me. "You should have your breakfast before it gets cold."

Sorsha arched an eyebrow at me. "Are you sure?"

I stole one last kiss. "I have everything I need. For now."

We emerged from the bedroom to find that Ruse had laid out his bounty on the RV's table—and Omen had returned to join us. The hellhound shifter had gone off on his own again not long after we'd finished questioning Gloam, who'd had no contact with the shadowkind named Ruby either, at least as far as he'd admitted. From our leader's stern expression, I suspected his independent search hadn't turned up any new information either.

Sorsha must have made the same assessment. "No sign of our mysterious Ruby?" she said as she slid onto the sofa-bench. I sat beside her and picked up a particularly delectable-smelling pastry with syrupy cherries in the middle.

Omen sighed. "As far as I can tell, none of the shadowkind in the city even *saw* her, let alone noticed any catastrophe she caused. It could be that the Highest's lackeys cleared out any other being who'd been drawn into her schemes... but I'd have expected there to at least be rumors of that kind of round-up."

"Perhaps it was a false rumor that brought them here to begin with," Thorn suggested. "Or a piece of information they thought was related to her but wasn't after all. We don't know how many cities they conducted a more intensive search in. The fact that they did here, where Sorsha was born, might not be that great a coincidence."

"True enough. For all we know, they harassed shadowkind across every metropolitan area in this half of the country." The hellhound shifter's next breath came out in a huff. "I suppose there's no point in continuing to go out of our way looking for Ruby. Whatever trail there was is long cold. We'll have to make do with what we have. Rex's hacker thought the command center of the Company was located in San Francisco. We'll scope them out and decide how to proceed from there."

Sorsha had picked up a wrap stuffed with cheesy scrambled eggs. She stopped in mid-bite, her stance tensing, and lowered her meal with an audible gulp. "You want us to leave now?"

Omen eyed her across the table. "It seems we've achieved all we can here. We have a basic sense of how you came to be what you are and no way of quickly determining any of the details. Did you really think we'd forget about our primary mission while we searched out the key to an incident that no shadowkind I've ever heard of has stumbled on before or since?"

"It might not be *that* hard to figure out. How many shadowkind have wanted to have kids anyway? I thought

I'd at least talk to the local Fund branch again. Klaus might remember more if I ask him some leading questions. And we could use their help *with* that primary mission too."

Omen made a scoffing sound at that idea. "It was hard enough getting the humans who knew you to contribute when we were in their own city, Disaster. What are these mortals going to do for us when we take on San Francisco?"

"I don't know. It just seems worth a try. Trying did get us somewhere more than once before, as you've admitted yourself." She waggled the wrap at him.

"And let's hope I never have to again," he said dryly. "They have your contact information if they feel spurred to action, don't they?"

"Well, yes, but—" Sorsha hesitated, the fierceness in her eyes dimming. I was about to put down my pastry and reach out to her when she found her voice again. "We still don't know why my powers have been acting up. I don't know how much help *I'm* going to be if I can't be sure I'll burn up the right people when people need burning."

Omen propped himself against the kitchen counter, looking unconcerned. "I think we've got enough of an answer for that. Obviously your human parts are having trouble accepting the shadowkind parts. It's the conflict of our species all over again."

"Wonderful explanation, but it doesn't help me avoid setting myself on fire."

"Sorsha." Omen's gaze turned momentarily intent, his tone serious enough that my ears pricked to even closer attention. "The fools in the Fund won't be able to help you with this. You can handle it. *We* can handle it. I'll just keep training your impossible self until your control improves. I'm not letting you go down in flames. All right? I'd just like us to take the training sessions in the direction of our ultimate goal so we can tackle more than one bird with the same stone."

Sorsha blinked at him. "Oh. Okay." Then her smile came back. "As long as these training sessions don't involve pummeling me into a pulp like you've attempted in the past."

Omen rolled his eyes skyward. "I think I can manage to keep you safe from that threat as well."

I inhaled slowly, tasting the energy that shivered through the air between them. It was such an odd mix of antagonism, comradery, and amusement that I had trouble knowing what to make of the stew. It wasn't at all like the steady vibe of fondness and support that flowed between Sorsha and Thorn or the sensual heat she and Ruse could spark with just a glance, but it held echoes of both of those flavors along with so many others.

Maybe they didn't know where to go with that chaos of emotions either.

"I'd still like to touch base with the Fund people here, even if it's just briefly," Sorsha was saying when her phone beeped with some sort of alert. She picked it up and read something off the screen. As her face fell, my heart sank too.

"What's happened?" I asked.

"It's—" She swiped her hand over her mouth as if trying to push away her frown, but it didn't quite work.

"It shouldn't really matter. I didn't expect anything. Ellen from back home just texted me. She's decided that as far as our conflict with the Company goes, she and the rest of the Fund members from my old branch are staying out of it completely."

20

Sorsha

A spurt of flame leapt up from the ball hurtling toward me—and at the same time, a crackling heat washed over my hand. As I dodged out of the way of the now fiery projectile, I clapped my fingers against my shirt and restrained a wince at the stinging.

"You're not keeping your focus," Omen said from where he'd leaned against the wall of the batting cage a few feet away. "You can't expect to maintain control if you're not even paying attention."

"Sorry for having a few other things on my mind the day after I discovered I'm some kind of never-before-heard-of human-shadowkind fusion," I shot back, and waved my hand in the air to dispel any lingering heat.

"If you're not up to continuing, we can leave things here."

"I didn't say *that*." Imagine the party he'd throw if I ever admitted I couldn't meet one of his challenges. Oh, no, this gal was in it to win it. Even if I wasn't totally sure what "winning it" would look like. Not frying myself at random, presumably.

The batting cage training session had actually gone pretty well at first. As Omen had set up the ball launcher to, well, launch balls in the approximate direction of my face, the other shadowkind had come out to watch. With Antic's eager cheers, Ruse's sly praise, and Thorn's and Snap's quieter but powerful support, I'd been able to put what I'd learned about my history and Ellen's refusal from my mind.

But now the daylight was dwindling. The time was creeping closer to the Fund meeting Omen was grudgingly agreeing to let me attend, and it was getting harder to tune out the niggling uncertainties.

And look what that got me. Scalded fingers—nice work, Sorsha.

I squared my shoulders and readied myself for the next ball. The machine chucked it at me with all the intensity of a nuclear missile launch.

My eyes narrowed, and the leather surface burst into flames. The ball streaked through the air like a meteorite, dissolving into ash just before it reached me. As the charred remains pattered to the ground with a whiff of smoke, I braced myself for a matching singe across my skin, but none came. Thank buttery boom sticks. For once, my trainer couldn't complain.

"Better," Omen said. "You *can* pull it off—now you just have to keep doing that."

"Thanks for the excellent coaching, boss. Where would I be without your sage wisdom?"

The corner of his mouth curved slightly upward. "Searing yourself to a crisp, I've gathered."

Before I could come up with an acceptable retort, Thorn emerged from the shadows, back from a quick patrol of the area. We must have been safe from marauding hunters and actual missile launchers, because his expression was... if not *happy*, because Thorn rarely managed to look anything other than serious, then at least semi-relaxed.

"Maybe our mortal has put in enough work for the day," he suggested mildly. "No one can focus well once they're worn out."

I dragged in a breath and found my muscles were starting to get a bit trembly from the effort I'd been exerting for the last few hours. "You have a point. I want to be sharp for this meeting, too." I glanced at Omen with a quirk of my eyebrow. "Unless you have any objections, dog breath?"

The shifter smiled thinly at me, but his gaze wasn't anywhere near as icy as it'd been when he'd first attempted to train me weeks ago. It might even have been a tiny bit warm. "Have a break then, Disaster. But don't expect me to cut the human side of you any slack."

He stalked back to the Everymobile. I rolled my shoulders, walking in a circuit of the arena to stretch my legs at the same time. When I came around to my original spot, Thorn had lingered there, waiting for me.

"These recent events—they're weighing on you," he said.

The gentle concern that came through his low voice sent a flutter through my chest. There was nothing quite like the reminder that one of my greatest marvels had been melting this warrior's stern demeanor.

"It's a lot," I said. "Especially when all I've got now is more questions. If it'd turned out my parents had a shadowkind work magic on me or whatever, that would have been a little easier to wrap my head around. And everything with the Fund..." I rubbed my arms and let out a little laugh. "I guess I really did burn those bridges right to the ground. Maybe it's a *good* thing I'm making tonight's appeal to people who barely know me."

Thorn let out a rumbling sound. "I don't think your behavior necessarily dictated how your former colleagues responded to your request for help, m'lady."

"No? They sure acted like it had."

"I've observed—there's a way all beings tend toward —" He paused, glancing around. The other shadowkind had left as far as I could tell, but either someone had stuck around in the shadows or Thorn felt we were too close to our home base for comfort. He motioned for me to follow him.

We meandered around the rusting fence surrounding the rundown facility and on toward the river, much farther down than we'd been parked before. I scooped up a pebble from the sidewalk and tossed it at the water, accomplishing a whole one skip before it sank with a ring of ripples.

Thorn gazed solemnly toward the opposite bank with its concrete barrier. "I saw it often during the wars," he said. His expression and his tone told me he had to be talking about the vicious battles fought several centuries ago, in which the wingéd had divided to support opposing factions of humans and battled each other. "We were always trying to stir up other shadowkind to our cause, as I suppose our brethren who opposed us must have as well, but rarely did they join in even if they voiced agreement."

"To be fair, there were quite a bit more people *dying* in that conflict than have in our 'war' against the Company so far," I had to point out.

"Perhaps. But one truth I have seen across my time is that beings will almost always retreat from a fight unless they are dragged into it by a motivation much deeper than a plea to their generosity. I fought because I couldn't turn away from my brethren when they called on me, because at least for some time I thought that if I fought well enough, fewer of us would die..."

When he lapsed into silence, I tucked my hand around his powerful arm. I'd heard the warrior voice regrets that he hadn't been there for his comrades enough, but never with the hint of doubt that had come into his tone now.

"Are you thinking you might have been wrong about that?" I asked.

Thorn's jaw worked. "The things I've seen and learned over the past few weeks have made me question many things, including my own judgments of the past. I'm starting to wonder if perhaps we would all have been better off if we hadn't been so quick to leap to each other's aid at arms but instead had stopped to discuss just how necessary the warring was to begin with."

I leaned into him, pressing a quick peck to his

shoulder. "You're turning into a pacifist on me. I'm shocked."

"I wouldn't go *quite* that far." He eased his arm right around me and traced a line of heat up and down my side with the stroke of his fingers. "I will defend you and the rest of our companions by whatever means necessary as long as breath remains in this body. But do you know... I never was even certain of what we were fighting *for*, or why our brothers who rose up against us were so convinced they needed to strike out at us. How many of us leapt into the fray so ignorantly? What if most of those deaths could have been avoided?" He shook himself. "But we're getting away from your concerns of the present."

"That's okay. I get to be concerned about you too. And it sounds like it's a good thing you're questioning the past. Better now than never. I still think the Fund doesn't have anywhere near as much an excuse for staying out of our battles. Their whole purpose is supposed to be helping the shadowkind—and they've heard plenty about why we're fighting the Company."

"Well, there are other, less honorable reasons one might avoid conflict too." Thorn's hand stilled against me. "When I first heard that the Company's presence extends into Europe, I must confess that something in me balked. To return to the lands where I fought before, or at least close to them—But it isn't as if much remains of that time anyway. It's only in my mind that the uneasiness dwells. The few of us remaining wingéd scattered far and wide after the slaughter. We're closer now to one of my former companions than I might ever be across the ocean."

I raised my head. "There's another wingéd around here? Where've you been hiding them away?"

Thorn chuckled grimly. "With so few of us remaining, we're attuned to each other's presence. I couldn't tell you how many exist in the entire world, but a few hours before arriving in this city, I could tell there was another of my kind some distance to the west. Perhaps even in San Francisco."

I was about to point out how that could potentially come in handy when Ruse hollered from the direction of the distant RV. "Oh, Sorsha! You've got a gentleman caller."

Thorn frowned. I gave his arm a tug. "Come on, let's see what he's going on about."

It didn't take long to figure out. When we reached the Everymobile, the rest of our group was standing on the pavement outside it, in a loose ring around a lanky figure with floppy black hair and pointed ears. Gloam the elf had come to visit.

If it hadn't been for the hair and the ears, I might not have recognized him. The evening was settling in around us, but Gloam was glancing around with far more pep than I would have imagined he could exude. His hair no longer drooped but swished with the movement of his head. He rubbed his hands together and shot a wide grin my way.

Maybe I was hallucinating? But Omen, Ruse, and the others were all staring at the elf with equal amounts of bemusement.

"I've come to join your quest," Gloam said with a playful bow. "You mentioned that you were looking for more shadowkind to help you tackle these enemies of all of us. How can I hide away when adventure calls?"

I just barely held myself back from gaping at him. Antic bounded around him, jerking at his clothes and poking him here and there, her mouth twisting at a puzzled angle.

"What's the big deal?" she demanded. "You got two beings in the same body or something?"

"Just the one." He smiled at her too as if oblivious to her prodding.

She turned to the rest of us and jabbed her thumb at him. "No way is this the same guy we met in the sewers. Maybe toxic waste mutated a twin!"

"Oh!" Gloam said with a lilting laugh. "I see the confusion. I apologize for how downcast you must have found me yesterday. You see, I'm a *night* elf. When the stars and moon are out, I'm rejuvenated. During the daylight hours, I haven't much energy to put on a good face."

Understatement of the year. But having now met the perky version of Gloam, I could believe Luna had been best buds with him.

"I don't suppose you bring any special combat skills or potent magic to the table?" Omen asked.

Gloam shrugged with the same buoyant grin. "I can cast my own darkness."

"In more ways than one," Ruse remarked, smirking.

"We're glad to have you on board," I said, half afraid the others' skepticism would send him back into his previously depressed state. "You made it just in time. We're going to be heading out any minute now."

Antic was still eyeing the elf suspiciously, but she snapped her fingers and darted toward the RV. "Come on. I'll show you where *you* can make a spot for yourself. Just remember, any pranks or tricks, I call the shots."

Omen caught my eye as the rest of us moved to follow them. His voice came out cool, but he couldn't totally flatten the amusement in it. "How is it that you manage to conscript the most useless beings to our cause, Disaster?"

I held up my hands, matching his tone. "Don't blame this on me, boss man. *You're* the one who mentioned our grand crusade to him."

Omen's expression twitched as he must have realized I was right. "I didn't *invite* him," he said. "But I suppose I can't blame you if he invited himself. Other than your optimism might have influenced me into mentioning it at all."

I swatted him. "Sure, I'll take the blame, as long as I also get the credit when he ends up foiling the Company on our behalf."

"Rather than waiting on the chance of that, you'd better keep practicing that self-control. A little of me has to rub off on *you* eventually."

"Hey, my amazing abilities are thanks to me alone."

"And aren't we all grateful for that," Omen muttered, climbing the steps, but I thought I caught a flicker of a smile.

He hadn't needed to practice with me today. He hadn't needed to dedicate himself to helping me control my powers at all. I wouldn't have expected it to necessarily matter to him if one human—well, half-human—burnt herself up as long as I burned down the baddies in the process. But apparently he did, and that softened any snappy retorts I might have tossed at him.

However much he'd come to value my contributions, it didn't stop Omen from tossing out a little more snark when Ruse parked down the street from the gaming store. "Make your plea and be back here in ten, or maybe we'll leave you with these bozos."

"You'd better leave me Darlene, then, since you won't be needing her without my mortal ass around," I informed him on my way out.

I'd texted Monica to give her a heads up that I'd be stopping by. Apparently the Austin branch of the Fund was particularly cautious about people infiltrating their secret lair: the password had already changed, to "Yoshitaka." I gave it to the same dude behind the counter and strolled on in to the evening meeting.

A couple more people had shown up for this one: a slight, middle-aged woman with a Tinkerbell pixie cut and a young man whose not-entirely-successful attempt at growing a moustache looked like tufts of grass poking up from a desert plain. Klaus was standing at the foot of the table, waving his arms emphatically as he made some point about, "...might be the only real chance we get."

Everyone looked over when I came in, and a smile leapt to Klaus's face. "I think we're all decided," he said before turning back to the others. "Are we?"

Monica nodded slowly, the Man in Black and the scraggly moustache dude more emphatically. Klaus beamed, the rosiness in his rounded cheeks making him look even more like Saint Nick.

"That's great," I said. "Er... What are you decided about?"

"You made it clear there's a menace lurking that's a threat to both the shadowkind and those of us trying to help them. We can't look the other way. Let us know where you need us and what we can do, and we'll pitch in however we can."

I'd expected to have a debate on my hands, but apparently it'd already happened without me, spearheaded by Father Christmas himself. And it wasn't anywhere near December 25th. I'd still take this gift, thank you very much.

I grinned back at him. "Okay, I take back my 'great' and raise it to 'awesome.' We're definitely going to need all the help we can get. I can't stay very long because we're about to head out, but we'll be regrouping in San Francisco. If any of you are willing to make the trip and help us on the ground, maybe even just coordinating with the Fund branch there, that'd be huge. But even doing some information gathering or similar from afar would be useful."

Klaus rubbed his hands together. "I haven't been out to the west coast in years. A vacation and a campaign of righteousness in one—sounds good to me. I'll just have to check the flights." He glanced around at his companions. "Who's with me? You've got to figure out your own way there, but I can cover an AirBNB big enough for all of us."

"I've got the time off already," the Man in Black said. "Count me in."

The pixie woman raised her hand. "I think I can

make it work. I'll just have to make a couple of calls."

"Same here," Monica said, and inclined her head to me. "Keep me in the loop with what's going on and what else you discover. If you could email me a full run-down of how you've tackled these people so far so we can start our own strategizing, that would be great."

I wasn't sure I really wanted them knowing that our strategy so far had involved a lot of torn-off heads, disemboweled torsos, and charbroiled corpses. As the memories darted through my head, a wavering heat shot over my arms—and a flame shot up over the knuckles of my right hand.

It was barely a flash of light, there and then gone as I jerked my hand against my side. I bit my tongue at the stinging sensation but held in my yelp. Still, spontaneously catching on fire is the sort of thing it's difficult to keep on the down-low. When I looked up, several of the eyes watching me had widened.

Time to divert and refocus! "Of course," I said quickly, clasping my hands in front of me as if nothing at all unusual had sparked from them. "It'll be a bit of a novel, but I can give you the gist with all the important stuff."

"Excellent." Monica smiled, which I hoped meant everything was still a-okay. I had the feeling apologizing for my near-combustion would only make things worse.

"I'll get started on that then. And reach out once we're in San Francisco so we can meet up. Don't you lose my number." I wagged a finger at the group at large and hightailed it out of there before my prickling nerves could let loose any further supernatural special effects.

21

Sorsha

When I came out in the morning to grab breakfast, Gloam was drooping over the table like a plant that had wilted with too much sun. The downcast nature that consumed him by day made it hard to believe he'd been gleefully discussing favorite mortal desserts with Snap yesterday night.

Antic perched on the counter across from him, holding the new map book Ruse had picked up for her. A vibrant pink sticky note poked from the top of the cover announcing *This Way Up*. I wasn't sure trusting her to give directions even with that safeguard was the best idea.

She looked up from the book to stick out her tongue at the night elf. Her skinny legs swung against the cabinets. "I keep telling him he should take that sour face into the shadows where at least we won't have to look at it."

Gloam sighed. "I know it isn't pleasant to observe my dejection. I can remove myself if that's what you'd all prefer."

I shot a warning look at Antic and sat down across from him with the muffin I'd picked up. "Don't be silly. You are the way you are, and if you'd rather stay in physical form, that's up to you. Anyone who doesn't like looking at you can just point their eyes in another direction."

The imp huffed and hopped down from the counter to stand closer to Ruse, who was back on driving duty. "In another, I'd say, ten miles we're taking an exit south." She turned the book sideways and then her head sideways to match, which didn't exactly add to my confidence.

Even with shadowkind drivers who had no need for sleep, we weren't going to make it to the Golden Gate City until tonight. At least we had our lovely home on wheels to enjoy for the journey. And we hadn't even stolen it or conned it out of anyone—legitimate rides for the win!

As I bit into the doughy sweetness of my muffin, Gloam raised his head enough to peer at me from beneath his thin eyebrows. "There's so much more Luna was hiding from me than I ever could have guessed. *You* came from a human and an ifrit..." He stopped there, just staring, as if the impossibility of it had rendered him mute.

"Hey, no one's more surprised than me," I said. "She raised me for thirteen years and never made a peep about me potentially having voodoo skills or anything like that."

Really, a warning would have been nice. What if I'd accidentally set one of my high school teachers up in flames for disparaging my essay-writing attempts or what have you? Not that I was thinking of anyone in particular who might have deserved it...

"I never thought such a thing could have happened. I suppose that just shows how little I truly understand this world."

I had to restrain myself from rolling my eyes at his insistence in making the insanity of *my* existence all about *his* failings. "I'm sure it wasn't easy. Omen has been around for, like, a thousand years or something and he's never heard of anyone managing it."

Somehow my reassurance only turned Gloam gloomier. He looked down at his hands. "They must have wanted you an incredible amount to try so hard to bring you into being. I can't imagine anyone will ever care that much about *my* being."

No wonder Luna had only hung out with this guy during the night. I was starting to rethink my rebuke to Antic. But his comment stirred up a trickle of warmth too, one that spread through my chest as I soaked it in. For the first time since Ellen had texted to say she and the rest of that part of the Fund were out, my nerves completely settled.

"They did," I said. "Love me a lot. I remember..." My recollections of my parents were vague, but every impression I had of my mother's face framed by her ruddy hair was beaming with affection. In the note they'd left for me, they'd called me their "treasure." And Luna had believed in their commitment to each other and to having a child enough to not only help them with their search for a solution but to devote her life to me for more than a decade after their deaths.

So what if I was an impossibility? Yeah, I was a freak of nature who still had a lot of work to do when it came to controlling her hocus pocus. But I'd also been born out of the most immense love I could ever have imagined.

My parents and Luna had believed I deserved to be brought into this world—that I'd make things here better rather than worse. I had to believe in myself at least as much in their honor.

The Everymobile swayed as Ruse changed lanes, to no honks just this once. "We're officially halfway there!" he called back to us.

"Woohoo!" I raised my arm in a fist-pump. A moment like that called for a song. "We're as spry as a tiger; we're as chill as a kite, rising up to the challenge on arrival!" I belted out.

Gloam blinked at me with a bewildered expression, but Antic giggled and did a little jig with the map book.

Omen materialized next to the table with his arms folded over his chest. "If you want to actually 'rise' to that 'challenge' without barbequing yourself any more than you already have, I'm thinking another training session might be in order. If you think you can manage not to burn down Darlene around us?"

I stuffed the last of my muffin into my mouth with a quick nod. How many challenges had I already tackled and lived to tell the tale? I'd get the hang of this. If my mom and dad had managed to get their differing natures to cooperate enough to produce an entirely new being, I could talk the opposing sides of myself into getting along.

Swiping my hands together, I got up. "All right. Let's do this." I paused, considering our limited options for training space. "Maybe not right here near the driver's seat, since I can't promise a flame or two won't get a *little* out of hand. And I'd rather not make a bonfire out of my own bed, so... the master bedroom?"

"I could just stuff you into the bathroom, since no one else here needs that."

"Yeah, but there'd be no room for you to join me in there to boss me around."

I marched past him to the narrow doorway at the very back of the RV. I'd only gone in there once before, when Gisele had been curled up on the bed unconscious from her battle wounds. Apparently she'd wanted to shake that memory too by changing the surroundings—the bedspread was different, a dark blue that twinkled here and there like stars. She must have gotten Bow to scrounge up a new one for her.

"All right," I said. "What's on the menu today? Any sparkly things you'd like scorched out of existence?"

Omen cast a baleful look around at the bedroom, which had more surfaces that shimmered than not. Even the ceiling had been dabbed with patches of gold glitter like a shiny hurricane was about to descend on us.

The unicorn shifter's taste in décor was unmistakable. It really was too bad she and Luna had never gotten the chance to meet.

"I thought we'd go back to the first trick that worked." Omen brandished a handful of torn strips of paper he'd pulled from his pocket. "Simple and easy to work with in a confined space. But first—I thought back to when I originally decided I needed to temper my, ah, temper. We can try a few centering and calming techniques that might help you stay cool while you're summoning your fire."

Anything that reduced the chances of me ending up in cinders sounded good. "I'm ready. Teach away!"

Omen talked me through a couple of mental exercises involving measured breathing and visualization. I decided it was wisest not to mention that his instructions sounded an awful lot like the yoga guru meditations Vivi's mom was addicted to.

Who was I to poke fun, anyway? Picturing a serene stretch of still ocean water, I could compel its imagined cooling sensation all the way across my skin. Of course, what really mattered was whether my mental imagery would continue to hold water once very real flames came out to play.

"Do you think you've got a good enough grip on yourself now?" Omen asked. After several minutes of pacing while he lectured, he'd finally allowed himself to sit on the edge of the bed—a foot away from me, but even when I closed my eyes, the heated power of his presence tickled over my skin.

"I'd better be," I said. "Bring out the papers!"

He got up again to stand in front of me and held one pinched between his fingers about two feet from my face. The bedroom, for all its impressiveness, *was* still an RV bedroom, and we didn't have a whole lot of room to work with. He waggled the paper slip so it swayed above his grasp. "You should feel honored. I'm trusting your aim enough to put my hand in harm's way."

"Of course, what that actually means is you still don't believe I could actually incinerate you."

He really smiled then, with a cocky slant to it that abruptly made me wish I was getting a grip on *him*. "Glass half full, glass half empty—it's up to you how you see it."

He shouldn't be tempting me, or one of these days my uneasiness about the energy that sometimes rose up inside me would be outweighed by my desire to teach him a lesson about underestimating humans... or half-humans... whatever.

I focused my gaze on the paper. Imagined that serene ocean landscape spread out through my body—and a jolt of my inner heat leaping up through that, aimed only at my target. *Burn!*

The paper went up in flames. If they stung Omen's fingers, he didn't let on. Still smiling, he closed his hand around the fire to snuff it out and then brushed away the ashes that remained. "Excellent. Now we just need to do that a thousand or so more times."

I restrained a groan. "Suddenly I feel like I've become your personal shredder. I'll have lots of practice if I ever want to take a job in covering up paper trails when all this is over."

"There you go. I'm setting you up for new and exciting career opportunities too." He paused, and the wry tone left his voice. "Did it feel all right? You didn't burn yourself at all?"

"All good. Perfectly cool and oceanic." I made a

beckoning gesture. "Let's get on with the rest of that practice, or we'll be in Uruguay by the time I'm done."

By taking a moment to center myself and bring up the calming imagery before each blast of flame, I managed to barbeque four more small slips of paper and then a couple of larger ones without any ill effects. Were we going to work all the way up to a complete encyclopedia set?

Of course, when I needed to extend my voodoo in the middle of a fight, I wasn't necessarily going to have time to perform a little meditation before I jumped into the action, or I might get barbequed by our attackers in the meantime. My visualizations weren't going to deflect bullets or daggers or laser whips.

As Omen prepped his next target, I dragged in a breath and let the cooling sensation wash through me again, as thoroughly as I could summon it. I needed to see how long the effect would last if I didn't keep bolstering it with every surge of power.

The hellhound shifter started mixing things up by crumpling one paper into a ball, letting another wave as he dangled it, and whatever else he could think of to vary the practice. I blasted each of them one-by-one, not letting myself hesitate to gather my emotions this time. Pretend we were in the midst of the fray, and each of those scraps was a Company asshole about to slaughter me or my shadowkind allies. *Burn. Burn. Burn it all...*

A sharper flare of heat shot through my chest, and a flame licked up across my forearm at the same instant as Omen's paper caught fire. I slapped my arm against the bedspread, an ache already spreading through my flesh. When I checked it, the skin gleamed dark pink.

"Fuck finicky flapjacks," I muttered.

Omen grabbed a bottle of aloe he'd had on hand, proving he hadn't really trusted my control all that much. "Were you concentrating?" he demanded.

"Yes, yes. But I had to pick up the pace. My powers aren't going to do us much good if I'm stopping to praise the seas while some prick is stabbing a knife into me."

"I'm sure you'll get there. You're rushing it."

I made a face at him. "Right, I have no idea why I feel any time pressure at all. It's not as if dozens, maybe even hundreds of shadowkind are being tortured as we speak, all to develop some sickness that'll kill the lot of you."

"You won't accomplish much to stop the Company if you're too busy scalding yourself."

Rather than handing the bottle to me, he squeezed a dollop onto his own fingers and sat next to me to smooth the gel over my burnt skin. At least the shadowkind part of me seemed to heal the wounds it dealt me faster than any human would have recovered.

The real cool of the aloe spread over my arm. As the pain drew back, other sensations came into more vivid awareness. Like the brush of Omen's fingers, unexpectedly gentle, as he finished his administrations. Like the not-at-all unpleasant heat emanating from him where he was now poised just inches away.

As he let my arm go, I gave in to the urge to poke one of his substantial pecs. "Who would have thought the hellhound could be so sweet?"

Omen snorted. "Yes, my preference that you remain

uncharred so you can actually participate in those upcoming battles is clearly a sign of boundless devotion."

"There you go," I said, cheerfully ignoring the sarcasm dripping from his voice, and leaned back on my hands. "I knew underneath all the rancor you adored me."

The shifter's gaze skimmed over my breasts and down the rest of my body, the flicker of orange light in it kindling a very different flame all through me. Then he pushed away from the bed with a jerk, that familiar ice forming in his eyes. Any good humor flattened from his tone. "You should get back to practice. With a minimum of burnt flesh this time, if you can manage that?"

I glowered at him. "Why do you have to revert back to being Bossypants the Asshole? Is it that hard to admit that you care at least a tiny bit what happens to me beyond my usefulness to your cause? And, y'know, to act like it for more than a few seconds at a time?"

"We've talked about this. I'm not interested in being another one of your fuckbuddies. I can't see any way that won't just lead to more disaster."

"I'm going to have to point out that *you're* the one who brought up fucking. I'm not even asking you to kiss me. All I'm talking about is a little more consistency in the respect and compassion department. Or do you figure since I'm only half shadowkind, I'm only half worth caring about?"

He bared his teeth. "I certainly didn't come here to make friends with mortals."

"I'm not 'mortals'—I'm *me*. And I think I've proven that I'm nothing like the ones you hate."

"I never said you were like them."

I threw my hands in the air. "Then what's the problem? You know I'm in this to the end. I've given up pretty much everything I had before you all crashed into my life to see this mission through. Why are you still so convinced that being a little friendly will ruin *your* life somehow?"

"Who says it's my life I'm worried about ruining?" Omen said, with an edge of a snarl. "Do you really think getting more wrapped up in my business is going to turn out so hot for you?"

How could I resist an opening that good? I peered at him through my eyelashes. "Yes, actually I expect it'd be incredibly hot."

The hellhound shifter let out a strangled sound. "And of course you have to turn things around like that. I don't for one second think you'll be the one hitting the brakes if I stopped doing it."

"So what you're saying is you don't trust your own self-control, and you're blaming me for it."

"That's not— I know what you're like. I've seen how you've drawn the others in, even if there was nothing malicious about it. Don't try to pretend this is all about making friends, because I see *you*."

He said the words like an accusation, but the deeper truth of them rippled through me, dispelling most of my frustration. My fingers relaxed where they'd clenched the bedspread as we'd argued. One corner of my mouth lifted in a crooked smile.

"Yeah," I said. "You do. Not just like that. You're the only one who saw that I was more than human when even I was turning a blind eye. You see what I'm capable of, and you see when I'm struggling—and you like me at least enough to push me or bandage me up as I need it. That's why *I* like you, or at least why I'm trying to through all the hot-and-cold routines you pull."

At my change in tone, Omen's stance had gone rigid. "What are *you* trying to pull now?"

Huh, it looked like kindness pissed off the hellhound shifter even more than snark did. Because it got under his emotional armor more than he liked?

I shrugged, keeping the same calm attitude. "I'm simmering things down—which doesn't mean I'm *backing* down. I just don't see the need to keep throwing insults at each other. Call me a disaster all you want, but no one's ever believed in me as much as you do."

Another flicker of flame passed through Omen's eyes. His hands balled at his sides, and his voice came out terse. "I believe you're a fucking headache."

"Nope. I'm not doing this. The bickering has been fun, but aren't you getting tired of it? If we're going back to practicing, then it's with the understanding that I know you're doing this to help me, because it matters to you that I come out of this mess okay."

"You don't get to announce how I feel."

I gave him a wry smile. "I'll agree to that rule if we also make one that you don't get to pretend you've got no feelings at all."

"Don't go all Dr. Phil on me," Omen snapped. When I didn't respond, he took a swipe at my shoulder, knocking it just enough to make my body sway. "Where's your fight, Disaster? Aren't you always going on about all the incredible strength you're holding back?"

"I don't want to fight you. And frankly, I think it shows a lot more strength to own up to what you really want than to walk around with some tough-guy front."

"It's a hell of a lot more than a front." Omen took a jab at my other shoulder. "If you think I'm some kind of puppy dog, you're sorely mistaken. Do I need to show you just how hellish I can be?"

"Better that than the Ice-Cold Bastard," I said. "Who said I wanted a puppy dog anyway?"

"Then show you can take on the hound."

He shoved me more roughly, his eyes flaring, his hair rumpling like it always did when his temper emerged. I wasn't going to give him the satisfaction of pushing back.

I raised my arms in a gesture of surrender instead, and that enraged him to the point of blazing. His fangs came out, the magma glow and lava darkness coursing over his skin.

With a full snarl, he slammed me back on the bed. His hands pinned my wrists to the mattress with a prick where one of his claws nicked my skin. He clamped his jaws around my throat. His fangs nicked my flesh with a sliver of pain. And all that dangerous, delicious heat flooded over me.

If he thought he could push me into giving him the fight he wanted instead of the fondness I'd been offering, he hadn't seen quite enough.

"I trust *you,*" I said quietly. "Whether you want me to or not. You can't scare me enough to make me run away."

A growl reverberated up from Omen's chest,

transforming into a groan as it spilled across my throat. His body hovered over mine, his muscles tensed. Then his tongue swiped across the sensitive skin he'd been threatening, drawing a rush of pleasure with it.

My breath caught with a gasp taut with desire. I dared to raise my hand to that wild tawny hair—

And he wrenched his mouth from my neck to my mouth, claiming me with a kiss of scorching breath and searing tongue.

My fingernails scratched across his scalp. His fangs were still out, his hellhound heat radiating all across his otherwise mostly human form, but damn if that didn't make the embrace that much more intoxicating.

I arched up toward him, the need to meld with that heat clanging through me like a fire alarm. Without breaking the kiss, Omen dragged me farther up the bed, his hips pushing between my thighs. The hottest part of him, long and hard, pressed between my legs, setting off a shock of bliss. I let out a very undignified whine.

There wasn't anything dignified at all about the collision of our bodies. It was all savage fury. Our mouths crashed together again and again, a metallic tang creeping across my tongue where his fangs had scraped my lip. I tore at his shirt, and he flung it the rest of the way off so violently it smacked a china figurine off the dresser to smash on the floor.

More veins of orange glow blazed across his chest. When he lowered himself again, my shirt crackled with the raging heat. As the fabric charred and fell away like soot, he might have blistered the skin beneath it, but I instinctively called up my own fire to meet him. The flames of our beings danced together between us, searing away the rest of our clothes but licking against my flesh with only the most ecstatic of burns.

Apparently I could also avoid incinerating myself in painful ways if I was in the process of being thoroughly fucked. Good to know.

My legs splayed farther apart with a need too overwhelming to deny, and Omen didn't require any further invitation. His cock rammed into me, sending pleasure sizzling through my nerves.

As he plunged deeper, he grasped my thigh as if to haul us even closer together than we were already joined. My body bucked with his of its own volition, urging him faster, harder. With each forceful thrust, ecstasy roared through me in a growing inferno.

Omen tore his mouth from mine to ravage the side of my neck and the curve of my shoulder. "*You,*" he growled, but if he was pissed off about what we were doing, it wasn't enough to stop. Stopping was a concept that had burned away with our clothes and any common sense I'd still possessed. Why the fuck had we waited so long to *start*?

It might not have been the wisest act I'd ever taken part in. Leaving aside the whole fiery destruction element, there was our new discovery about shadowkind fertility—but if my parents had needed some unknown magic to perform the impossible feat of my conception, the possibility of it happening by accident felt far too distant to wrench me from this bliss.

An unexpected sensation slid across my calf, like the teasing of a finger—except Omen's fingers were currently tangled in my hair and clutching my jaw to yank my lips back to his.

An inkling crept through my pleasure-hazed mind. I groped across the sculpted planes of his blazing back to the even more tempting ass I'd admired through his slacks on more than one occasion, and found out just how much those slacks had been hiding.

He *did* have a tail even in his unshifted form—the one shadowkind feature he couldn't lose when otherwise in his full mortal guise. A tail that shivered as my hand closed around its warm, sinuous length.

My touch must have sparked something enjoyable for Omen, because one of those groaned growls pealed out of him. It reverberated into me with a fresh rush of delight. The tail's devil-pointed tip traced another giddy line up my leg and then along my side in its own caress.

Just how much control did he have over *that* part of his body—and when would I get to test that out?

I wasn't going to ask him now, both because I wasn't sure any request wouldn't knock him out of the furor of the moment and back into his frigid restraint and because I was skyrocketing toward my orgasm too swiftly now to let out more than a moan.

Omen pounded into me with all that fiery intensity, his tail flicking along my ass. With another moan bursting from my lips, I crackled apart like a firework, ecstasy singing through every part of my heat-flooded body.

I dug my fingers into Omen's back, and a ragged breath stuttered out of him. Even more heat pulsed into me as he reached his own climax.

And then it was done. I was lying there on the bed

with the hellhound shifter poised over me, coming down from the high of what he'd just minutes ago sworn he never wanted to happen. Uncertainty dampened the afterglow.

Did I want to look into his eyes and see what reaction was waiting for me there?

I might have been bold to a fault, but that didn't mean I couldn't procrastinate. My gaze slid first to the bedspread beside us, and a giggle tickled up my throat.

The fabric was scorched black. When Omen eased back, withdrawing from me, the charred area disintegrated into flaky cinders.

"Well," I said, "I guess we're going to have to find the equines a new bedspread. Maybe if it's twice as twinkly, they won't mind."

I dared to glance up at Omen then. He was staring down at me, his skin returned to its normal pinkish human shade and his eyes their mortal blue. Any bits of his short-cropped hair that weren't sticking up were plastered to his forehead with sweat from that rather intensive workout with bonus flames.

His expression wasn't exactly warm, but it wasn't hostile or horrified either. He ran a finger across my collarbone and rubbed the soot he'd wiped off my skin against his thumb. "It's a mess all around. Still a disaster."

His tone was even enough that I felt comfortable trailing my hand across his pecs to smear the effects of our merging there too. "I'm pretty sure the burning was at least as much your fault as mine, demon dog. Not that I'm complaining. I don't think I'd consider what we just did a catastrophe. The world hasn't ended yet, has it?"

Omen's shoulders relaxed incrementally. "No, not yet," he said, and there was definitely a droll note in his voice now.

"I didn't intend for us to end up like this, you know."

"I know. If you had, it wouldn't have happened." He exhaled with a rough sound that pinched at my gut.

"Then I hope we can move forward without any regrets," I said.

"We'll see how I feel about it when you're attempting to yank my chain again." He gave me a sharp look. "Even if you kept up with my fire after all, that doesn't mean you're getting out of the rest of your training."

My heart swelled with relief and perhaps even affection. I bobbed up to steal a quick kiss before he decided to set himself off limits again. "Well, I think the one who can recreate his outfit in the shadows and move between rooms unseen should grab me some new clothes from the other bedroom. Then you can train away."

"I'm going to hold you to that, Disaster," he said with what might have been a smirk before he vanished into the darkness.

22

Sorsha

The one thing we did occasionally have to stop for was gas. Around noon, Ruse pulled into a station that had a pizza place next door. While he cajoled free gas out of the station staff, I grabbed my wallet to head over to the pizza place, figuring it wouldn't be a horrible thing to actually pay for what we were going to consume now and then.

"Bleeding heart," Omen said lightly as he stepped out into the midday sun behind me.

"Talk like that, and I'll order pineapple across the whole thing," I replied, anticipating his grimace. One definitive thing I had learned on our road trip so far: the hellhound shifter didn't approve of citrus on his cheesy pies, the poor soul.

"Heavy on the pepperoni, and maybe I'll forgive you anyway. Just—"

"Make it snappy—I know, I know."

The guy at the counter told me it'd be a fifteen-minute wait for the three pizzas I ordered—only one sprinkled with the pride of Hawaii, since I was feeling kindly—so I stepped out of the humid seating area to bask in the warm early fall breeze and the greasy scents wafting from the kitchen vent.

Apparently Gloam had felt the need to stretch his legs too, because he came trudging over in his typical daytime slouched stance.

"I doubt the pizza we get here will compare to what they offer in the city," he said with equally typical gloom.

I gave him an encouraging smile even though I knew the effort was likely in vain. "I subscribe to the idea that all pizza is good pizza."

He made a humming sound and drifted toward the alley between the pizza place and the gas station shop. A moment later, a clang of metal colliding carried through the restaurant's windows. Antic popped into view in the alley with a distinctly guilty expression.

"The chefs looked so bored, I thought I could cheer them up a little," she said. "I guess I didn't set the prank up well enough. It all just slipped..."

I raised my eyebrows at her. "As long as you didn't ruin our pizza."

"Oh, no, it was all empty pans! I was going to roll them across the floor." She made a sweeping motion with her scrawny arm to demonstrate.

Okay, so maybe I couldn't blame Omen for being skeptical about how much these two would add to our master plan. I motioned to the RV. "Why don't you go get the table set up with drinks and napkins and stuff? I'm sure you can find something fun to do with them."

A glint danced in her eyes. "Oh, yes, I can do that! You're going to love this." She darted off, blinking invisible again after her first few steps.

Our pizzas were ready at fifteen minutes on the dot. As I carted them to the RV, the spicy scent of the pepperoni set my mouth watering. The hellhound shifter had better not mind if I grabbed a slice or two of his pie.

Antic had formed a leaning tower of pop cans on the table. I laughed, and she did a jig of delight on the sofa-bench. Snap came hustling over for the food but first gave me a peck on the side of my neck as if in thank you. We all dug in, the devourer's eyes gleaming neon with pleasure, more slices vanishing as Ruse and Gloam rejoined us. The night elf didn't even complain about the slice he slowly nibbled at.

Ruse tucked his arm around me in a casually affectionate gesture, letting his fingers trail across my shoulder to enticing effect. "Thorn decided he needed to patrol, naturally," he told me. "Omen must have gone with him, probably to make sure he doesn't take the whole day at it. I suppose we should save a slice or two for them."

"That seems wise," I agreed, and reached to pet Pickle, who'd hopped up on the sofa beside me.

The little dragon flinched at the motion of my hand. As he took me in, his wings came down, but his body stayed tensed as I scratched his shoulder. Despite the deliciousness filling my stomach, a pinch of sadness ran through my gut. Was he ever going to be completely comfortable with me again?

"You feel a bit tense, Miss Blaze," the incubus said. "Let's see if we can't work that out of you."

He shifted his pose to set his thumbs against the admittedly tight muscles along my spine. A massage *while* eating pizza—could there be anything more heavenly? I wasn't sure what in blue blazes I'd done to deserve this doting, but I wasn't going to say no.

Snap watched this development with a glimmer of consternation. He stroked my knee under the table and motioned to the tower of pop cans. "Would you like something to drink? If nothing here is quite right, there was a large selection in the store."

"I'm good, thank you." I nudged his knee with mine and leaned back into Ruse's hands. "What's with the spoiling me all of a sudden?"

"You've been working hard," Ruse said in his sly voice. "Don't you deserve to be spoiled? We could make a competition out of it. See if the devourer can keep up with an incubus."

At the determined light that flared in Snap's eyes, I gave Ruse a light kick. "I'm not sure I'd survive that competition, even if it'd be a spectacular way to die. You've been doing such a good job of sharing—it'd be a shame to ruin that."

"Hmm. I suppose it would." He leaned in to press a brief but tender kiss above my ear. Apparently satisfied that his devotion wasn't being questioned, Snap returned to his meal, leaving an only slightly possessive hand on my thigh.

A matching tenderness tightened my throat. Omen might have seen more in me than anyone else, but my original shadowkind trio had been there for me in their diverse ways from the very beginning. How quickly one's romantic fortunes could change. A few months ago, I hadn't been sure I could manage to handle even a friends-with-benefits arrangement without it going sideways—and not in the way you'd hope to end up sideways as a benefit.

Now I had two gorgeously monstrous men vying for the chance to pamper me the most—and a third out there patrolling with an unshakeable determination to ensure my safety. I must have done something very, very right in a past life I couldn't remember. I tipped my head to offer Ruse a kiss over my shoulder, which he accepted with delight, and hooked my ankle around Snap's in an effort to show how much affection I held for them both in return.

As Ruse worked over my back, I offered Pickle a bit of bacon off one of the pizzas, but he wasn't inclined to fully forgive me yet. The dragon nipped it from my fingers with a squeaky snort—and promptly scuttled to the other side of the table.

Before I could ply him with more meaty delicacies, my ringtone pealed out. I swiped sauce off my fingers and groped for my phone. Ruse released me but left his hand resting on the back of my neck.

The call was from Klaus. "Sorsha, I'm glad I could reach you," he said, his normally deep but jovial voice more hesitant than usual. He didn't sound particularly glad.

The pinch in my gut turned into a knot. "What's up? Are you still planning on flying into San Francisco this afternoon?"

"Oh, yes, everything's covered there. *I'm* good to go. The trouble is... the rest of my colleagues are backing out."

The knots were now multiplying like bunnies. "What? I thought they were on board—most of them, anyway. They just had a change of heart?"

He sighed. "It seems they felt you were behaving a little oddly at the end of our last meeting... Monica reached out to your original branch of the Fund to check in about you. Apparently the things they told her left her rather disturbed."

"Oh." I swallowed thickly. Huyen—or maybe even Ellen—had given these people the idea that I was some kind of menace? Or just off my rocker? They didn't know about my fire powers... but they could have shared plenty about the destruction that had followed me across the city. "Everything that happened back home—we didn't have much choice if we wanted to take on the Company of Light. They're way too vicious to just sit down and negotiate with or something."

"I can imagine. And I'm not judging you. I've been around in this scene longer than any of the others—I've seen how horrible we mortals can be to each other and to the shadowkind." He paused with a rustling sound as if he was rubbing his beard. "I don't know what exactly you've gotten yourself into, Sorsha, but I know your father was a good man, and I think you deserve a chance. And I wouldn't be here at all if it wasn't for the shadowkind who had the kindness to stop and help when my wife and I got lost on a trip through the desert ages ago, so I figure they deserve whatever I can offer too."

"Thank you," I said around the constricting of my throat. "I appreciate it."

"I wish I could convince the others, but youth do like to dismiss their elders. You'll at least have me, and I'll do what I can. I think your Fund leaders might have reached out to the branch in San Francisco as well, so I'm not sure you can expect much help from that quarter either, but I may be able to weasel my way in there without them realizing I'm working with you. I told my people I'd cancelled my plans so they wouldn't pass on any additional warnings."

That was something. I summoned all the gratitude I could manage into my voice. "We'll make the best of it. Thanks again—I mean it."

"Of course. I'll touch base once I've touched *down* on the west coast."

My fingers clenched around the phone before I dropped it back into my purse. As I drew my hand back into my lap, a burst of sparks leapt from my palm, prickling across my thigh. I squeezed my hand into a fist to snuff any lingering ones out.

I *was* a menace, wasn't I? The Fund folks back home might not have known exactly why people should be cautious of me, but they hadn't exactly been wrong.

Omen was going to be just ecstatic when he heard this news. I could already hear the "I told you so" lilt that would creep into his voice. Damn it.

Damn Huyen and Ellen and the rest of them who

hadn't even wanted to try. That was what the Company relied on, wasn't it? The fact that everyone who might have supported the shadowkind they were set on eradicating was too scared to tackle enemies as big and brutal as they'd built themselves up to be.

Snap was watching me, a half-eaten pizza slice dangling, shockingly forgotten, from his hand. "What happened?"

I opened my mouth, and Thorn materialized by the door. I braced myself for the hellhound shifter to join him, pulling together the words to reveal yet another failing of mortal kind. But Thorn strode over alone.

"Where's Omen?" I asked.

The warrior frowned. "Is he not here? He was when I left."

Ruse's forehead furrowed. "We assumed he went with you. I haven't seen him since just after we pulled in here."

"Same." I glanced at Snap and the others.

The devourer shook his head, his mouth slanting at a worried angle that looked all wrong on his beautiful face. Antic scrambled up with a sharp salute. "I can go looking for him!"

Thorn considered her with unveiled skepticism. "I think you'd better stay here and let me do the searching, little one." He glanced around at the rest of us. "I'm sure he can't have gone far. Perhaps he discovered something nearby that caught his interest."

As Thorn vanished into the shadows, an uneasy tremor ran over my skin. If my stomach had been knotted before, now it might as well have been one solid lump of limestone.

It wasn't like Omen to get distracted, and he'd been determined to make it to San Francisco as quickly as possible. Even if he'd wandered off for some bizarre reason, I'd have expected him to be back by now, if only to let the rest of us know something needed our attention.

Had the Company managed to capture him again? But it wasn't their style to stealthily scoop up just one of us if they could easily see where the whole squad was. I couldn't imagine the hellhound shifter being caught without a major fight that *one* of us would surely have noticed.

Snap set his pizza down, the first time I'd ever seen him lose his appetite. He tucked his hand around mine instead, but I was too on edge to take much comfort from the gesture or Ruse's squeeze of my shoulder.

It felt like ages before Thorn returned the second time, but the slice I was forcing myself to nibble at hadn't even gotten cold when he appeared with no ice-cold bastard beside him. He looked even graver than when he'd talked about failing to protect his boss the first time, before we'd rescued Omen.

"I can find no sign of him," he said. "I can't imagine where he would have gone."

My heart ached for the warrior even as a twisting sensation ran through my chest. The only thing I could think of that had happened recently and might have affected Omen's mood was our scorching interlude in the bedroom this morning. He'd seemed like he accepted what had happened, even if he wasn't crowing from the roof about hitting a home run with me. He'd hassled me when we'd gotten here like I'd have expected him to.

But who really knew what was going on behind those icy eyes and his carefully constructed self-control? Had he gotten angry at me for provoking him—had he gotten angry with himself for giving in to his lust? Would he really have compromised our mission just to go cool himself off?

Maybe, if he felt he was fraying enough to warrant it.

Ruse had been tapping at his phone. "I'm not getting any response the mortal way. He might be in the shadows. Phones don't work there."

"He wouldn't have *left* us," Snap said, but he looked at his companions for them to confirm that was a fact.

The incubus chuckled. "And miss out on the chance to call the shots for the grand finale of our trip? I can't imagine it." But the worried crease hadn't left his brow.

We picked at the rest of the pizza until the incubus declared a ceasefire and packed the rest of it into the RV's tiny fridge. With each passing minute, Omen's absence weighed heavier. Finally, Thorn cleared his throat.

"We know what Omen wanted us to do—to continue to San Francisco as swiftly as this vehicle can convey us. He knows if we're not here, that's where we should be heading. And he may be able to arrive there even faster than us making use of the rifts through the shadow realm. I say we move out. The longer we linger here, the more likely we'll draw the attention of the wrong people."

That was true. I nodded despite the lump in my throat, which seemed to have spawned from my stomach.

Ruse swiped his hand across his mouth. "Just watch.

We'll pull up to the city limits, and he'll be standing there ready to chide us for taking so damn long."

His jaunty tone fell flat. My original trio had gone on without their leader before, but then they'd known what had happened to him and had some idea of how to get him back. Now, we didn't have a clue how to help Omen or whether he even needed help.

And after the way I'd been losing us allies left and right, I had to admit that whatever had happened to him, chances were I wasn't totally blameless.

23

Thorn

With every passing minute after we'd left our last stop behind us, Omen's disappearance gnawed at me more perniciously. I stalked the length of the RV—physically and through the shadows and then back into my solid body again—but I couldn't wear out the uneasiness winding through my nerves.

It'd been my suggestion to move on without our commander. I stood by that suggestion without a single doubt. It was what he would have wanted, regardless of what had happened to him. Whether he was with us or not, the Company of Light still needed to be demolished.

But it was so unlike him to abandon us without a word. I couldn't imagine how our enemies could have attacked and seized him without my coming across any trace of that incident in my patrols. The mystery of it loomed over me in a way that was, well, ominous.

As the incubus drove us onward to the city that was

the Company's base of operations on this side of the ocean, my faint awareness of the other wingéd presence thickened too. It didn't tug or gnaw but simply spread through my chest like a pang of recognition on seeing an old friend you barely recognized.

The one who dwelled out here couldn't be any actual friend of mine, though. The brethren I'd been close enough to that I'd have considered them friends as well as comrades had all fallen in the war. This one might not even have fought on the same side as I had... not that I was certain I could have distinguished who'd belonged to one party or the other after all these centuries.

We were going to pass the spot where that one must be dwelling, though. The pang came with a vague sense of direction—northwest of our current position, shifting closer to pure north the farther we traveled along the highway. I paused to gaze out the window as if I might see a sweep of vast wings in the distance.

"You made the right call," Sorsha said to me, observing my pensiveness but not being aware of the full source. "Omen knows where we're heading. We won't be hard to find once we're in the city. Maybe this is another one of his beloved tests."

Her smile looked tight around the edges, and she didn't sound as though she were as relaxed about the situation as her words were meant to imply. She'd said very little at all since we'd pulled away from the fuel station.

What if Omen *wasn't* in the city when we arrived? What if he never returned to us at all? I had trouble conceiving of that possibility, but we needed to be prepared. I'd committed myself to this cause, and I wouldn't let it fall apart while I was still standing.

My gaze skimmed over my other companions: Ruse humming with disconcerting merriness behind the steering wheel, Snap stroking Sorsha's hair comfortingly, the imp dancing invisibly through the air with ridiculous attempts to provoke our mortal into a smile, and the downcast presence that was the night elf lurking in the shadows beneath the table.

Could we take on the highest level of the Company with just our current allies? Tackling even a less powerful leader had required one of our equine companions and more than a dozen shadowkind helpers from a local criminal syndicate—and we'd had Omen with us too.

I looked toward the window again. My kin was almost directly north of us now. Another road veered away from our highway up ahead, dust billowing behind a speeding car's tires as it raced that way.

My muscles tensed all through my body. But my own discomforts mattered far less than our mission. I meant to see us emerge victorious from this war no matter the cost to myself.

"We should make a brief diversion," I said abruptly.

The incubus glanced back at me. "Not satisfied with patrolling the vehicle, my overeager warrior? I promise you we'll be safer driving in a straight line at the highest possible speed."

"It's not to patrol. There's someone I think I might be able to persuade to join our cause. And it seems now more than ever we should attempt to gain every possible ally. Take that next right turn."

Sorsha was studying me with a glimmer of understanding in her eyes. I'd mentioned my awareness of the nearby wingéd to her. She was respectful enough of my preference for keeping my nature secret not to speak up, though. A flutter of gratitude passed through me even as I prepared to end that secrecy myself.

Ruse pulled onto the narrower, dustier road, but he wasn't as mindful of his own tongue. "And what makes you think this random potential ally will have any interest in joining our wild and crazy mission?"

"It's not random. This is one of my own kind. One of the few remaining. If anyone can make an appeal that will succeed, it'll be me."

Snap's expression turned more alert at that statement, his head cocking with curiosity. The imp ceased her endless bounding about to solidify in the middle of the table.

"Oooh," she said, placing hands on her hips. "We're going to find out what the big scary shadowkind is."

Ruse swiveled right around to look at me, leaving me thankful that the road ahead of him was so barren. "Are you actually going to put an end to the guessing game? I should have started a betting pool."

"You don't have to do this," Sorsha said softly. "If you think it's worth it, I'm all for it—but we'll manage with the help we've got."

My tenacious lover could be so tender when she wanted to be. Her acceptance of my hesitations made me all the more sure that it was time to end them. If I was going to reveal myself for any reason, it should be to ensure I'd done everything I could to make sure *she* survived the upcoming battle.

"We'll manage better with more," I said. "I'm not certain how this member of my brethren will react to being approached, though... Perhaps I should prepare you. You'll want to pull over to the shoulder, incubus, so you don't risk crashing our means of transportation."

"You think very highly of the shock value of your secret identity," Ruse teased, but he did as I'd asked.

When the vehicle was parked, he got right out of his seat and propped himself against the wall just beyond it, watching me expectantly. Antic bobbed on her toes with excitement.

Suddenly the act felt too momentous. I hadn't intended to build it into some earth-shattering announcement. What would the others make of me when they saw what I was? Sorsha had taken my full physical form in stride—but she didn't have the same awareness of the history most of the shadowkind would, and besides, she was hardly a typical example of *her* kind.

But then, none of the beings around me were quite typical, were they? They wouldn't have joined this crusade to begin with if they'd been your standard shadowkind. I had to assume any goodwill I'd garnered with my contributions over the recent months would hold out against their feelings about my kind.

I inhaled deeply and allowed the energies I usually kept tamped down within this mortal body to rise to the surface.

My limbs and torso expanded. My eyes prickled as the heated darkness came over them, not hazing my vision but sharpening it to every movement around me. My feathered wings flared up from below my shoulders, arcing as high as the Everymobile's ceiling and as wide as its windows even only partly open. This space was too confining to show my true shadowkind form in its full glory, but that might be for the best.

No snarky remarks came from the incubus. His lips had parted with the slackening of his jaw. He collected himself with a rough chuckle, but he kept staring. "Holy hell. I should have guessed. Of all the damned beings out there—" He shook his head in disbelief.

The imp had cowered back to the corner of the sofa-bench. Not the reaction I'd wanted to provoke, but an unsurprising one. She peeked at me through her fingers.

"I have no interest in hurting you," I told her, my wingéd voice resonating from my lungs.

A scrabbling sound drew my attention behind me. Sorsha's tiny dragon had emerged from the bathroom where he'd built his nest. At the sight of me, he stiffened, letting out a squeak with a flare of his nostrils. Then he flexed his wings as if to say, *I've got those things too.*

He didn't scramble away, but he didn't come any closer either. This might be the end of my amity with the little creature.

One of our number wasn't taken aback, though. The devourer smiled at me, his wide eyes offering nothing but awe. "Of course you wouldn't hurt any of us. You've been hurt *yourself* so many times to protect us. Your form is marvelous. Why didn't you show us it before?"

Ruse let out another short laugh. "You never heard

about the wingéd, huh, devourer? They have an... interesting reputation."

His gaze had definitely become warier. I could accept that. It wasn't as if we'd been the closest of comrades before. He hadn't fled for the hills or hurled cutting remarks my way, which I could count as a victory.

"I'd prefer not to be judged based on events long past," I said. "We all have questionable moments in our histories, don't we?"

"Most don't have moments that involve an entire war that nearly exterminated your own race—but by all means, let us focus on the present." The incubus offered a grin that looked more like his usual playful self, and just this once, I was glad to see it. "You've stuck to smiting the right people as long as I've known you. I'll trust that you'll continue to do so."

The imp had lowered her hands. Snap glanced over his shoulder toward the window. "The shadowkind we're going to see—they're another 'wingéd' like you?"

I nodded. "The only one I've come close enough to recognize in well over a century. Let us hope time has mellowed him as it has me."

Ruse muffled what might have been a snort of disagreement with his hand, but he returned to the wheel. "Direct away, oh angelic one."

There. It was done, and the world hadn't crumbled apart around me. Relief washed through me so abruptly I had to pause to catch my breath. With a tug of my will, I pulled my features back in to leave only my mortal-appearing form on display.

"Drive onward," I said. "I'll inform you when we need to deviate from that course."

The pang in my chest grew stronger with each mile that passed beneath the wheels. When a dirt road even more desolate than the one we were on veered off to the left, I directed Ruse down it. Finally, a shack that looked as if it had been put together out of discarded, beaten-up planks of wood came into view in the midst of a plain that was otherwise all hard-baked earth and tufts of yellow grass.

No road or even pathway led from the one we were on to that building. Ruse parked, and we studied the shack through the windows.

"I think you'd all best stay here—as much as you might enjoy spectating," I said, adding the last piece when Ruse started to open his mouth with what I suspected would be a protest. "No one lives so far away from civilization because they enjoy company."

"Fair enough," the incubus said with an air of resignation. "But I'm certainly going to watch as much of the show as I can from in here." He plopped himself down at Sorsha's other side and promptly twined his fingers with hers.

I caught our mortal's gaze for a brief moment, hoping I could convey with mine my thanks for her faith in me—in this and so many other things. Then I moved through the shadows onto the barren plain and strode toward the shack.

My fellow wingéd would have been able to sense my approach as well as I'd sensed what I was approaching. A small part of me worried that I might find the place abandoned and feel the presence dashing away from this intrusion, but our kind didn't tend toward fleeing. The sense of his presence remained steady until I was only a few feet from the shack's crooked door. Then a figure formed out of the patch of shadows there.

As was to be expected, the wingéd who emerged before me matched me in stature: tall and broad with much muscle filling out his powerful frame. His knuckles were similarly hardened, but with ridges of a ruddy hue that looked more like copper than crystal. His eyes gleamed the same metallic shade beneath straggling gray hair that fell past his shoulders and shadowed his brow.

"What business do you have here?" he demanded. "I have no interest in reuniting with the remnants of our kind."

"Only one remnant at the moment," I said. "My companions are... various other sorts. And this isn't about reunification." I studied him and the shack. "You've lived a long time in this part of the mortal realm."

"So that I could remain undisturbed. In the emptiness, I can meditate on the failings that led me to continue to be in existence at all."

My companions might rib me about my severity at times, but I didn't believe I'd ever put forth attitudes quite that grim. If I had, it was a wonder none of them had shoved me back through a rift. Although I supposed my stature might have had something to do with that as well.

As somber as the disgraced warrior was being, however, I did at least understand the sentiment he was expressing. It was only a darker shade of the guilt and regret I'd recently begun to shed.

"What if I could offer you something better than that?" I asked.

He scowled at me. "That you would even think any of us deserve better—"

I held up my hand to stop him. "Not in that way. In the way that you might be able to make amends for the errors of the past by contributing to a new struggle with even greater stakes. We're in dire need of assistance."

My kin didn't stop frowning, but I thought his eyes brightened just a little. He shifted his weight and folded his bulging arms over his chest. "How can you be sure we won't simply bring about an even more horrible fate than before?"

That question had haunted me ever since Omen had first come calling. I hadn't always been confident in my answer. But here, thinking of his leadership even if he wasn't with us in the flesh, of the deeper understanding of my capabilities and flaws that Sorsha had brought out in me, and of the cause we'd all come together for, the words came to my lips without a hint of hesitation.

"One can never be sure," I said. "But I've seen enough to believe that in this conflict, I can make a difference for the good of all shadowkind. I can save far more lives than were ever lost in the wars of the past. And you could too, if you'll lend your instincts and your fists."

The other wingéd was silent for a long spell, considering me. Then he said, in a tone that ignited a flicker of hope within me, "Tell me more about this new war."

24

Sorsha

When we came up on the San Francisco city limits, I found myself drifting to the front of the Everymobile to watch the buildings whip past us through the windshield. Their lights and the glow of the streetlamps streaked in the growing darkness. My gaze snagged on every figure we passed.

None of them were Omen. I hadn't *really* expected him to be standing waiting for us to turn up with his impatient glare and his authoritarian stance. Still, I couldn't help being a little disappointed that he wasn't. I'd have taken a heaping of criticism about our discipline and arrival time just to know where the hell he'd gone.

"I suppose we should find some cozy nook where we can settle in for the night," Ruse said in his usual flippant tone, but his expression looked a tad weary. I'd bet the incubus could last for days between the sheets without losing energy—a wager I wouldn't mind taking to the bed one of these days, just to confirm—but he wasn't made for driving mortal roads for hours on end.

"Where would Omen think to look for us?" Snap asked, coming up behind me. "We should pick a spot where it'd be easy for him to find us."

"But not likely that the Company will notice our arrival," Thorn put in.

"Yeah." I sucked my lower lip under my teeth. "We've usually had the best luck finding areas without much mortal activity around the fringes of the cities. Let's ramble through the suburbs and see what we turn up."

If that didn't work... Post an ad in the Missed Connections section of a newspaper? Put out an emergency bulletin over the public TV? Hire a plane to skywrite a message? He'd be most likely to see that last one, but then, so would every other person in the city, Company assholes included.

In the end, Ruse found a vacant lot between a couple of faded warehouses and parked the RV there in cargo van guise. Thorn stayed up to continue discussing the situation with his new wingéd friend, whose name—Flint—matched his appearance better than any shadowkind I'd met yet, and I tugged the incubus and the devourer into the bedroom with me.

They came without complaint and settled in on either side of me. I was too tangled up to want to conduct any experiments in stamina right now, but with Ruse brushing his fingers down my back in a fond caress and

Snap tucking his chin over my forehead to encompass me with his fresh scent, I was able to sink into sleep faster than I'd thought.

My two lovers were still there when I woke up. As I stirred, Snap pressed a kiss to the top of my head and Ruse let his fingers skim over my waist. "Anything we can do to make this a happy morning for you, Miss Blaze?" the incubus murmured.

I tipped my head up to kiss Snap on the lips and then rolled over to offer the same to Ruse. His claiming of my mouth was so fervently tender that my pulse fluttered. I might have given in to the temptation to rediscover all the other sensations he could rouse with his touch if the absence of my most recent paramour hadn't been hanging over us.

"What would make me happy is to see the entire Company going up in flames," I said. "Then maybe we can spark a few metaphorical fires around here."

"I will happily take that rain check."

I had the urge to pass some of that loving on to Thorn too, but when we emerged into the RV, there was no sign of him. Flint sat at one end of the sofa-bench looking at a mug in front of him as if he wasn't quite sure whether to drink from it or crush it with his rock-like fist. Gloam was meandering through the hall in full droop-mode. Antic flashed into visibility at the sight of me, balancing on one hand on the edge of the counter with her spindly legs wheeling in the air.

I cracked a smile mostly so that she'd be satisfied that she'd gotten a reaction from me and quit goofing around.

"The first big dude went off to check for bad guys," she said as she flipped onto her feet, anticipating my question.

"Thorn said he would return shortly," Flint added. I'd always thought Thorn's voice was low and rumbling, but compared to Flint's thunderous tones, our original wingéd was a soprano.

I plopped down onto the sofa across from him and nodded to the coffee cooling in his mug. "Typically that stuff is better enjoyed hot."

He gave it a skeptical glance. "I have not consumed mortal provisions in many centuries. I hesitate to begin now."

Antic bobbed beside us as if debating snatching the mug for herself but seemed to decide it wasn't worth the possibility of pissing off a shadowkind of Flint's stature. She settled for pouring some out of the pot into two new mugs, splashing the brown liquid liberally on the floor and counter alike, and plunking one of those down in front of me.

"What's the plan?" she asked in an intrepid tone, taking a noisy swig from her mug.

What *was* the plan? We'd been going to figure that out once we got here, assuming Omen would have plenty to contribute. Now...

I might have suggested we wait and see if Thorn's patrol turned up the hellhound shifter, but before I could speak, the warrior emerged from the shadows, his mouth set at a pained angle. My heart sank. No luck in that respect, clearly.

We had to go forward without Omen then. If he didn't like the plans we made in his absence, then he shouldn't have fucking absented himself.

I dragged in a breath and looked around the table. All of my shadowkind companions were watching me. Somehow I'd become the substitute boss when the regular one was away. No pressure there.

My gaze caught Flint's metallic brown eyes—and a hail of impressions burst in my head.

I wasn't in the RV anymore but in the middle of a battlefield scattered with bloody bodies, more figures charging over them with blades gleaming. The stink of gore flooded my nose, and clangs and groans filled my ears. Someone hurtled right past me, knocking me to the side hard enough to make my arm throb—

And I was back on the sofa, gasping and shaking as my mind reeled.

"Sorsha!" Thorn grasped my shoulder and stared at his comrade. The other wingéd grimaced, lowering his gaze.

"My apologies, mortal," he said in that deepest of deep voices. "My particular talent is to spark visions of horror—I would generally only apply it to my enemies. I've used it so little in so long, I'm no longer as used to moderating it. I didn't intend to aim that memory toward you."

A memory. So that was one glimpse of the brutality he and Thorn had managed to survive, to their apparent disappointment. I set my hand over my warrior's, letting his touch steady me. My heart was still racing, but a sharper sense of determination rose through the dwindling panic.

That kind of brutality wasn't so different from how we'd approached our conflicts with the Company so far. Rush in, burn them to cinders or rip their heads from their necks—y'know, whatever suited our particular skill set best. But we'd found another way back in Chicago. Sure, the plan I'd suggested there had ended with a fiery skirmish anyway, but there'd been at least a little less death and destruction than before. Give me a little credit for a partial win, won't you?

I might have been part shadowkind, and I might have accepted the fact that I enjoyed laying down with monsters, but that didn't mean we had to prove the stereotypes right. We could use the same tactics as in Chicago, only on a bigger and better scale. Show all the jerks who were too scared to help us that the Company could be decimated without a single drop of blood spilled.

Okay, maybe that was a little too optimistic. We could probably manage it without more than a bucket of blood, though. That'd still be a step up from the torrents the shadowkind had unleashed when we'd stormed Victor Bane's mansion back home.

I didn't think Omen would like my continued resistance to carnage at all, but he was welcome to show up any time and tell me about that.

I leaned my elbows onto the table. "We need to figure out who here is running the North American operations of the Company, right? But destroying them isn't going to fix anything. The real leader is off in Europe somewhere.

What if instead of trying to burn everything down, we figure out a way to get to that guy and use *him* to get to the man in charge overseas."

Ruse cocked his head. "Interesting. Go on."

I motioned to him. "You can work your charm over the phone. All we've got to do is convince the head guy here to put us in touch with *his* boss, and then you can bend the ear of the guy who controls everything the Company does. Imagine all the things you could convince him to do."

A smirk curved the incubus's lips. "Oh, there are many, many acts I'd like to talk him into committing. But starting with having *him* destroy the Company from the inside out sounds ideal."

Thorn frowned where he was still standing over me. "Would that work? Could you maintain enough control over him to compel him to cause that level of destruction?"

"That's the thing," I said. "The head honcho wouldn't need to destroy anything in a physical way. He must have access to all the Company data—we can get him to wipe it off the networks. We can have him call up the regional leaders and disband the branches. Maybe we'd need to force him to act in some crazy way to convince his followers that he's been wrong all along so they don't start things up again. I'm sure we can figure out the details once we have a hold on him."

Antic swung her little fists in the air. "Or we could just go across the sea and give him what-for the traditional way."

"But that might not work," Snap said, understanding

lighting in his face. "We keep destroying parts of the Company, and more of these people rise up in their place. The fact that we're destroying them convinces them that they need to keep fighting us."

I snapped my fingers. "Exactly. Knock off one leader and someone else will step up to take his place. I think it's over-ambitious to assume we can eradicate the people who hate shadowkind and all the work they've done by picking them off bit by bit, and we can't tackle them all at once. But whoever's running the show—he can. And if we play this right, he can tie all the loose ends in a bow for us too."

One by one, the heads around the table nodded. Gloam was the last, caught in despondent hesitation. "It sounds very grand—I don't see how I could contribute."

An inkling about that had already started to form in my head. I made a reassuring gesture toward the night elf. "Oh, I'm nothing if not resourceful. I'll find a way for even you to pitch in; don't worry."

Flint stirred in his seat. "This plan sounds worth the attempt. How do we begin?"

I patted my purse. "The one guy who's on our side in the Fund was able to talk to some of the local members last night. Klaus couldn't find out a lot, but one of the things he did put together was a probable hunting location where the Company has been collecting shadowkind near one of the rifts. We grab one of those Company hunters, and then we can follow the trail that one gives us to another and another until we get our hands on someone who can point us to the big gun."

"Of course, we don't know how often they stake out that spot," Thorn pointed out.

I smiled at him. "So we'll just have to make a little mischief there to draw them out."

25

Sorsha

For once, the Company of Light played right into our hands. Less than an hour after Antic had darted through the park near the rift invisibly, making chess pieces fly through the air over the stone tables and leading people on wild goose chases after hats that appeared to have taken on minds of their own, a white van with an exterminator logo pulled into the public lot. How very fitting.

Four men tramped out, their silver-and-iron protective gear hidden under thick hazmat suits, which I guessed they could pass off as being protection from the supposed wild animal they were here to contain. Any mortal not watching for the glint of metal would have missed the edges of the helmets and vests beneath.

They strode to the area near the rift where the imp had pulled off her pranks and hollered for the nearby patrons to leave for their own safety. When all witnesses had dispersed—other than my shadowkind allies watching from various patches of darkness and me in my perch hidden on the roof of a historic cottage in view of the clearing—they drew out their shiny nets and whips and stalked through the area.

Of course, we didn't need—or want—them to catch Antic, or any other shadowkind for that matter. We'd only needed them to come. After a thorough search, a vigil while they waited to see if the shadowkind would emerge if they gave it some space, and another scouring of the area, they packed up into their van, muttering about how inconvenient this monster had been.

Little did they know that a few of said monsters were hitching a ride in the shadows attached to their vehicle.

I kept my phone at my side as I waited for the first stage of our plan to come to fruition. Half an hour of pacing later, a text from Ruse appeared on the screen.

We've got a loner. He took off the worst of the gear but is still wearing a badge. Come on by and steal it off him for us, my lovely thief?

My pleasure, I wrote back, and passed on the address he gave me to the Uber I hailed.

It was a simple enough operation. I knocked on the door of the guy's apartment like I just needed to borrow a cup of flour. The moment he opened it, Ruse leapt out of the shadows next to him. The guy startled, his head jerking around, and before he could even see me moving, I'd kicked his legs out from under him. Thorn and Flint emerged to pin his limbs to the floor while I yanked open his button-up to uncover the silver-and-iron badge he'd fixed to his undershirt.

Borrowing my tricks—tsk tsk.

As soon as I'd tossed the toxic metals aside, Ruse started talking in his cajoling tone. "Good day to you, my friend. I'm so sorry about the sudden intrusion. If you'll give me a moment, I'll get this all straightened away to attend to your best interests."

Within minutes, he had our captive laughing at his jokes and beaming eagerly when the incubus told him we desperately needed his help. "I don't know who's giving the orders," he said. "But I can tell you a few locations we've worked out of. Maybe someone at one of them can tell you more."

Ruse smiled. "Perfect. We so appreciate anything you can contribute. I'll be sure to inform your colleagues what a team player you were."

We hopped from lead to lead across the afternoon and into the evening. The first several Company dupes had no idea where the big boss might live, but they all knew someone else who was connected to the Company. Finally, our game of leapfrog led us to a woman who'd worked on our Very Important Person's security detail. After chatting with Ruse for a bit, she coughed up an address in the Financial District, as well as some other choice information.

"I never got the guy's name," she said. "Never even saw him. He lives in the penthouse, and I worked outer security, patrolling the block outside. Never had any trouble, but I guess you can't be too careful with these monsters, especially when he's helping keep the whole Company organized." She sighed. "It was an easy gig, that's for sure. But I got bored and asked to be in on more of the action. Kind of regret it now."

"We've got the building," Snap said eagerly when we were back in the RV. "Does that mean we can carry out the rest of Sorsha's plan now?"

"We've got to investigate the place first and determine our best point of access," Thorn said. "It doesn't sound as though reaching this man will be a simple matter, even knowing his location."

I shot a fond smile at the incubus, who was back behind the wheel. "We need Ruse to get a hold of one of the head honcho's current security people. That should be our ticket in."

The Financial District was a forest of skyscrapers, concrete faces and gleaming windows towering so high they looked as if they really might touch the clouds. Ruse cruised by the condo building our contact had indicated. I definitely wasn't scaling that slick face from the outside. But that didn't matter when we could charm ourselves an inside man—or woman. We'd gotten this far, hadn't we?

"Every blame you lay," I sang as we rounded the corner, "every sprite you slay, we'll be watching you."

Antic shuddered as if she thought I was anticipating some slaying going on tonight. "Don't worry," I said. "If it looks like anyone's getting slain, we'll do a lot more than watch."

"I'd like to slay *them*," she muttered. "Big bullies."

We parked several blocks from the building with a mind to how thoroughly the Company tended to guard their more prominent members. After setting the RV to look like a tour bus that had every business parking downtown, Ruse, Thorn, and Snap went to scope out the big boss's place, the three of them insisting that Flint stay back with me in case we had to deal with Company attackers after all.

I paced the narrow hall, trying not to fidget and carefully avoiding looking directly into the wingéd's eyes. Antic bounced between twisting my discarded shirts into ridiculous poses and chattering with Gloam, who'd shed his despondency with the sinking of the sun.

My trio returned with matching pensive expressions.

"We could only go so far up," Thorn reported. "The highest floor had silver and iron panels built into the walls and floor—possibly the ceiling too."

Snap nodded. "We couldn't check it very closely, because the floor underneath was totally vacant. Very bright lights all across the ceiling, making sure there were no shadows for us to travel through, and cameras watching for intruders. I didn't pick up any useful impressions from the areas we could reach."

"The main elevator doesn't go up to the penthouse," Ruse added. "The only access we could identify was through a secondary elevator on that shiny sub-penthouse floor. There aren't any guards there, although that may cause more problems than it solves. We don't know who's working 'internal' security with him. From what our recent friend told us, the external folks don't know much about getting to this guy."

I exhaled slowly. "All right. Then we wait, and we watch. Unless this guy's got all his security living with him twenty-four seven, *someone's* got to come out of there eventually. We see who it is, track them until we can get to them alone, and prep them for Ruse's charm like we did the others. We've made it this far. No rushing, or it could all fall apart."

Thorn and Snap left again, Thorn to keep watch over the brightly-lit buffer floor and Snap to test the public areas of the building for any impressions that could point us in the right direction. I touched base with Klaus, who had nothing further to report.

"If you want me getting in on anything other than information-gathering, just let me know what I can do," he said.

I grimaced at the ceiling. After everything we'd been through with the Fund, I was uneasy even with him knowing we were in San Francisco. I wasn't sure I wanted to tip him off to our exact location. What if he had his own change of heart?

"We're covered for now," I said. "The best thing you can do is keep an eye on the local Fund and let us know if they seem to be on the lookout for us."

Night fell with no sightings of the head honcho's inside men. Finally, I curled up on my bed to get some sleep. I wasn't going to be much use to my companions if I was zombified with exhaustion by the time they needed me.

It was Thorn who woke me, but not in the way I'd have liked one of my lovers to come to my bed in the wee hours of the morning. He cleared his throat, and that yanked me out of sleep with a jolt through my nerves. When I looked up at him, it was still dark, only a little artificial light filtering through the small window to catch on his white-blond hair.

"We have our guard," he said. "I believe now may be an excellent opportunity to prepare him."

"Right, right." I shoved myself out from under the covers, finger-combed my hair back into a messy ponytail, and allowed myself the small indulgence of tapping the warrior's impressive chest. "Next time you wake me up, I expect it to come with benefits, not work."

His dark eyes gleamed. "We might have a moment for a brief benefit if it would raise your spirits to the task."

"Perfect way of looking at it." I gripped his tunic and rose up on my toes to kiss him. Thorn returned the gesture, his mouth so hard and hot it left no doubt that there would be *plenty* of benefits to come when the time was right.

Ruse had driven the Everymobile to new digs while I'd slept. I stepped out into the quiet of a residential street, bungalows and two-storey houses set behind small, neat lawns. The incubus emerged from the shadows by one of the smaller places down the block and beckoned me over silently.

When I reached him, he tipped his head toward the house, his voice dropping to a whisper. "We were hoping you could keep your beauty sleep, but he wears his damned helmet to *bed*. The boss man must have made these lackeys awfully paranoid."

"Yep," I said. "Clearly they have no reason at all to worry about shadowkind descending on them in the middle of the night."

"Well, not before now. You want to put those thieving skills to further use?"

I didn't have my lock picks with me, but I didn't need

them. The guard's security wasn't quite that tight. I crept through the backyards to make a discreet approach, and Ruse slipped into the shadows around the back door to unlock it from the inside. When he eased it open, I slunk in past him. He pointed me to the door that led to our target's bedroom.

As I stepped inside, I almost started feeling bad for the dude. He must have had a softer side in him somewhere: his walls were adorned with posters of cartoon ponies frolicking with their magical friends. He even had a plastic figurine of a purple one watching over him from the bedside table.

That said, he was still a shadowkind-hating prick. And now he'd get to experience a truly magical friendship.

Ruse hadn't lied—the guy had his silver-and-iron helmet pulled tight over his head, covering it from his forehead down his temples to just above his ears. It looked as if he'd added some padding to it, but it still couldn't be all that comfortable. He was either very dedicated or very exhausted.

He had a badge pinned to his nightshirt as well, I saw—it poked just above the sheet that slanted across his chest. That would be easy enough to deal with, thank holy hand grenades.

I padded across the floor, breathing silent and shallow. With cautious fingers, I peeled the sheet down far enough that I could grasp the badge. This maneuver called for delicacy rather than speed. Just my luck that I was familiar with both.

A few twists of my fingers detached the clasp. I set

the badge on the bedside table and motioned to where I assumed Ruse was watching from the doorway, not risking taking my eyes off our target. As I reached for his helmet, the guy made a muttering sound and rolled over.

Fine, I'd just have to lean farther over the bed. As soon as I had it off, Ruse could work his voodoo. We could forget delicacy now.

I set my hands against the cool metal surface, readied myself, and heaved as hard as I could.

The dude yelped and flailed. I darted backward, carrying the helmet with me, and Ruse swept in, his smooth, chocolatey voice already lilting from his lips.

"Hello there, my friend! Nothing to be disturbed about. This is the moment you've been waiting for all this time."

He must have read something in the guard's emotions to suggest a solid angle for his charm. As he talked on, I shoved the helmet into the closet, made an apologetic gesture to the poster ponies staring at me wide-eyed, and stepped back to join Thorn, Snap, and Flint, who'd emerged from the shadows.

Ruse could always tell when he had his subject eating out of his hand. It wasn't long before the incubus offered a simpering smile and said, "All we need to know is when we can expect your boss to leave his fine abode."

"Oh." The lackey's face fell with obvious distress. "I don't think I can help you there."

After all this, we still hadn't found someone with answers? I restrained a groan.

"Why not?" the incubus asked.

"Well, he just... never leaves. We come and go in

shifts during the day, but in the year I've worked there, I've only seen him leave maybe three times. He had an essential appointment a few weeks back, so I doubt there'll be anything else for months unless something special comes up. Anything he needs, he has delivered."

"If I could even talk to him on the phone—"

The guy shook his head. "He's on his phone a lot, that's for sure, but I don't have the number for it. If I was ever going to be late for or miss a shift, I'm supposed to tell the head of the team, and they just send someone else."

My stomach sank. It wasn't that this guy didn't have answers—it was that the answers he had sucked donkey balls. If we couldn't lure his boss out of his apartment with its shell of toxic metals to somewhere Ruse could get his ear, the incubus wouldn't be able to charm the man we most needed to reach.

I stepped closer again. "Can't you think of *anything* he'd be willing to leave for?"

"I'm sorry. I wish I could do more."

I paused, feeling the weight of my companions' attention on me. This had been my plan, and now I had to salvage it before all our efforts had to be chucked in the trash.

A glimmer of inspiration lit in my head. It might not work—but it was worth a shot. Story of my life.

With a thin smile, I propped myself against the dresser. "Actually, I think there is one more thing you could do to prove your loyalty to the cause. Listen carefully."

26

Omen

There were times when the frequent sunlight of the mortal world became wearying, and I missed the constant dim of the shadow realm. The cycle of days and nights did have its benefits, though. For example, if I'd had more than this constant dimness during my long wait for the Highest to offer their attention, I might have some idea how long that wait had been.

It felt like an eternity or so at this point. Apparently the most ancient of shadowkind had decided to give the DMV a run for their money. Or maybe it only seemed like days on end because I didn't have much to think about besides what trouble my crew might be getting into in my absence.

I hoped that they'd at least had the sense to keep moving and scope out the situation in San Francisco so we could jump right into action when I returned. And also that their scoping out hadn't involved too much action on its own. Maybe it was too much to wish for both rather than one or the other, especially with our fiery not-quite-mortal in the mix.

My mind veered in that direction now and then of its own accord. To her scarlet hair and the defiance in her bright eyes… to the heated taste of her on my tongue and the feel of her matching my heat flame for flame…

I had no physical presence here, but the memory managed to stir a flare of lust all the same.

I hadn't meant to give in to that temptation—but possibly it was all right. The world *hadn't* ended because we'd fucked. I'd enjoyed it, and so had she, and she'd still been the same mouthy but frustratingly appealing nuisance afterward as she'd been before. It hadn't been a vow or a nuptial. Releasing all that pent-up desire had eased the tensions inside me in a way I could actually appreciate.

It might not even be such a bad thing if we did it again. In moderation.

That was, if I could sort out whether I was more unsettled or gratified by the realization that no matter how much I'd insisted that I'd seen *her*, I now couldn't shake the sense of how much she saw *me*. More of me than I'd have wanted anyone in all the realms to see. She'd struck straight through all my best intentions with the tenderness in her voice and those knowing eyes…

I should have been furious. I *had* been furious. But at the same time, the memory of her proclamation that I couldn't scare her sent an odd twinge of longing through me.

Of course, none of that would matter if the Highest decided to keep me on hold until the end of time.

I shifted my awareness, searching for the lackey that had instructed me to wait here. If I bit that being's head off, would the Highest decide it was time to turn their attention my way? The lackey didn't appear to have lingered, though, and neither had the fiercer beings who'd caught me by the gas station and insisted I return with them to the nearest rift at once.

I could have taken down even the four of them if they'd been sent by anyone else. Damn the Highest and their fucking deals.

The call finally came, wordless but insistent, with a constricting tug around my neck. I sprang forward, wanting to shed that sensation as quickly as possible. The less I was reminded of my ties to these bastards, the better.

The deep, dark hollow roiled with an uneasy energy I hadn't felt there before. The Highest loomed as monumental as always, but the sharpness of their attention now that they had deigned to lower it to me prickled through to my soul.

"Hellhound," one intoned. "There you are." As if I hadn't been waiting on their doorstep for the last decade or so.

"Here I am," I agreed. "What do you want, oh ancient ones?"

The thicker thrum that echoed through the air suggested the edge that had crept into my tone hadn't gone unnoticed. The Highest let it slide, though, which should have been all the warning I needed right there.

"We've heard reports from your travels," another said, her voice reverberating through every particle of my being. "More than one shadowkind have claimed you are working with a human woman who can work shadowkind powers."

Fucking hell, not that complaint again. I'd known as soon as Rex's crew got a glimpse of Sorsha in action, word would start to get out. The Highest would just *love* the idea that I might be collaborating with a sorcerer. Those mortal miscreants were little better than the hunters and collectors, the way they used our kind.

It seemed simpler to circumvent the complicated full story and stick to a half-truth. I shook my head, as much as I had one in this space, in feigned exasperation. "You bought into that story? I'd sooner disembowel myself than ally with a sorcerer. No, all of my comrades are shadowkind. One of them made a joke to a few rather dim-witted beings about being human—the humor must have gone over their heads."

They studied me with more of that prickling intensity. "You've had no associations with any humans or being at times presenting themselves as human?"

What was that second bit supposed to mean?

"Not at all," I said. "Plenty of our own kind to call on as I need to." Not that many of them had responded to that call, but the Highest didn't give a rat's ass how my mission was going, as they'd made very clear during my last visit.

The tug at my throat came again, along with a jab of pain. I didn't give them the satisfaction of a wince. They could yank my chain all they wanted, but their hold over me couldn't stop me from lying as seemed necessary. I had at least that much freedom left.

"The reports were somewhat disjointed," one of the Highest allowed after a moment. "The less experienced shadowkind are not always as astute as would be ideal. No matter. We have another subject to discuss with you."

Joy of all joys. "Let me have it." Then I could get back to my crew and leave these giant bastards behind.

"Seeing as you are spending so much time mortal-side as it is, and given your familiarity with that world and your earlier interest, we have decided on the final favor you will carry out for us."

My spirits leapt with a wash of exhilaration I couldn't have contained if I'd wanted to.

They could call it a favor all they wanted, but what it really amounted to was slave labor. Ten tasks, anything they demanded, was what I'd agreed to carry out for them in exchange for not ending up a savaged corpse like Tempest. The most generous favor my former partner-in-crime had ever offered *me* was the lesson of just how badly things could go once the Highest's wrath came down on you if you didn't think quickly enough.

Ten tasks, and I'd jumped at the snap of their fingers nine times already—the last more than a century ago. They'd taken a good long while deciding how they could best use me this final time.

As soon as the terms of my deal with them were fulfilled, I was slipping this leash and running free, and they could forget it if they thought they'd ever get a reason to have me kowtowing to them again.

"I'm at your service," I said. It might disrupt our plans

to take on the Company in the moment, but that would be worth it to shake off my shackles. "What is it you need?"

"We would like you to find the being named Ruby and inform us of her location."

Ah. Well, that was good news in that I'd have liked to find that being too, but less so in that I'd already given it a pretty good go and had little to no luck so far. No one seemed to even know Ruby had ever existed except the Highest themselves and the shadowkind they'd informed of the fact. Were they setting me up on an impossible task so they could keep me chained to their will forever?

I resisted the urge to produce my fangs and dipped my head in acknowledgement instead. "I'd be happy to do so. I'll be able to accomplish that task faster if you could let me know her last known location and any other details you have about her appearance and behavior."

The Highest made a grumbling sound between them as if they were offended by my request, but they obviously wanted this Ruby more than they cared about any impudence they thought I was expressing.

"She slipped through our fingers many years ago, shortly after we first became aware of her existence. We've had no further information since. That is your responsibility. As for the rest, you must be aware that she is highly dangerous, although she may not appear to be at first. Avoid direct contact at all costs. As soon as you have identified her, come straight to us."

Oh ye of so little faith. I sighed. "That's really not much to go on. Presumably if this shadowkind is so adept at hiding herself, she won't be going by the name you've been asking after her by anymore. What type of being is she? What mortal appearance does she take? What are these horribly dangerous secret powers of hers?"

There was more grumbling as the Highest appeared to confer with one another. Had they really thought they could send me off on this ridiculous quest without giving me a single hint about who I was looking for?

Probably, yes.

Finally, someone else spoke up from their immense huddle. "We can tell you more, but if we discover that you have spoken of this matter to any other being, our deal will be forfeit and you will be at our mercy."

Oh, for fuck's sake. "Yes, yes," I said. "That's fine. Just tell me." It wasn't as if I hadn't kept plenty of other secrets—like the fact that the Highest had any sort of grip on me at all—from my companions.

"Very well. The one named Ruby may not appear to be a shadowkind at all. That is part of what makes her so treacherous. When a shadowkind abases themselves to a mortal level, it is in rare circumstances possible for them to bear a child with a mortal. As few beings would lower themselves in such a way to begin with, we are aware of only three such unions in all existence. The first two we were able to deal with promptly. With this third, we have been foiled so far."

A nauseous chill started to unfurl in my gut. "And this Ruby... is the shadowkind who produced that child?"

A harsh sort of chuckle echoed through the space. "No. That one and her mortal partner met the fates they deserved. But some accomplice of theirs escaped with the child. That is Ruby—the name they gave her. As if she were a jewel and not a menace to all existence."

I tried to find the words, but for a moment I could barely think, let alone speak. They couldn't really mean—Sorsha had never given me the impression she thought she'd had another name. That was the sort of thing that would have come up while searching out her history. And from what I'd seen, she was more a danger to her own existence than to anyone else's.

Had we gotten the wrong information somewhere in our search? Mixed wires that had crossed her history with this shadowkind-human hybrid? But she *did* have powers no full human should have been able to possess.

"I hope you'll forgive my confusion," I managed, gathering myself. "But wouldn't a creature born of shadowkind nature mingled with humanity be *weaker* than a pure shadowkind, not stronger?"

"One would wish it was so, but that is not the case. Do *not* approach and especially do not provoke this being when you come across her. The unnatural bond in her natures creates a connection to both realms. She can inflict all the damage her powers allow on both without bringing any harm to herself from either side. If we could have snuffed out that alchemy when she was a mere infant... Now it will have had time to grow within her. All it will take is a little fuel, and she will set our realm and theirs alight in the most searing flames."

The Highest had been wrong about a lot of things in their time. Their understanding of the mortal realm was utterly second-hand, and they'd admitted themselves that the only other two hybrid beings they were aware of, they'd slaughtered in infancy. But their words brought back the momentary terror I'd seen in Sorsha's expression now and then when we'd fought. Her warnings that she might be able to hurt me more than I could imagine.

She'd sensed something in herself, something more than I'd been able to see. Maybe I shouldn't have dismissed her fears so quickly.

But still—how could I wrap my head around the idea that the sassy thief who liked nothing more than to tease the beast out of me and sing songs to her own lyrics was some kind of destructive force on a global scale?

I couldn't, not yet. Maybe when I saw her again, knowing what the Highest had told me—

And then what? They'd called in their last favor. I would never be free until I fulfilled it. They would never believe I'd fulfilled it until they were sure "Ruby" was dead. Even speaking of what I'd learned today might mean I met the same fate as Tempest after all this time despite everything I'd sacrificed.

I reined in that inner turmoil. I couldn't make the decision now in front of these ancient goliaths—that much I was sure of.

"I understand," I said, even though there was a hell of a lot I still didn't, and then another thought struck me, slicing straight through the core of me. I gathered myself and forced out one more question. "If this hybrid mortal-shadowkind has had time to mature... might she not have created children of her own?"

Could the fiery union I'd remembered fondly be an even bigger disaster waiting to happen?

"We are unsure if this monstrosity would even be

fertile. If she has mated with another human, perhaps it is possible, but their offspring would not have the same balance of powers that gives her such potency. You could destroy those without threat to yourself."

"And if she's mated with another shadowkind?"

The Highest who'd spoken let out a sound like a huff. "That would require the same ceremony of abasement as that of her mother. We expect that to be exceedingly unlikely—and even if so, the balance would again be skewed. Ruby herself should be your primary concern."

And so she was. I had to assume this ceremony was more than simply allowing oneself to mash genitals with a mortal, or there'd be a hell of a lot more hybrids running around just of my stock, not to mention the many incubi and succubi of all existence. I was safe from hellhound pups for the time being, apparently. That hardly solved my larger problem.

I made a gesture of deference. "Any trace I discover of her, I'll pass on to you as soon as I hear of it."

"We will be waiting," another of the Highest said in a tone that sounded more like a threat than a promise, and I felt their dismissal with a lightening of the constriction around my neck.

As I made my way through the shadows, my thoughts whirled, but I didn't try to pin down any one thread. An insistent pull drew me onward—not to one of the rifts that would have spilled me out into the San Francisco area, but one that would return me to Austin.

I tore through the boundary between shadow and mortal realms with the quivering electricity the transition always provoked. Roaming from shadow to shadow, I made my way to the office that held the city's records. The one where Sorsha had tried and failed to find evidence of her birth.

If I couldn't find anything either, it wouldn't mean much. Her parents might never have registered her, given their situation. But if I did...

The office was closed for the night. I slipped beneath the door and found a computer that booted up without any special commands.

We'd celebrated her birthday only a little more than a week ago. I knew what date it was supposed to be.

The names rippled by, none of them familiar. Then a tickle of sensation passed over my eyes. I paused, studying the screen.

A fae glamour was embedded in the data, just as it'd been in Sorsha's memories.

With my stomach clenching, I willed a bolt of my power at the illusion. The magic crackled and fell away. And there, glowing before my eyes, were the damning words.

Twenty-eight years ago on September 4th, Philip Woodsen had registered the birth of his daughter, Ruby.

27

Sorsha

The spoils our guard handed over after his shift in the penthouse didn't look like much of a bounty. He'd gathered them in a shopping bag so that his body wouldn't tarnish the impressions on the objects with his own thoughts and feelings, and it held only a crumpled, ketchup-stained paper napkin, a dried-up pen that was slightly gnawed at the end, and the severed plastic packaging from a... Tibetan singing bowl set?

I guessed we could hope the big boss had been meditating on his sins.

"Sorry," the charmed young man said. "That was all he had in the garbage can by the end of my shift. I had to knock over his wine carafe just to fill up the bin so I'd have an excuse to take out the trash."

"That's okay," I said, deftly picking out a few spare shards of glass that clung to the packaging. We'd specifically instructed him to stick to the garbage so that there'd be no thefts to alert his boss to our scheme. "If we can't get anything out of this, we'll just try again. He didn't seem at all suspicious about the accident?"

The guard shook his head. "He really had left the carafe too close to the edge of the counter. I made sure he was watching so he'd see all I did was walk by it."

Ruse patted him on the shoulder. "You've done excellent work. I'll see that you're properly rewarded when all this is over."

Snap was waiting for us back in the RV. He sat up straighter on the sofa at the sight of the bag. "Those are the head man's things?"

The incubus tossed the bag onto the table. "Yep. Ripe for the tasting. See what you can slurp out of them."

As Snap eased open the bag, our other companions emerged from the shadows to observe more directly. The Everymobile's living area was becoming a tight fit, especially with the second hulking wingéd in the mix... even without Omen here.

That thought twisted my stomach. Shoving down my uneasiness about our own boss's continued absence, I squeezed over to the sofa and sat down there. Pickle scuttled beneath the table, hopped up beside me—and for the first time in days, scrambled right onto my lap. A little of my apprehension melted as I tickled his chin.

If my dragon could get over my failings and come back to me, then surely everything else could turn out all right too.

"The pen might provide the most information,"

Thorn suggested, peering at the small collection of items. "The other objects would have been used much more temporarily, would they not?"

Antic bobbed on her feet, only able to make out the surface of the table when her heels left the ground. "Yes! The pen first." With her last bounce, she sprang right onto the edge of the table but kept swaying there, adrift on waves of excitement.

Snap took the pen in his slender hands and brought it to his face. His forked tongue flicked out, skimming through the air just above its surface.

I'd seen him work his subtler devourer magic plenty of times, but the distance that came into his expression as he sorted through the impressions he'd gleaned from the past still sent a tiny shiver up my spine. To be able to know so much about a person just by testing something they'd touched... Say whatever you wanted about the whole soul-devouring thing, *this* was damned amazing.

His tongue flicked out a few more times, but the pen didn't have much surface area to test. As his eyes refocused on us, his mouth settled into a frown. "I'm not sure anything I sensed will give us a strategy to encourage the boss out of his home. The main impression I get from his use of the pen is boredom. He used it for writing numbers into boxes in some sort of game? And also words in other boxes in a different game. Nothing he felt very strongly about."

Yeah, I didn't think Sudoku or crossword puzzles were going to be our ticket to luring the boss man away from his protective walls so Ruse could work his voodoo.

"That's okay. What about those?" I tipped my head toward the other two items without a huge amount of hope. Maybe we were waiting to launch our grand plan until our charmed guard could take out another haul of trash.

Snap picked up the ketchup-y napkin gingerly and tested all around it. A hint of a smile curled his lips, but not for the reasons we'd have wanted.

"He had a very delicious meal," the devourer reported. "One of those burgers of ham, very juicy with seeds on the bun." He paused. "And he became frustrated because of a call that interrupted his meal. But he put the napkin down when he answered. I don't know what it was about."

At least Snap had gotten some second-hand deliciousness out of that one. I restrained a sigh as he picked up the torn packaging.

It was the largest of the items, so it took several minutes before the devourer had checked it over thoroughly. He lingered on one spot, his tongue flicking here and there around a seam in the plastic. A glint of neon flashed in his eyes.

I straightened my posture, watching him. *Something* had caught his interest, and in a different way from the burger.

"It was a long time ago," Snap said, slowly and softly. "But he remembers it sometimes at odd moments. He didn't realize how much this set would look like the one she showed him..."

"Who showed him what?" Antic demanded,

practically tap dancing across the table in her eager impatience.

I waved her silent. Snap took another taste of the impressions attached to the packaging. "A young woman he cared about a lot. He had asked her to connect her life with his—he gave her a ring." He glanced at me.

"Humans exchange rings when they get engaged to be married," I said. "It's basically the highest form of commitment any person offers anyone else."

The devourer hummed to himself. "Yes. That. But there is much sadness when he thinks about her. I think it must have been a very long time ago, years and years, but it still hurts him a lot. And—there is anger too. Something dark and large with vicious teeth... Blood..." His forehead furrowed. "I think perhaps she was killed by a shadowkind. That could be why he would want to kill us, couldn't it?"

"Not that I think one murder excuses attempted genocide, but yeah, that could do it." I rubbed my mouth. If this guy still thought so much about his long-lost fiancé, she might help us prevent that genocide. "Did you see anything else about her? What she looked like, her name...?"

"Yes. Yes, there was—" His tongue flicked. "Carmen. That was her name. Her voice is very soft in his memories... She called him 'Isaac'."

The pieces were starting to interlock in my head to form a rather impressive picture, if I did say so myself. Ruse leaned in and tugged on my ponytail. "I like that sly look on you, Miss Blaze."

Snap peered at me hopefully. "You can use that?"

"It might be perfect," I said. "The ring you saw... Was the impression clear enough that if you went to a store with lots of rings, you could recognize which one was the most like it?"

The gleam came back into Snap's eyes. "I think so."

"Is there anything else you'd require, m'lady?" Thorn asked.

"A wig," I said. "Since he's probably been warned about a redhead running with the monsters by now. With that and a ring—we can make this happen tonight."

The wig wasn't the most comfortable thing I'd ever worn. My shadowkind companions—who were becoming as adept as thieves as I was, with the additional benefit of being able to sneak into just about any building without any need for tools—had found me a good quality one, thick black waves that looked natural once my real hair was all tucked underneath. But the edges still itched at my skin. I didn't want to fix it on completely until it was actually time to head out.

I took one last look at my transformed self in the mirror and then tugged the wig off. The plan was to move out in a little more than an hour. We wanted to be sure the business day had begun in Europe before we grabbed the boss here, because we couldn't count on keeping our hands on him for all that long once we had him. Get in there, pull him and then *his* boss under Ruse's spell, and end the Company for good—as fast as we could manage it.

All our running and fighting might be over tonight. It was too bad Omen wasn't here to see it. Of course, maybe he'd have argued every detail of my scheme.

I'd found a part for each of us to play. Antic had brought in our first Company lackey; Snap had found the ticket to the boss. The rest of us would tackle that boss tonight. Our combined if very different skills were going to bring this all together... as long as I hadn't miscalculated in any way.

As long as all those pieces lined up just right when it mattered most. And as long as the powers lurking inside me didn't act up at the wrong moment in the wrong way.

I inhaled slowly, reminding myself of the inner cooling techniques Omen had talked me through, and someone knocked on the bedroom door. I could tell it was Ruse from the jaunty rhythm of it before he even spoke. "I hope that black monstrosity hasn't swallowed you whole, Miss Blaze."

I opened the door. "I wouldn't call it a monstrosity. It's actually not a bad look. Maybe I'll have to keep it when all this is done."

Ruse made a scoffing sound and curled a stray red strand around his fingers, his chuckles caressing my jaw. "You can't be Miss Blaze without this."

"The actual fire that can pour out of my body isn't enough to justify the nickname?"

"I suppose I might make a temporary exception." He stroked the side of my face again, a whiff of his bittersweet scent reaching my nose. The gentleness of the gesture woke up a flutter in my chest alongside the heat that always came with his touch. "Shouldn't you be getting a little more sleep before the big play?"

I grimaced. "I tried—and I managed a little. I don't think I'll be able to totally relax until this is over."

"It should be simple enough, shouldn't it? You coax the Man In Charge onto that elevator, and the second you're out on the floor below, we pop out to distract him while you yank off any protections he brought with him. Then I'll get him eating out of my hand." The incubus smirked. "Possibly literally, if we have time for that."

"Right. Piece of cake." But I'd thought that plenty of times in the past, and ever since these shadowkind had entered my life, my ability to judge hadn't been quite as sharp as it'd used to be. Too much chaos in the mix.

Leaning into his caress, I rested my hand on his chest just below the collar of his sleek button-up shirt. "The plan does put a lot of the burden on you."

"Do you hear me complaining?" The incubus slid his fingertips along my jaw to tilt up my chin, his warm hazel eyes holding mine. "I never expected to be the cornerstone of any operation we carried out here, Sorsha. I figured I'd be a convenient tool to smooth along the larger plans. Turns out I'm good for more than that after all—and I'm flattered that you believed that before it ever occurred to me."

I couldn't help smiling back at him with a playful tug of his collar. "I do have a talent for spotting valuable objects. Very handy in my usual line of work." My good humor faded as I considered the point of uncertainty our entire plan rested on. "We don't know what kind of personal protections he might be wearing, though. It won't necessarily be as simple as luring him out and snapping off a badge. If you all jump out at him too early..."

"Then we decide on a signal for you to give us as our cue."

"That won't work if I need you to spring out the second the elevator opens. And even if I don't, anything odd I say or do might tip him off. He'll already be on edge."

Frowning, I dropped my gaze. If we could have used radio gear, I might have been able to make a subtler signal that way, but electronics wouldn't function in the shadows. If only there was some way I could have passed on the message essentially invisibly—

I hesitated, my hand stilling against Ruse. There *was* a way, wasn't there? The thought sent a momentary flicker of panic through me, but it petered out as quickly as it had risen up. I gazed up into the incubus's face again, and the answer came to me clear as anything.

I'd seen who he was. I trusted him. This monstrous man had stood by me and stood up for me in so many ways, and I didn't have a particle of fear left that he'd ever intend to harm me.

"Yes?" Ruse said, meeting my gaze with one eyebrow arched.

"I know how we can time it perfectly without the Company boss having a clue." I reached to unclasp the silver-and-iron badge of my own and set it on the dresser with a clink. Lately I'd been wearing it more from habit than any real sense that I needed it. "As soon as we're out of his apartment, you'll be able to look inside my head and sense how I'm feeling—whether I'm confident and ready to go or still scrambling to work out the best approach. Go by that, and we're golden."

Ruse stared at me, the nonchalance I was so used to in his roguish face broken by shock. "Just to be clear, you're giving me permission—"

"I'm *asking* you to read my emotions," I said. "It's the best possible option. And—when I made the rules before, I didn't really know you. I do now. And I know you'd never use this opening against me. I don't just believe in your skills. I believe in *you*."

The incubus blinked at me once more, and then he was pulling me to him, branding my mouth with a kiss so hot and giddying that I nearly melted on the spot. I barely had time to kiss him back before he'd eased away just an inch, his breath tingling over the lips he'd left tender with his embrace.

"I love you," he said in a voice both stiff with tension and ringing with sincerity. "I realize—from an incubus, it may not be—and of course I couldn't expect—"

My heart swelled with an ache of affection so great that I lost my breath. I touched his cheek, swallowing the lump that had risen in my throat. I wouldn't have been able to let him in as much as I was offering if this hadn't been true. It was easier saying it the second time.

"I love you too."

Ruse let out a rough sound and yanked my mouth

back to his. This time the kiss stretched on and on, sending tingles all through my body and setting my skin alight. Without breaking it, he slid his hands down my sides and grasped my hips to lift me onto the edge of the dresser. More heat flooded me as our bodies aligned even more tightly.

He drew his lips from mine only to mark a scorching path along my jaw and down my neck. "I want to toss you onto that bed and ravish you until you've come a million times," he murmured against my skin, each brush of his lips sparking new pleasures. "But we have a kingpin to topple, so that'll have to wait. But I'll be damned if I'm not going to have you at least once right now. It's been too long since I was last inside you."

No arguments here. I tucked my legs around his thighs, urging him even closer. "You have me. Let's see what you can do with me, lover boy."

He laughed, the sound thick with promise, and reclaimed my mouth. As he drew every ounce of pleasure from my lips, he worked my blouse free from my skirt. With what seemed like magical speed, he whipped it off over my head, unhooked my bra, and cupped my breasts.

His deft thumbs rolled over both nipples simultaneously, and the surge of bliss made me whimper against his mouth. He smiled into our next kiss, working me over with skillful strokes until I was dying with need.

My teeth nicked his lip as I kissed him harder. I arched into him, burning for more.

"Give me the incubus," I said, knowing he'd understand what I meant.

Ruse grinned, no protests about my ability to handle

him in his full shadowkind form now. And apparently while he'd been teaching Snap a few tricks, he'd picked up one from the devourer. As he closed his eyes, his clothes blinked away, giving me an instant view of his transformation.

The golden sheen glowed from his skin. His horns curled farther out of his hair. And down below, his already rigid cock curved upward at that angle I knew could send me soaring in a matter of seconds, his pubic bone jutting just far enough to stimulate my clit as well.

In every sense, he was made for fucking—and making a fucking miracle out of that intimate act.

When his eyes caught mine again, they gleamed as gold as the rest of him. He captured my mouth with an even headier kiss, and his hands skimmed up my thighs.

Never had I been so glad to be wearing a skirt. I'd chosen it for the Company boss's benefit, figuring a feminine look would work in my favor, but it was definitely benefiting *me* right now. Ruse yanked the fabric up to my hips in one smooth gesture and divested me of my panties with another. Then his glorious erection was pressing right up against my sex.

I managed to keep my senses enough to remember the caution that had come over me with Snap—and just how much I did *not* want to add a baby to this mix any time soon. "Condom," I gasped out, groping for my purse, expecting Ruse to laugh.

But no doubt the incubus had gotten the same request from an awful lot of his conquests in recent decades. He delved inside my purse to produce one as if it'd never have occurred to him not to.

The second he drove into me, as if his cock were meant to be nowhere else, all thought of the ridiculousness of safe sex with an incubus flew out of my mind with the rush of bliss. I matched Ruse's thrusts, the dresser rattling beneath me. His glow seeped through every pore in my body. Everywhere it touched, more desire flared.

The head of his cock pulsed against the sweet spot inside me. He hit it again and again, grazing my clit at the same time, his mouth on my lips and then my neck and then my shoulder, his hands seemingly everywhere. I wrapped one arm around him for balance and let the other tease up into his hair to grasp one of his horns.

Ruse groaned and plunged into me even harder. Pleasure crackled through me, whiting out my vision. I came, gasping and moaning and deeply glad that his incubus sound-proofing magic would keep my cries of ecstasy from alerting the entire Everymobile to what we'd gotten up to.

"I love you," I mumbled again, wanting to say it unprompted, and those three words tipped Ruse over the edge after me. He came with a heave of his hips and a guttural sound that rang through me with a burst of afterglow.

I clung to him as his rhythm slowed and his body came to rest against me, soaking in every bit of that glow that I could.

I might have lost one of my lovers, but I still had the three who'd dedicated themselves to me from the very beginning. Yeah, okay, you could call them monsters, but they'd looked out for me and stood by me more than any human in my life had ever managed to. They'd accepted both my mortality and my own monstrousness without hesitation.

If they believed in *me*, who the hell would I be not to?

28

Sorsha

I approached the Big Bad Boss the same way our charmed guard had said delivery people did—and you might say I *was* delivering something to his doorstep. Chaos? Hocus pocus? Retribution? A little of all three, really.

Of course, I'd imagine his typical deliveries didn't arrive at five in the morning, but that might have worked in my favor. When I brandished the courier envelope I'd slapped several *Priority* stickers on for emphasis, the lobby security dude gave me a slightly glazed look before waving me on to the elevators. Then it was simply a matter of punching the button for the top floor the main elevator let out onto.

As the elevator car hurtled upward, I stuffed the empty envelope into my purse and palmed the ring Snap had procured—round setting, 1-carat diamond, white gold. With something that simple, I could hope the big boss's own memory wouldn't be so exact as to notice any tiny differences. Sweet summer sandwiches, let him not have gotten the original one engraved.

The wig didn't itch now that I'd fixed it on properly, but I couldn't shake my awareness of its weight on my head. I resisted the urge to tug at it and rocked on my feet instead, singing a little tune to keep my energy pumped up. "If I blow there will be rubble; if I slay there will be double. So come on my little foe."

The elevator dinged, letting me out on the sub-penthouse floor. The blaze of light from the glaring panels set all across the ceiling made my eyes water. Strips of more fluorescent light beamed along the baseboards, and the seamless floor was polished like a mirror to reflect all of it. What the hell did a regular delivery person make of this funhouse hall?

It was a good thing we'd been prepared for this in advance. My shadowkind allies who'd snuck with me onto the elevator unseen would have been shit out of luck for darkness to conceal themselves in out here—if it wasn't for the skill our night elf possessed that Omen had scoffed at.

Gloam could produce his own darkness. As I walked down the hall to the private elevator at the far end, a streak of shadow trailed along the edge of the floor, long enough to accommodate all my allies but so thin I could barely see it unless I looked hard. Here was hoping that meant it wouldn't show up on the security cams mounted at intervals along the ceiling.

One of those cameras was pointed at the spot directly in front of the private elevator that only moved between this floor and the penthouse above. Our new friend had told us that one of the two guards always on duty would be keeping an eye on that feed at all times.

To catch that dude's attention, I gestured wildly, setting my face in a fraught expression. Then, as if frantic to get my message across, I snatched a paper out of my purse and pretended to scrawl a message I'd actually written ahead of time. I held it up to the camera with both hands and a pleading gaze.

I MUST SPEAK TO ISAAC. IT'S ABOUT CARMEN. PLEASE!!!!!

Very important to add the multiple exclamation marks. Each one could serve as a little jab of guilt over my apparent desperation.

I held my breath. If the strangeness of my arrival and the message wasn't enough to prompt the guard to wake up his boss and ask for guidance, and instead the guy came down to chase me off without checking in, the situation would become ten times more complicated. But our charmed guard had said that his boss didn't like them taking their own initiative, and this time that worked against the head honcho rather than for him.

I waited there, holding up the sign and waggling it now and then, for long enough that my shoulders started to twinge from keeping them in position. Mr. Big Bad would have plenty to think about, faced with my message. How had anyone connected his real first name to the condo where he didn't even let his direct employees identify him as anything other than "boss"? How had I found out about his long-ago fiancé? What could I possibly know about her that would bring me to his doorstep?

He might be wary, but we were counting on the questions eating at him too deeply for him to dismiss. He had no reason to suspect that this intrusion could have anything to do with the gore-and-fire-happy monsters who'd ransacked various laboratory facilities belonging to the Company in cities far away.

Finally, a thrumming sound carried through the wall. I lowered the sign, my body tensing.

The door opened to reveal not the silver-buzzcut, square-jawed guy our charmed guard had described as his boss, but a muscle-bound woman who looked only a little older than me. She pointed a gun at me, her other hand at a whip hanging in a coil from her belt, and jerked her head toward the shiny elevator car she was standing in.

"Get on. The boss will see you. No funny stuff—hands to yourself, avoid sudden movements. Understood?"

I nodded meekly. We'd expected the process of roping in the boss man to go something like this. I might have piqued his curiosity, but he'd want to indulge that curiosity in the comfort of his well-shielded home. The *real* trick was going to be convincing him I had a legitimate enough cause to get him out of that home and vulnerable enough for us to make our move.

Leaving my shadowkind allies behind, I stepped into the elevator. They couldn't follow me up into that realm of silver and iron without it shattering their disguises and their strength. However much monster I had in me, I was still that much human.

As the door slid closed, the guard patted me over from shoulders to feet. She rifled through my purse too, but I'd emptied that of anything unusual. Finally, she motioned for me to open my mouth and peered into it. Satisfied I wasn't carrying weapons anywhere accessible on my person, she wiped her hands together and pressed the control button.

A faint vibration ran through the polished floor as the elevator whisked us upward. Its doors whispered apart, and I found myself face-to-face with Isaac, last name unknown, grandmaster over the North American Company of Light.

From the guard's description, I'd expected his jaw to be a little squarer, his buzzcut a little more severe. The man of fifty-something years who was staring at me somewhat blearily could have passed for a college professor easier than the military general I'd pictured him as. The clearly hastily-thrown-on button-up and slacks, rumpled where he'd stuffed the former into the waist of the latter, didn't help.

But then, as he looked me up and down with a tightening of that jaw, I caught a steely vibe that removed any doubts about this guy's claim to authority.

One of the most important things he'd have been watching for was how I reacted to entering his condo. The sheets of silver and iron I knew were built into his walls didn't affect me at all, as he could no doubt observe.

I hugged myself as if nervous for totally normal

human reasons, still clutching my sign. Isaac's gaze dropped to it, and his shoulders went even more rigid. He'd worked very hard to keep so much of himself private from his employees. That worked in our favor now too. What did he want to protect more: his identity and the details of his past, or his current presence from whatever threat he thought some shivering stranger might pose.

"You checked her over?" Isaac asked the guard standing next to me. Another, a middle-aged man, stood behind his boss in the entry hall.

The woman gave a brisk nod. "I wouldn't have let her up if I found anything to be concerned about."

"All right. Retire to the surveillance room—both of you. If she comes any closer to me or I move to leave the hall without first giving you the okay signal, intervene. Otherwise, leave us be."

The man looked startled. "Sir?"

"You heard me. This is a matter I need to handle on my own." A hint of a sneer curled his lips as he looked me over again. "And I think I should have no trouble handling her at all."

Was that so? He was lucky he wasn't meeting my cat burglar, pyromaniac self just yet.

The guards left without another word. Obedient sorts, obviously. No doubt he'd picked them with that criteria in mind. One more choice that would no longer work in his favor.

I'd gotten the hook down his gullet. All that was left was to reel him in.

The boss man waited several seconds after his lackeys had vanished to give them time to get out of earshot. Then he said, low and curt, "Who are you?"

"A friend of Carmen's," I said.

A muscle in his cheek twitched. "That's impossible."

I let the words spill out as if in an anxious rush. "You thought she was dead. They wanted you to think that, the horrible creatures. Some of them can cast illusions—you know that, don't you? Ones that can fool all sorts of people for ages. That's all it was."

"And how would you know this? How did you know to come here? What is it you *want*?"

I gazed at him from beneath my fake black waves with widened eyes. "They had me too. She told me everything. How much she wished she could find her way back to you. The bond she still felt must have mingled with their magic somehow—she started having visions; she saw this building. We managed to break free and come here, but she's ill. I'm afraid to try and move her, so I told her I'd come get you."

"Then she's here? She's waiting—" He shook himself, and his tone hardened again. "No. It can't be. I *buried* her."

"You buried an illusion. I swear it. She *needs* you, now." I held out my hand, showing him the ring. "She gave me this so you'd know it was her."

Isaac froze. Then he reached out and took the ring from me, holding it up to the light. His throat bobbed. "She really... She managed to hold on to this all this time?"

"Nothing meant more to her," I said softly.

"And those monsters—" His voice shook with more fury than it could hold.

An answering anger flared inside me. What about all the monsters he'd ordered tortured and slaughtered who'd never harmed a single mortal? Did none of their lives count while he acted out his revenge for the savage one that had ripped his fiancé from him?

Heat prickled through my chest—and I yanked it back with a hitch of breath I couldn't quite hide. Cool waves, a salty breeze, the rhythmic hiss of the ocean. Focus on that. Focus on that and keep my fire in, or so many more monsters would die under this man's orders because I'd screwed up our one chance to stop him.

My emotions settled with an ache around my heart. I could do this. I could stay in control. At least as long as I didn't *need* to fling any fire around and could keep all of it inside.

The big boss was watching me again. "Are you all right?" he said carefully.

"I'm not totally well either," I said as if embarrassed to admit it. "But it's Carmen who kept me going all this time—I had to do this for her. Will you come to her? She's nearby—it won't take five minutes. I don't want to leave her too long. If she sees anyone but you, I think she might run."

So don't call up someone else to handle this. You don't really want to anyway, not when it shows so much of the life you've tried to keep away from all your colleagues' eyes.

Resolve flashed in his eyes. Something I'd said or done had gotten through. He spun on his heel and hollered to his guards. "Is there anyone at all in the lower hall or any report of trouble from the lobby?"

An intercom crackled. "No, sir," the woman replied. "It's been totally quiet all night except your guest."

He wavered but only for a second this time. Then he gave a brisk nod, made a gesture toward the camera, and strode off. He returned moments later pulling on a suit jacket that he stuffed a phone into the pocket of. Something about the way it hung on him pinged understanding in my brain.

"That's a good one," I said, eyeing the jacket with feigned approval. "It's got strips of silver and iron sewn right into it? I knew a lady who had a dress made like that." I patted the lapel, just a brush of my fingertips to prove to him that I didn't shy away from those metals. And to get a feel for the fabric. Sooner rather than later, I was going to have to wrench this thing off him.

"I believe in taking every precaution," he said. "Let's go. You and Carmen will be safe from the fiends in here. I can bring in doctors and whatever else you need."

He opened the door to the elevator, leaving his guards behind. Leaving them watching the surveillance feeds. Fresh tension wound through my body as I followed him in.

We'd thought he might bring his lackeys with him, so that Thorn and Flint would need to bash their helmeted heads right off their bodies when we emerged into the hall. It looked like we wouldn't be able to stage our ambush there after all. If we attacked just him, the guards would see and come running to the rescue.

The others would have to wait until we were out of the hall below. Actually, better that we weren't even in the building, since I knew for sure he had his phone. We couldn't rely on this going so smoothly that the building's own security wouldn't notice and interfere.

Ruse would be relying on his read on my emotions to tell him all of that. I concentrated on the worry of them acting too soon, my longing to be somewhere out of the cameras' view. *Not yet. Not yet.* And woven through all that was my hope that he'd understand.

The elevator door slid open on the brilliant hall of light. No shadowkind leapt from their constructed patch of darkness. And how terrible it would be if they did just yet. I let that horror fill me all the way to the second elevator, even as I studied Isaac from the corner of my eye. To get the jacket off him as quickly as possible, I'd need to stand—yeah, just like that would be fine.

No one had used the main elevator since I'd gotten off. The door opened the second he pushed the button. We stepped on, and I kept the same anxiety racing through my veins. Oh, to be out in the open air, away from *any* potential prying eyes.

We descended without interruption. I hurried through the lobby a step ahead of the big boss, both to maintain my story that I was worried about the supposed Carmen and to get on with the part of the plan that didn't rest entirely on me.

"This way," I said on the sidewalk, hustling a few buildings over and then ducking away from the streetlamps down a driveway currently closed off with a thick chain. A tarry smell drifted in the darkened air.

When I paused, Isaac came up beside me. His head swiveled. "Is this where she was? We have to—"

As he spoke, I placed myself at his right flank, braced myself, and let relief and urgency wash through me. *We're in the clear. Let's do this!*

My feelings must have pealed through loud and clear. Ruse, Snap, Thorn, and Flint sprang into being around us.

The boss man startled with a fearful cry, and I grasped his suit jacket by the collar. With one sharp yank, I'd pulled it to his elbows—but then he connected one of those elbows with my forehead.

The impact radiated through my skull, sending my thoughts reeling. I clung on, but he was twisting around to strike another blow, and while he had the jacket on him my allies could barely touch him—

I could use my fire. I could control it enough to have it do my bidding down to the letter. I *could*.

Through a hasty swell of ocean imagery, I coaxed my flames from my hands and into the fabric of Isaac's jacket.

He let out a hiss of shock. The wool melted into cinders, the sagging strips of metal pattered to the pavement—and there he was, naked of protections, the fabric of his dress shirt only faintly singed.

The emotion that hit me then was nothing less than elation. I could have hugged the dude I'd just traumatized for staying uncrispified if he wouldn't have tried to punch my nose in again.

Ruse shot me the swiftest of winks, already talking

with the full force of his power thrumming through his voice. "We're so glad you could join us, my friend. We have the answers to destroying the monsters you wish to exterminate. Unfortunately, you've been helping them rather than hindering them. Because of you, so many more young women like your fiancé have fallen."

The big boss pressed his hands to his head. "What are you talking about? I've—that can't be true."

"Oh, but it is. We've been watching, and we've seen. What you don't know, what your bosses don't know, is that the entire Company of Light is a trick dreamed up by the monsters themselves. They set this whole thing in motion, made the first crusaders feel they had to come together to fight back. But the truth is that they *need* your anger and fear to continue passing into this world. Every bit of evidence about them you take down in your computers, every order anyone gives to capture or kill them, it allows the pathways between the realms to remain strong."

"I can show you," Flint said with that voice like a roll of thunder. He fixed his gaze on Isaac's. An eerie light flickered into being in the depths of his eyes, and the color drained from our target's face.

We hadn't been sure if even Ruse's charm could win the boss man over convincingly enough. But Flint—Flint could show him the supposed horrors the Company of Light was enabling in vivid reality, as if he were standing in the midst of the worst of it. We'd determined that his ability could work across great distances as long as he could look into the other person's eyes. As soon as we got the biggest boss of all on the phone, Ruse was going to cajole him into a video call.

By the time the vision the second wingéd stirred up had faded away, Isaac was trembling. He swiped his hand across his mouth, looking as though he might vomit. "I never realized—I had no idea..."

"None of you did," Ruse said with false sympathy. "The worst of it is, you're the only ones left who even understand that the monsters exist. If *you* stopped all your activities around them, wiped clean all the data you've collected on them—their pathways to this world would close up, and they'd never threaten another mortal again."

The key, Ruse had said once, was to give the person you were charming what they'd wanted in the first place. Those ideas took hold like nothing else. And what Isaac wanted more than anything in existence was to rid this realm of monsters.

"My God," he said. "We have to—I'll do whatever I can, but I don't have control over everything. I'll start reaching out—"

"First," Ruse said smoothly, "we should talk to the man who gives you *your* orders. Otherwise he may not understand and might even stand in your way while you try to set this right. You have the means to contact him, don't you?"

The boss man dragged in a breath. "Yes. I have a way to indicate to him that I need him to call me. He'll want to know immediately."

As he fumbled for his phone, Ruse caught my gaze over Isaac's shoulder. The corner of his mouth quirked with the start of a smirk, his eyes glowing with triumph. I couldn't help grinning back at him.

We had the Company by the throat, and in just a few minutes, we were going to snap its neck so hard not one piece of it would ever rise again.

29

Sorsha

If you've never partied with shadowkind, I've got to say I highly recommend finding an opportunity to do so.

I was running on about three hours of sleep, but the rush of our victory and the energy humming through the air inside the RV from the beings who didn't need sleep to begin with pepped me up no problem. Ruse and Snap had "liberated" a large amount of snack food and some very nice champagne from a couple of stores downtown. Now we were all full of frothy alcohol and bubbling over with laughter and jubilant remarks.

Ruse had managed to find an '80s station on the RV's radio, sending bouncy notes careening through the narrow space. He spun me around and sent me flying into Snap's arms, who stole a kiss while he danced with his usual sinuous grace. Thorn and Flint toasted each other—a little carefully after their earlier attempts had resulted in several cracked glasses. Pickle darted around on the table with energetic little hops, managing to stir a smile even from Gloam after he'd sunk into his usual daytime despondency.

"The look on that mortal's face when I showed him a vision of the destruction his Company would bring about," Flint said, his thunderous voice sounding almost jovial, and let out a chuckle that vibrated through the room.

Ruse smirked. "He couldn't demolish his own work fast enough. And we accomplished all that from thousands of miles away. I do enjoy modern mortal technology."

"There will still be the independent hunters and collectors," Thorn pointed out, even though he was smiling too.

I dismissed that concern with a wave. "We can deal with them like we always have. No big deal. And with those last tidbits Ruse planted in the big bosses' heads, they'll have the Company cracking down on *anyone* who's doing business around the shadowkind from now on. After all, who else will they have to blame when the shadowkind don't vanish completely after the Company is disbanded?"

I paused to take another swig of champagne—and two figures popped from the shadows so abruptly I almost choked.

Antic's arrival wasn't a surprise. She'd insisted on being the one to go off and collect some more refreshments, restless after standing back so long after her initial contribution to our plan. But standing next to her, in all his tight-jawed, icy-eyed glory, was our missing hellhound shifter.

With a sputtered cough, I set down my glass, my mouth already stretching into a welcoming grin. My heart had skipped a beat both startled and ecstatic. But as I took in the stern set of Omen's mouth and the way he was looking at me, as if I'd created some new catastrophe even worse than the ones he'd accused me of before, my pulse hitched again in a much less pleasant way. I found myself glancing around to confirm that I hadn't somehow burned the Everymobile to the ground without noticing.

Everyone else had fallen momentarily silent. Ruse found his tongue first. "Omen! Very convenient of you to skip out while we did all the work and only return for the victory party."

The hellhound shifter's gaze slid from me to the incubus. "The imp told me about your scheme—and that, miracle of all miracles, you pulled it off. So, you managed to topple the Company without me. Not a bad day's work."

I folded my arms over my chest. "You don't sound all that happy about it." Was he upset that we hadn't waited for him to show up before taking action, even though we'd accomplished more than he could have even been hoping?

"Oh, I'm very glad to know that particular thorn is no longer in our side. Ecstatic, even. It just hasn't had time to sink in. And I've had more pressing concerns on my mind."

"More pressing than bringing down a massive

organization dedicated to exterminating all shadowkind?"

"They could have been ignored for a few days without total disaster. This might not." He glanced around, noting the second wingéd in our midst with only the barest flicker of surprise. "Out. All of you except the mortal. *Now*."

Antic squeaked and darted into the shadows. Gloam's mouth dropped open, but a second later he followed her.

Flint stood, his solemn face reaching new levels of stony grimness that Thorn could only have aspired to. "If there is some concern with—"

"I'm not *concerned*," the hellhound shifter growled. "I just want you all out. I assume you know how to follow orders?"

The warrior winced and vanished. Omen swiveled to consider the three remaining shadowkind, who'd drawn closer around me rather than departing.

"What's going on, Omen?" Ruse asked.

Thorn inclined his head. "I would prefer to remain and hear the news you've brought, given the option."

Omen glared at them. "I wasn't giving options. When I said 'all of you except the mortal,' I meant the three of you as well. Get going."

"Hey," I broke in. "You should know by now that *I* don't jump just because you say so. If you make them take off, I'm leaving too. Whatever's going on, they deserve to know." And I wanted them here, especially when Omen was looking at me like that.

His cool eyes pierced mine and held there. I stared

right back at him, all my celebratory elation fading away behind my defiance.

"Fine," he muttered. "They'll end up finding out soon enough anyway." He made a curt gesture. "Disaster, you've mentioned a note your parents wrote to you. Would you let me have a look at that?"

Snap peered at him wide-eyed. "Are you going to tell us where you've been first?"

"The Highest called me in for a talk I couldn't refuse," Omen said flatly. "They weren't very prompt about their invitation." He raised his eyebrows at me. "Well?"

"Yeah, of course, I can get it." I swiveled, slightly dizzy from both the champagne and the sudden change in atmosphere, and hurried over to the bedroom to grab the pearly trinket box.

Had he found out something else about my parents—from the Highest shadowkind or somewhere else on his way back? What could be so urgent about people who were *dead*? And why wouldn't he have wanted the other shadowkind hearing about it?

When I returned with the box, Ruse and Snap had sat down on the sofa-bench. Omen was leaning against the table, his face the same stern mask it'd been since he'd arrived. Thorn stepped to flank me as I approached, as if to guard me. I'd have felt better about that if I'd had any idea what he might be guarding me from. I didn't think even *he* knew that yet.

Omen snapped open the box's lid and withdrew the folded notepaper. His mouth twisted into a crooked smile. "As I thought."

"What?" I demanded, leaning closer and ignoring the heat that rose up between our bodies with our arms nearly touching.

The note looked the same to me as it always had with its few lines about how much my parents had loved me and how sorry they were not to be with me now. But Omen flicked his fingers toward my name scrawled at the top of the page.

"What about that?" I started to ask—and the ink shifted before my eyes. The letters wavered and reformed. My back stiffened, and any other words I might have said died in my throat.

There'd been a glamour on the letter, just like whatever ones Luna had fixed in my memories. She'd altered this piece of my past too. Now Omen had broken it, and the name I'd thought was mine had vanished.

In its place, the curving lines of ink formed a new one I couldn't wrap my head around: *Ruby*.

My mouth opened and closed and opened again. "I—But—The note wasn't for me?"

Omen gave me a penetrating look. "Of course it's for you. Your parents didn't name you Sorsha. *You* are Ruby. I'd imagine your fae guardian must have worked some awfully complex glamour repressing all memory of that name from your mind, woven into your thoughts so thoroughly so long ago I couldn't have picked up on the magic."

Thorn shifted his weight behind me. "How can this be? Not even Sorsha was aware of her powers until recently. She was a small child the last time she was in

Austin. How could she have done something to cause such a hunt from the Highest?"

Very good questions, and I was glad he'd asked, since I was still having trouble formulating full sentences.

Omen grimaced. "The Highest didn't want people to know what exactly they were looking for or why. Ruby hadn't done anything except come into existence—and escape their attempt to end that existence."

He paused and met my eyes again. There might have been something a little sad behind the ice now. "It wasn't hunters who killed your parents. It was shadowkind. The Highest sent their warrior minions to slaughter the three of you. The fae woman got you out of there and was clever enough to ensure they never caught wind of your location again."

My parents... had been killed by *shadowkind*? Shadowkind who'd meant to kill three-year-old me as well? Just when I thought I was starting to get a grip on his revelations, another one threw me for a loop.

I curled my fingers around the edge of the table to hold myself steady. "Why? I mean, I know a mortal and a shadowkind managing to have a kid is pretty much unheard of, but—is it really such a horrible thing, enough that they'd want us all dead?"

"As far as I could tell, it's about the most horrible thing the Highest can conceive of."

"Why should it be?" Snap spoke up, unusually fierce. "If that was what Sorsha's parents wanted—no harm came out of it—"

"That's where you might be wrong," Omen said. His voice had gone taut. "The Highest believe that a union between a mortal and a shadowkind would create a being of incredibly destructive power—enough power to ruin both this world and ours." He studied me. "You've felt it. I didn't believe you when you told me, but it seems you might have been right to be wary of what lurks inside you."

The fire I'd managed to control so well just hours ago? It flared in my chest now, prickling hot and jittering, but I willed it down, swallowing hard. "I just—I just need to practice more, to get a total handle on it, like *you've* always said. I haven't done anything that awful with it."

"Not yet. They think you will if you're allowed to live long enough." He tucked the notepaper back into the trinket box and set the box down on the table. "Whatever exactly you are, the most ancient and powerful beings among all the shadowkind are absolutely terrified of you."

The absurdity of that statement left me lost for words again. Pickle crept over and nuzzled my hand, but I couldn't take a whole lot of comfort from his gesture of solidarity in the face of this discovery. All of the celebratory joy had drained out of me.

The Highest shadowkind wanted me dead. I might contain some kind of world-shattering power. How was I supposed to respond to that? What were we going to *do* about it?

I might have asked one or both of those things, except before I could recover my voice, Omen's phone rang.

His head jerked down, and he frowned at his pocket for a second before reaching to answer it. Obviously he hadn't been expecting a call. Did shadowkind have to deal with spammy telemarketers just like the rest of us? This one couldn't have had worse timing.

Omen's frown deepened as he took in the screen. I was standing close enough to him to see no number or name was showing up on the display, not even a note of *Unknown Caller*—it was totally blank. But his ringtone sounded again.

Cautiously, he hit the answer button and lifted the phone. "Hello? Who is this?"

A sharp laugh pealed from the speaker, so loudly that the hellhound shifter yanked the phone away from his ear. "Omen," an equally sharp female voice said, as clearly as if he'd put her on speakerphone. "I knew I'd get you."

Omen's posture went rigid. He stared at the phone as if he'd suddenly realized he was holding a viper. "Who is this?" he asked again, but with a slight hesitation that suggested he was bracing for an answer he already expected.

"My goodness. I recognize *your* voice after all this time. Do you really not know your favorite associate in all things havoc-raising? I'm wounded."

A chill shot down my spine, my own troubles briefly forgotten. What was the name of that formidable shadowkind Omen had said he'd harassed mortals with ages ago?

He offered it up hoarsely, his knuckles whitening where he was gripping the phone. "Tempest. You—I watched a squad of wingéd *murder* you."

"You watched them *attempt* to murder me. I must have put on a very convincing show of being murdered. It was necessary, you know, to get those stuffy windbags that call themselves the Highest off my back, and once I had the freedom of being supposedly dead, I didn't really want to give it up. I'm sorry if you've grieved for me across all these years."

From the set of Omen's mouth, I suspected he was more likely to be grieving her return. "You had to do what you had to do," he said, evening out his tone with his usual strict composure. "Why are you honoring me with the secret now?"

The sphinx tsked. "It seems you've been making mischief for the wrong side. Nearly putting all my diligent work to waste. Thankfully I caught on and knocked the delusions out of my good friend's head before he blew up the entire Company of Light."

I wouldn't have thought I could get any more stunned, but that comment smacked me right through speechless and out the other end. "*You're* working with the Company of Light?"

"One of your new friends, Omen? She catches on quick. Although I'm not so much working for them as *they're* working for me. Tempest the sphinx bows to no one."

"If I could interject," Ruse said, looking as discombobulated as I felt. "I don't know who you are, but you're obviously shadowkind. Why in blue blazes are you running a 'company' set on destroying the lot of us?"

"Oh, you haven't told the stories of our glory days, Omen?" Tempest sighed with exaggerated dramatics. "No matter. I can assure you the mortals won't manage to wipe us out no matter what they do—at least, not those of us smart enough to deserve this life. If you'd like to discuss the matter further, I won't make it hard to find me. You remember that architectural dream of mine? I got to make it come true."

Omen froze and then gave a disbelieving chuckle. "You didn't—"

"Oh, I did. The king was only too happy to oblige when I nudged him in all the right directions. I suppose I'll see you there shortly. I'd appreciate it if you'd leave my sycophants alone until then. You've already caused me enough of a headache."

The connection cut off as abruptly as her voice had first blared out. For several seconds, we all just gaped at Omen, who was trying valiantly not to gape at his phone and not entirely succeeding.

A fresh wave of heat swelled inside me. "A *shadowkind* is convincing people to torture and slay the rest of you?" We'd made that claim to the big bosses just hours ago—but nothing I'd actually heard from any of my companions would have indicated it was true. And the damage the Company had done to untold numbers of shadowkind certainly wasn't make-believe.

"She always did care more about sowing chaos for her own satisfaction than anything or anyone else," Omen said in a shell-shocked tone.

A flame broke out across my forearm before I could suppress a surge of anger and betrayal. I slapped it against my side, but the hellhound shifter's gaze snapped to it.

He shook himself as if shedding all the bewilderment of the last few minutes and pushed himself away from the table. When his eyes met mine, something in them made the bottom drop out of my stomach.

"Dealing with her will have to wait until later. First we have to deal with you. I'm sorry."

My heart lurched. "Omen—"

He didn't give me a chance to plead or protest. As his name slipped from my lips, he lunged at me, his arm swinging faster than I could track.

With the slam of his fist into my temple, my mind spiraled into darkness.

Made in the USA
Monee, IL
19 February 2021